AWARD-WINNING AUTHOR
RUTH LOGAN HERNE

Try, Try Again

DEDICATION

To my beautiful daughter Sarah Blodgett Bermeo, who introduced me to Princeton, to St. Paul's Church and the delightful Msgr. Walter Nolan, pastor emeritus of St. Paul's Church. God blessed us with you as a precious baby... how wonderful to see the woman you've become!

ACKNOWLEDGEMENTS

Big thanks to Zach Blodgett for his always helpful insight on how to keep Conor's character real because this farm girl's experience with big city lawyers is somewhat lacking. Zach, thanks for the help and the encouragement! To Luke Blodgett whose advice about how companies work financially from within gave me solid ground. To Sarah Blodgett Bermeo for sharing her life in Princeton as she completed multiple degrees. How fun it was to walk the streets, eat ice cream at Thomas Sweets and meet the folks of St. Paul's Parish. And we only got pulled over by the local police once while driving our somewhat tired and worn red farm truck, so that's not a bad average, LOL!

To Msgr. Walter Nolan, formerly of St. Paul's parish in Princeton whose warmth, humor and great smile inspired the "Fr. Murphy" character in this book. Msgr. Nolan's common sense directives behind a warm grin brought my "Fr. Murphy" to life. God bless you Monsignor, for your life of dedication and holiness. You are a very special person.

To the NYPD who aren't afraid to specialize in things like "Bridge negotiators", special police skilled at saving lives of mentally fragile people. To Mandy, Paul, Beth and Jon for always stepping in to give me time to work, or time to run and play! And to all my children whose college experiences and careers have given me reason to visit East Coast cities and fall in love with America all over again.

Also thanks to Transiberian Orchestra's "The Lost Christmas Eve" which made me see this rich man for the lost soul he was, and to Emerson Drive for their music video "I've Had My Moments". I love when inspiration hits from multiple sources to become a final product. Your great music helped to inspire my story.

PROLOGUE

Wells, Terwilliger, Whickman and Bradstreet, LLP
One Financial Trade Center Plaza
New York, New York 10005
New York Los Angeles London Tokyo Beijing

FROM THE DESK OF CONOR BRADSTREET:

Note to self: Christmas list:
Send: Godiva chocolates and gift certificate to
Mom: ✓
Broadway tickets and checks to Addie and Kim: ✓
Flowers to female office staff: LeAnne, Dorothy, and
Kate: ✓
Saks gift card to Brennan and Sheldon: ✓
Suits to cleaners before they close: ✓
Call: Mom, wish her a Merry Christmas: ✓
Daughters, ditto: ✓ (Addie didn't pick up, left msg.
w/Kim)
Deposit sufficient funds in Alicia's account: ✓
Make stupid administrative assistant cry twice: ✓ ✓
Kick someone's dog: Unfortunately unavailable
Brighten everyone's day, take the bridge: ✓

Conor Bradstreet's Kenneth Cole shoes matched the silent night as he trudged the bridge's raised deck. The late hour coupled with the holiday to keep traffic sparse. City sounds and odors receded with less volume, allowing the smell of river water to mingle with cold December rain.

A real George Bailey moment, thought Conor as he pushed one foot after the other. Christmas Eve alone, no one to talk to. Share a meal with. Another Christmas missed and unmissed.

Most days he loved New York, the frantic pace, the pyramidal moneymaking schemes enacted behind closed doors or in full view on public streets. In the daily to and fro, the hustle and the bustle that *was* New York, he could pretend to be painfully busy and vital.

But not tonight, not this night. Never this night.

From the looks of Manhattan, the public had gone to bed. More power to them. Someone should be able to sleep. To dream. Especially on Christmas Eve.

He'd shrugged into his hat and scarf before he left his upscale downtown apartment to take a final dip. Now why did he do that? For comfort's sake, when he was planning to join Moby Dick beneath the waves? Sleep with the fishes? He needed a hat and scarf to protect him from whatever the swirling waters could give? Yeah. Lots of luck on that one, Einstein.

Or had he turned into such a city boy that he couldn't manage the bridge walk without proper headwear and foot gear? More likely. What a wuss.

He remembered a different boy in Pennsylvania, long ago, when life was sure. Happy. Running with his pals, chasing dogs, impervious to the bitter winds of winter.

Now the cold pierced to the core of his being. He hated the chill, the damp, the cold, the snow, the caustic loneliness of this night above all others.

Most of all, he hated himself.

The waters of the East River swirled and swished, tempting, courting, their whisper a Siren song to the sad and oppressed. *Woosh... Woosh... Woosh...*

Not unlike Frank Capra's famous fictional character, Conor figured a whole bunch of lives could be happier if he reduced himself to a generous life insurance settlement on top of his expansive portfolio. Kind of like an eighth grade mathematical equation, simple in its factuality. He was the money, the money was him. Very Zen.

He leaned beyond the rail, knowing he'd have to scale the cables to reach the granite and limestone tower. Jumping from the base ensured nothing but wet clothes. The towers? No one survived them, and he was a 'go big or stay home' kind of guy.

Eyeing the cable climb, he realized he should have worn his shorter coat. The placketed front of the Armani trench didn't allow full movement, and at forty, even in good shape, climbing the slippery cables wasn't the easiest option on a cold, damp night hampered by a long coat. Should he ditch the coat altogether, or enjoy his last minutes in well-fitted designer outerwear?

He'd be cold either way, then wet, then dead, so did it matter? He lifted one leg and shifted his gaze upward as he reached. Spotlights sparked a Grinch-green effect and the sting of the ice-cold steel cables made him suck a breath.

Conor loved the Grinch. He understood the Seuss icon. They were copasetic, peas in a pod. He couldn't approach December without dreading vapid lights, inane carols, false cheer and the crass commercialism which helped make him a rich man, but to what end?

He refused to think about Alicia with her dark auburn hair and gray/blue eyes, the dash of copper freckles sprinkled like cayenne pepper across the bridge of her nose, living with their two girls in New Jersey. The home they'd shared until...

The water called again, a moaning whisper, a temptress' hum, reaching for him. To him. *Conor... Conor... Conor...*

Homer understood the lure of the sea, as did Poe and his Annabel Lee. Definitive reasoning overpowered poetic license in feminizing the sea, Conor felt certain of it, mostly because he'd dealt with women. Some were deep, some were shallow, most were totally unpredictable, not unlike the gathered waters of the earth. The rolling motion beneath the bridge beckoned him, a strumpet calling, the thrust and push of the waves pulling at his very being. *Conor...*

His second foot began to follow the first, his hands stretching upward, grip tight. *Conor...*

"Got a light, Mister?"

"What?" Swinging around, Conor stepped back and jerked his hands into self-protective fists. His heart raced at the interruption, unexpected and unwelcome. A short, stocky man faced him, aged and battle-weary, shaggy gray-flecked dark hair framing a damp face beneath a worn, brimmed hat. "Get out of here, buddy, if you know what's good for you."

The old man regarded him through tired eyes. "Just need a match. Got a few cigarettes left to see in the holiday, but no match. You got one maybe?"

Of all the...

He'd had one foot up, arms reaching, ready to follow through, and out jumps a derelict on a mission for a smoke. Conor felt his coat pockets, then shrugged, a brow up. "None. Who are you?" A sudden thought occurred to him, considering the circumstances of the night. "No chance your name is Clarence, is it?"

The bum's faint smile said he got the correlation to George Bailey's second class angel, the first person to get Conor's jokes in a very long time.

"Name's Sarge." A jerk of his head indicated their surroundings. "This is my bridge."

"Really?" Conor regarded him, mentally scanning bits and pieces he'd read about the Big Apple's homeless. Not like their plight was one of his pet issues. Please. The idea was repugnant. Didn't he already offer a generous annual donation to his daughters' church and one, equally as liberal, to the Cancer Research Institute, hoping for a someday cure?

The homeless? One of many necessary evils tied to a big city. Just his luck, it stood representative before him, big as life and not as reclusive as he might have wished. "The mayor might take issue with that."

Sarge snorted, then swept the back of his hand across his face. "It was mine when the mayor was chasin' skirts on Long Island, it'll still be mine when he's hangin' out in Washington making rich men quake on Capitol Hill." The wreck of a man waved his thinning pack of smokes aloft. "I'm a New Yorker."

Conor's lip tugged up. Obviously the old-timer kept up on city affairs. At least those involving their mayor. Conor glanced around before studying the scruffed-up figure standing solid before him. "You live nearby?"

The old man narrowed his eyes. He nodded to the city behind Conor, his look wizened, his voice waxing sarcastic. "Third box on the right with the white colonial mailbox, just past the broken street light after the second Baby Gap."

His wit tweaked Conor's humor, rusty from disuse. Maybe corroded was a better word. "Funny."

"Not so much when it's true, Sonny-boy."

In a burst of realization, Conor unbelted his coat to probe an inner pocket.

The old man took a step back. "You fishin' for a gun?"

"No." Conor pulled out a box of matches and an expensive Cuban that one of the other partners had doled out to celebrate the birth of a grandson a few weeks previous. He handed both to his newfound friend. "Merry Christmas."

The words felt alien. When was the last time he'd wished anyone a Merry Christmas, other than his daughters? And his mom? No clue. Who cares?

"...the Grinch hated Christmas, the whole Christmas season, Now please don't ask why, no one quite knows the reason..."

Seuss's sing-song phrase squeezed Conor's heart tighter. Smaller.

The bum groped the matches greedily, his wet hands fumbling to strike the stick in the stiff wind. No luck.

"Here." Conor reached out and cupped his hands. "Let me help."

Once again the old man's eyes flicked to Conor's, the brief look sharp and shrewd, then he took a deep breath on his end. The match flickered, fainted, then brightened as the cigarette took hold in trembling hands. After a second puff, the old man eyed the expensive cigar Conor had offered, smiled and nodded. "Now that's a holiday right there."

Conor snorted. "A cigar?"

"Not just a cigar, my friend. A Trinidad Coloniale." The old guy waved the thing like a banner. "A gentleman's smoke, subtle and easy-going. Precious, Sonny-boy."

"You know Cubans?" Dubious, Conor eyed the stogie he'd handed to a derelict that most likely bore his full wardrobe on his person, layer by crusty layer.

"I know a good smoke," retorted Sarge. He tucked the cigar deep into the folds of clothing, his expression careful. He raised his eyes back to Conor. "The Missus don't let you smoke 'em in the house?"

The Missus. Conor's heart clenched and unclenched in spastic rhythm, remembering. He shook his head. "No wife."

"Kids?"

Conor nodded. "Two." Another stab of pain hit, somewhere in his mid-section. He swallowed hard, fighting it off. "Girls. Teenagers now."

"Got pictures?"

Conor straightened and stared at him. "It's the dead of night, Christmas Eve, we're standing on the bridge in the wind and rain, and you're wondering if I've got pictures of my girls?"

The lit end of the cigarette glowed bright as the old fellow drew a breath, then smiled, puffing smoke, as if the lit cigarette was the best gift known to man. "Good a time as any to get acquainted." He waved a hand toward the Manhattan side. "If we stand beneath the approach, we won't get so wet."

So wet? Conor contemplated how wet he planned to be and appreciated the irony. Obviously, dampness was subjective. "Sure, come on." Maybe if he led the old man to a safer place, he could get on with his mission. What was this, anyway? A guy couldn't even die in relative peace and obscurity on a rain-soaked Christmas Eve in the Big Apple. Was nothing sacred?

Impatient, Conor worked to match the old guy's shuffling gait. The least he could do was get the geezer to a warmer setting. Eyeing the other man's piled-on clothing, he guessed that washing facilities were scarce commodities among the box people.

"Over here." Following a lengthy walk, Sarge angled his head and led Conor beneath the bridge's Manhattan approach. "Not much, but it's dry."

"Kind of." Conor watched water sluice down a metal overhang, puddling at the far end.

"So we won't stand *there*." Sarge rolled his eyes. "The rest is dry enough, and that's all we need, hey, Sonny?"

His dad had called him Sonny-boy some thirty years past. His tone would be teasing. Fun. "*Hey, Sonny-boy, you call that a catch? Let your old man show you how it's done, Bradstreet-style.*"

Hank Bradstreet didn't have a mean bone in his body, which made Conor wonder where his came from. Or maybe he was just looking for someone to blame instead of himself. Unfortunately the candidates were few and far between.

"You smoke?" Sarge was attempting to light up again, his fingers clutching the match, box and a new cigarette. He turned to block the wind, then sucked deep.

"No."

"Drink?"

"On occasion."

The old man scrutinized him, the cigarette glow an orange-gold smudge against his salt and pepper beard. "Meth? Coke?"

"No, thanks, I'm a Pepsi man."

Faded gray eyes held a spark of twinkle. "A funny guy."

Conor leaned back against the bricked support. "Why all the questions, old man?"

"Not so many." He puffed again, his cheeks hollowing to drag in the smoke, as if he'd been waiting a long, long time. "Old habits die hard, I guess."

"Oh, yeah?" Conor shifted his weight and took the bait, fully aware. "What habits are those?"

"Cop."

"Ah." Conor knit his brow and scanned the old timer's appearance with a skeptic's look. "Not recently, I take it."

"No."

"So." Conor leveled his boardroom gaze at the old man, assessing the clothes, the dirt, the overall condition. "What brings you here, Sarge?"

"You."

"Me?" Conor shook his head. "I don't think so. Try again."

"No, it's definitely you," answered the bum, his tone nonchalant, his look offering too much understanding.

"And others like you." He took a draw on the filter, sucking deep. "Aren't the first, won't be the last."

Conor straightened. Glanced around. "Where are you staying tonight? Where'd you come from?"

Sarge waved the cigarette in the general direction of the city. "We got us a nice place in a rotunda near the station. We clear out by day to keep the city fathers happy, and they return the favor by leaving us alone at night. Not a bad setup, all told. The walls block the wind, 'less it's due East, then it's just plain cold unless you've got some good cardboard, you know, the waxed kind. Shortage of big boxes these days, though. Damn recycling."

"Diminished commodities affect market share and value." Conor thrust an eyebrow up, ever the cynic. "My guess is you're at the lower end of the trickle down theory."

"And my guess is those two girls of yours don't want your lifeless body dragged out of the river on Christmas Day." Sarge drew a deep, smoke-filled breath and met Conor's gaze. "But that's just a guess, of course."

Conor winced, his mind reeling. The old man waved toward the brackish water. "Dead body, identification, all those unanswered questions, Christmas day. Kind of puts a damper on things, you know? No pun intended."

Conor stared him down, tiny hairs rising along the nape of his neck. "You don't know what you're talking about."

"My assertion or my evaluation?"

Conor nailed him with a pinprick gaze. "Either."

"Really?" Another drag on the cigarette lit an insignificant corner of the wretchedly cold, wet night. "I say I'm dead on." Over the dwindling cigarette, he met Conor's eye. "Pun intended, that time."

"But—"

"I've had my moments, Sonny," Sarge offered, chin up, brows drawn. "My day in the sun. I still know a few things."

Was it his words or his look that stirred Conor's awareness? No clue. A gust of wind swirled the roadway's edge, misting them. The old man ducked back, unfazed. "Sorry. Forgot that happens sometimes."

Conor swiped his sleeve to his face. The wet fabric offered little help.

"So. You got them pictures? I ain't got all night."

An unexpected smile tugged the corner of Conor's mouth again. "I beg to differ. You've got all night, all day tomorrow, then that night, the next and on, ad infinitum."

Sarge fixed him a cop look above nicotine-stained whiskers. Conor hauled out his wallet, flipped past the single credit card with no limit, and edged further under the bridge approach to avoid wetting the images. "This is Kim. She just turned eighteen. Heading to college next fall."

The old man touched the picture with reverent hands. "Beautiful."

"And Addie. Adelaide," Conor corrected himself. "She's fifteen."

Sarge eyed her photo, then cast him a knowing grin. "This one's a corker, ain't she?"

He could tell that from one picture? Conor nodded. "Yes. And then some. How can you tell?"

The old timer gave an impatient snort. "Ya gotta see what's in front of your eyes, man. This one," he held up Kim's picture, a beautiful senior portrait done by an expensive New York photographer and worth every penny, "wants to please everyone. Strong, hard-working, smart, caring."

He shuffled back to Addie's photo and held it out. "This one says 'no way can I keep up with that, nor do

I want to, screw the whole thing, I'm my own person, no ifs, ands or buts.'"

"In a nutshell." Conor took Addie's picture and studied the profile of a dark-haired, saucy girl, eyes bright, a slightly crooked smile that no amount of orthodontia could correct. "But how did you know that from this?"

Sarge stared him down. "Because she looks like her daddy."

Conor gulped and clutched the picture a little tighter. Words became a struggle. "You think?"

"Spittin' image, 'cept for the hair color. Must've gotten that from her mama. Besides that, she's you, through and through."

The weight in Conor's chest shifted slightly right. "She doesn't talk to me."

Sarge shrugged. "She's fifteen. Give her time."

"And Kim." Conor held up his oldest daughter's picture in his left hand. "She's the peacemaker, always trying to make things right. Help her mom, help me."

"Perfection's a tough act to follow."

Wise words. Conor nodded. "I hadn't thought of it that way."

"When we're too busy thinking of ourselves, we rarely do."

Conor straightened his shoulders. "I'm paid to think. It's hard to turn it off."

"Learn." Sarge took a last puff on his cigarette, gave the butt a longing glance, and tossed the filtered stub to the ground. "You're young and smart. Lots of money, lots of choices. Use 'em."

"That easy?"

"Nope." Sarge turned toward the water, waved his hand. "*That's* easy. Chicken's way out. Don't have to face nothin', let everyone else pick up the pieces." He eyed Conor's coat, his shoes, the hat and scarf. "Since money's not a problem, I think you're a pretty boy who's lookin' for the easy road, probably for the first time in his life."

The chest weight shifted again, hard and cumbersome. Conor didn't trust himself to speak.

Sarge moved a step closer. "Seein' as how you're a rich and powerful kind of guy, I don't know why you don't just change things up. Make amends."

"Amends?" Conor thought of all that happened the last few years and shook his head. "I wouldn't know where to begin."

"Sure you do." The old man reached out an ancient hand and touched the photos still clenched in Conor's fingers. "You start right there."

"With the girls?"

"Your girls." The old man let his fingers lay against the protective wrapping of the pictures. "Girls need their daddy."

Something in his voice gave Conor a clue. "You got kids, Sarge?"

The old man shook his head, his face hard, his breath harsh. "No." For a moment he faced outward, his speckled beard ruffled by the wind, then he swung back, his expression softer. "You start there and you don't stop until them girls know you love them more than anything in this world, Sonny. You got that?"

Something in his voice told Conor there was no choice. "Yes."

Sarge looked at his watch, frowned, tapped it, then frowned again.

Conor hiked up his sleeve and shrugged. "Two-twenty."

"You're it, then, most likely."

Conor frowned. "What 'it'?"

Sarge ignored the question. "Good thing, too, because I'm feeling a mite tired."

Conor stepped forward. "Can I take you somewhere? Help you?"

The old man shook his head. "You go home. In the morning call those girls. Figure out where you hid your sense of humor, dust the ratty thing off and put it to use."

"But—"

"Opportune phrase: Go home." Sarge gave him a clap on the back. "And if you think of it now and again, you might want to slip a few bucks to someone down on their luck. If you get a little heavy on cash flow, that is."

"Like a shelter."

"Huh." Sarge gave a snort. "You ever been to one of them, Sonny?"

Conor thought of his ridiculously affluent lifestyle and shook his head. "Can't say I have."

Sarge leaned in, a brow cast up, his expression all business. "Thought not. Word of advice, a little business aside that a bright, savvy guy like you can understand: Best to avoid the middleman. Go to the source. Diminishes the loss of discretionary income that way."

"Lose less at the upper levels thereby ensuring adequate finances for the intended outreach."

"You got it, Sonny. Pure Wall Street. Very poetic."

One thing Conor had never been called was poetic. He was pretty sure the Sarge knew that. He groped his pockets, wishing he'd brought a little cash with him, but found nothing. A guy didn't carry a lot of loose change into the water. What would be the point? "I'd like to give you something, Sarge. Something to help, but I didn't bring any money along." A sudden thought occurred to Conor. He started to loosen the buttons of his coat. "Here. Take this. It'll block the wind."

Sarge took a step back. He swept a cryptic glance to Conor's larger frame, then his own short stature, before eyeing the long Armani. "I show up at the rotunda wearin' that, they're gonna think I rolled somebody, on Christmas, no less. Don't do to mess with a good reputation, Sonny. A bright guy like you should know that." He raised both hands, palms out, as he backed away. "Don't need nothin' except you makin' peace with those girls, but I thank you."

"But where can I find you?" Desperate, Conor moved forward, frowning.

"I'm here, I'm there." The old man's gaze encompassed the bridge, his expression tight. "Mostly here."

"Third box on the right?" Conor tried to lighten the moment with humor.

The old man smiled, nodded, and tipped his cap. "With the white colonial mailbox, just past the broken street light after the second Baby Gap."

Conor twitched a smile, his heart giving a queer twist in his chest. "I'll be in touch."

The Sarge waved a hand. "You do that, Sonny."

The rich guy meant well, but he wouldn't be in touch. The old cop knew that like he knew people, most times. He moved deep within the shadows and waited, watching until the well-dressed jumper moved up, onto the approach and turned...

Sarge watched, waiting, holding his breath, muttering prayers that sounded more like commands. "Go left, Sonny. Left." He glared upward, his tone demanding. "You got any spare angels up there, you'd best get them onto this bridge and turn this guy toward home. I ain't got all night, you know. Got things to do."

As Conor wavered, Sarge studied him, hands fisted, his voice a whisper. "Stay off that bridge, Sonny, or I'm going to get really—"

Reaching up, adjusting his hat, Conor turned left, toward Manhattan, his footsteps assured.

Sarge nodded, narrowed his eyes, sent a glance to the dark heavens and turned, shuffling further into the gloom, suddenly tired.

CHAPTER ONE

Present day Princeton

"Mom!"

Alicia Bradstreet hung the last scherenschnitte snowflake in an upper pane of the bay window as her oldest daughter burst through the back door. "In here, Kim."

"Which here?" Kim's voice echoed as she strode through the house, her feet tapping in business rhythm.

"Sitting room 'here'," called back her mother, smiling.

"This place is a freakin' mansion," Kim complained for at least the fifth time that year. "No one could possibly need all this space. Why don't you sell it? Move on?"

"You mean move out." Alicia copped her daughter a knowing look, climbed off the dining room chair that doubled as an impromptu stepstool, and held open her arms. "Quit complaining and come here. I've missed you."

Kim returned the hug. "Me, too. They've kept me swamped at work and there's precious little time to just relax and be me. Christmas is such a mixed bag for the foundation. Altruism is at an all-time high, which is great, but the holidays have a way of showing poor people all they're missing. Makes for tough conflict. A lot of mixed emotions."

"You could come home on weekends," her mother reminded her. "Bring Brian along. And Grayce. Take a break."

"Then I'm away from work if they need me," Kim reasoned. "Poverty is not exactly a Monday thru Friday, nine-to-five kind of gig, especially this time of year. But Brian loves coming down here, hobnobbing with the old money and the *nouveau riche* wannabes."

"How much really gets done on Saturday and Sunday?" Alicia wondered. She slanted a look Kim's way.

Kim shrugged. "You'd be surprised." She slid her gaze to include the paper snowflakes. "I still love these things. We've had them forever, haven't we?"

Alicia stood back, eyed the hand-fashioned snowflakes she'd razor cut on an old maple bread board as a financially stricken new bride, then re-climbed the chair to drop one down a smidge. "At least forever, and don't get me wrong, Kim. I'm proud of the work you do with the homeless foundation."

"*Homeward Bound.*"

Alicia nodded. "I just want to be sure you allow time for life to unfold. You're young. Beautiful. A lot of living to do."

"You're kidding, right? With Brian and Grayce around, trust me, I'm living. Juggling, actually. I can't imagine how working mothers do all they do."

"Not all jobs require the hours you seem expected to put in," Alicia noted, not trying to hide the hinted disapproval. She'd lived with a workaholic New Yorker. She understood the city's lure better than most, and disliked it for more reasons than she cared to count, but one in particular stood out: Conor lived there.

She tucked the chair back in place and headed toward the kitchen. "Come on back here. Let me make you a flavored coffee. I've got the world's greatest blend..."

"Fair trade?"

"Wouldn't think of buying anything else, sweetheart. Me and Small World." Alicia crossed her fingers in a show of solidarity with the popular Princeton coffee shops. "We're sympatico."

Kim laughed. "Where's Addie? I thought she was due in yesterday."

Alicia crossed to the espresso machine, frowned and shrugged. "Went to New York to spend a little time with your father."

"Oh." Kim pulled up a stool in the expansive ivory kitchen, the old-school glass-fronted cabinetry harking timeless good taste. "Good. That'll be a nice surprise for him. I don't think he was expecting her."

"No." Alicia recognized the internal homicidal tendencies that surged whenever Conor was brought up. Thoughts of life in prison without artisan bread and coffee had held her in check so far or she'd have done him in a while back. Bare-handed, most likely. More satisfying that way. Getting a grip on her emotions, she glanced over her shoulder at Kim. "Addie had a great third semester and wanted to tell him personally."

"Ooooo." Kim gave a sage nod. "That will please him no end. I always figured she was a chip off the old block and her law school performance confirms it."

"Right." Alicia nodded, made a face and pursed her mouth as she ticked a list of Addie's attributes on her fingers. "Except she's nice, kind, honest, caring, sympathetic, empathetic and good to animals."

"Mom." Kim laughed out loud. "You know Dad's made substantial improvements over the years. Might want to cut him some slack."

"Great." Alicia threw her a look of encouragement. "Take out an ad, we'll post it in the 'Singles' column. Maybe he'll get lucky. *DWM, late-forties, filthy rich, indiscriminate in his taste for women, dishonest, mean-spirited workaholic, completely soulless. Ability to cheat on spouse as necessary. Send picture and resume to yaddi yaddi yadda, The Daily Princetonian."*

Kim perched one hip on the edge of the kitchen table and arched a brow. "Ouch. What brought all this up? I haven't heard you go off on Dad in years. And let me just add, it's been a nice break. From a kid's perspective, that is."

Alicia leaned over and slapped a folded sheet of paper in front of Kim. "Right there, Sugar-beans. Read it and weep. I did. And no, it's got absolutely nothing to do with your father. He's just an easy target."

The Zoning Board of Princeton Borough regrets to inform you that your application for restaurant zoning regarding the property at 101-105 Poole Street has been denied due to over-saturation of restaurant business in that specific locale. We thank you for your interest.

"But..." Kim eyed the form letter rejection, confused. "You want to open a book store."

"With coffee," added Alicia. "A Barnes and Noble type thing with legally addictive stimulants in the form of lattés, cappuccinos, frappes and, oh, yes, plain old coffee for the every day Joe who still calls Princeton home."

Kim swept the spacious stone home a look, her expression skeptical. "Not too many plain old Joe's around Princeton anymore, Mom."

Alicia couldn't disagree. Princeton wasn't exactly teeming with the every day middle class that populated most small towns. When a town boasts an Ivy League school that eats, drinks and breathes old money and Supper Clubs, the surroundings would be silly not to cater to that.

Nothing about Princeton, New Jersey was silly.

"Okay, you got me there. It's not like this," she splayed her hands to the side, indicating the house around her, "is the norm. This is the 'Dad has lots of money so Mom gets to live in high style since the divorce' syndrome."

"More normal than it should be these days." Kim drew a breath and picked up the rejection notice again. "I don't get this, though. What does coffee have to do with anything? Don't all bookshops offer coffee?"

Alicia scowled. "You're a child of a new millennium. In your lifetime, yes, most book shops have at least a coffee corner so that people can browse and lose themselves in the enticing scent of roasted beans, French vanilla and toasted hazelnut."

"So?" Kim frowned. "I'm still out of the loop."

"It wasn't always that way. A coffee shop was a coffee shop and a bookstore was a bookstore. The local zoning laws reflect that archaic reality."

"Seriously?"

Alicia nodded. "Once Starbucks coupled with Barnes and Noble, the idea caught on. Then every bookstore needed a coffee spot, big or small. To run the coffee side of the business, I had to apply for a restaurant permit from the town. That building is not slated for restaurant use, so I got a big, fat N-O."

"But that's ridiculous," argued Kim. The knot between her Morrissey eyebrows deepened, their dark line a contrast to the wheat-toned hair from Conor's side. "What's the big deal about serving coffee? Coffee's just..." she lifted a mug from the counter in salute, "coffee."

Her mother shook her head. "I don't think there is one. I think the big deal is that the University contracted for a humongous bookstore on Nassau Street to service students and staff with textbooks and pleasure reading. Guaranteed sales and proximity to campus. Therefore, I don't get to have one on Poole."

"But that's blocks away and a totally different clientele," argued Kim.

Her mother slapped a bottle of caramel syrup onto the counter next to a frothing wand. "Good girl. I knew that Bryn Mawr education would pay off in the long run."

"Oh, Mom." Kim's expression said she shared Alicia's disappointment. "I know how much you wanted to do this. And it would be such fun. Right up your alley. There's no other way? No other location?"

Alicia met Kim's gaze. "You know what retail space is like in this town."

"Non-existent."

"Pretty much. I could look out on Route 1, but that's not what I envisioned. I dreamed of a nice, neighborhood coffee shop-slash-bookstore where I could run library programs like I do now, and let people relax and unwind at the end of their day. Kid business during the week, adult customers at night and on weekends. Maybe even a seniors' group. That circular stairway arching into the upper level of the Poole Street property is perfect for this kind of thing. An ideal set-up. Seeing this," Alicia pointed to the letter on the antique oak table, "I assume they're going to say no to any location I might suggest. Carefully, of course."

"It's the kind of place grad students with families would eat up," Kim noted.

"The perfect demographic. I thought so too. Book clubs. And writers' groups. This area has all kinds of local writers from historians to sci fi and romance. A decent-sized book shop would be the perfect gathering spot for them with the ambiance of quiet culture."

"Any way to get them to budge?"

"You mean the Zoning Commission?" Alicia sent Kim a look that showed the unlikelihood of that possibility. "Not in this lifetime. The continuum of the town's grand plan is sacrosanct. No one messes with it. Like season tickets at a Penn State game, the plans are written in stone. You bequeathe them to your children when all is said and done."

Kim stared at her. "How on earth do you know anything about Penn State?"

Alicia turned back to the counter and foamed the heated milk/coffee/caramel combo. "Your father and I used to go."

Kim sank back into her chair. "Really?"

"When we were dating."

"Before Georgetown?"

"During." She gave a quick nod, carefully not mentioning that Kim was conceived after a really good game. Double overtime. The Nittany Lions won on a forty-nine yard field goal and clinched their division. Conor'd been beyond happy. Way beyond. Her cheeks flushed at the thought of that night, of the law student that soon became her husband and the child they shared as a result. Good night, all in all.

Then.

"It's hard to imagine you and Dad dating," Kim admitted. She gave a sniff of approval as her mother brought the hot drink to the table.

"Because most of what you remember isn't all that pleasant." Alicia set down the twin mugs, added whipped cream and a swish of caramel drizzle, then sat beside her daughter. "But we were happy then."

"So what ruined that?" Kim took a deep breath of the warm scents and settled back, her expression saying they needed to talk. "How do two people fall out of love? Was it because of Jonathan?"

Jonathan.

Alicia waited while her heart beat once. Twice. Three times. She usually avoided this topic at all costs. The pain of burying a small child, her only son, pierced on a regular basis despite the decade of time. He'd been a beautiful boy with Conor's eyes set in her face. Nice combination. "That was part of it. And your father's job. He was gone all the time with a whole separate life in New York. Eventually it became a life that didn't include us."

"But I remember he wanted us to come there," Kim mused. She took a sip of her drink, blew the heat from the foam, and sipped again. "For weekends and stuff. Before you split up."

Alicia shook her head. "That city is no place to raise two young, impressionable girls. I told him that, time and again, but he refused to listen." She didn't voice how hard it was to leave the church side graveyard, even for a weekend in New York. Who would tend Jon's grave? Trim the flowers? Bleach the spot of stubborn mildew that persisted on the stone's north side? No, those thoughts stayed buried. Tucked away. Safe. "Always so busy building business, eyeing the bottom line, making a name for himself."

"A skill he's very good at," remarked her daughter.

"But we got lost in the shuffle, honey." Alicia regarded her light-haired daughter and shrugged. "Listen, I'm glad you're getting along with your dad now, that's all well and good, but I'm not about to take the blame for his actions back then. He had a perfectly good family here in Princeton. He chose to wander. Not me."

Kim sat slightly forward, eyes down, as though weighing her next thought. "Did you ever think it might have been hard for him to come back here after the funeral? That maybe it felt better, staying away? Not facing that stone marker, week after week?"

"And I could no more abandon my time with that stone marker than with the boy himself, so I guess I don't understand those feelings."

"Mom." Kim paused and sighed. "I'm not trying to hurt you, I'm just trying to understand. Before Jon died were things okay? Were you happy?"

Alicia thought back and shrugged. "I wouldn't go straight to happy. We had good times and bad. Fairly normal."

"Did you ever want to have another baby? Try again?"

"To replace your brother?"

"No." Kim shook her head, the Morrissey brow wrinkled anew. "Not replace him, but just to bring joy back into your lives?"

"Well, honey, if nothing else, I've taught you the birds and the bees." Alicia gave her a frank look. "Your father would have had to come home now and again for that to happen, right?"

Kim squared her shoulders. "Or you could have gone there."

Alicia stood, her pride dented enough for one day. "He's done quite a number on you, Kimberly. Be sure to congratulate him for me."

"Mom."

Alicia raised a hand for quiet. "Enough. I don't mind talking to you about things, but I don't want to be blamed for choices I didn't make."

So. Kim didn't buy into her reasoning any longer. Not totally, anyway. When had she grown up so thoroughly, turned into this strong, stalwart, sensible woman?

"All I'm saying is that there are two sides to a story, and part of healing is seeing both sides. Giving them weight."

"So now you want me healed, huh?" Alicia angled Kim a look of exaggerated patience. "Will you psychoanalyze me forever, now that you have your degree, or can I come up for air from time to time? Draw a breath?"

Kim shook her head. "I'm not psycho-analyzing you, Mom, it's just that Brian and I are talking about the future, about our lives, and I..." Her voice tapered, her look frustrated.

Kim, run! Run now! Run for your life, my blessed girl!

Alicia bit down hard to fight the urge to warn her beautiful daughter away from the young financial wizard who appeared to have won her heart. She'd acted crazed enough for one day. Pulling her emotions into a nice, tight ball, she blew out a breath. "You don't want to make the same mistakes your father and I made."

"In a nutshell. I'm just wondering if there's some way to know if this is the real deal. If Brian and I have what it takes to make a go of things."

Alicia grasped Kim's hands. "Trust your heart, Kim."

"Like you did?"

Alicia frowned and pondered the durability of anti-wrinkle cream on a terrible, horrible, no good, very bad day. She felt like her forehead had been knit since the afternoon mail delivery. She gave Kim's hands a squeeze. "We loved each other then, Kim. What happened later..."

"Just happened."

"Yes."

"But—"

"Kim." Alicia faced her head on, her voice flat and direct, wishing she could soften her tone, knowing she couldn't. Something within snapped lean and raw whenever the subject of Conor and forever arose. "Love doesn't come with return policies, or money back guarantees. It comes packed with questions and problems, life and death, a Pandora's box, never knowing what might spring up next. It either lasts or it doesn't." She swung back to the counter, busying anxious hands by stowing away coffee clutter, something mundane and mindless to ease the inner ache, a pain she pretended didn't exist until something dredged it back up, unexpected and unsought. "Ours didn't."

CHAPTER TWO

Foster met Conor at the door, the quintessential butler's loyal service totally unnecessary at this late hour and unbelievably welcome after Conor's extended day of work and benefit appearances. He nodded toward the expansive living room as he accepted Conor's coat and hat. "Miss Adelaide, sir."

Addie? Today? Conor glared at his watch and frowned. "How long has she been here?"

"Since late afternoon."

"And you didn't call me?"

Foster inclined his chin, his appearance impeccable despite the hour, his gray hair in perfect array. "By her request, sir." He indicated the sofa with a slight nod. "A bit weary, I would say."

Conor remembered his second year of law school. The competition, the push, the reading, studying, learning at the feet of some of the greatest barristers of current times. He distinctly remembered being tired. A smile tugged his left cheek as he crossed to the spacious room sporting a must-see view of New York by night and Central Park by day.

"That you, Daddy?" The fatigue in Addie's voice took Conor back to a tumble-haired toddler clutching a pink satin blankie, huddled at the upper edge of the stairs, thumb in her mouth, waiting for her daddy to come home, then heading off to bed disappointed because business kept him in the city night after night. *Moron.*

"Yes." Conor bit back words of self-reproach for then and now. "Sorry, Ads. I didn't know you were here or I'd have come home earlier. And I'd have come in more quietly if I'd realized you were camped on the couch. Why didn't you call me? Let me know?"

"Figured you must be busy. You weren't exactly expecting me and I didn't want to interrupt your plans."

"Considerate."

"Or a total suck up." The admission made her twinkle up at him. "It *is* close to Christmas, after all."

Her honest response drew his grin. The light from the foyer backlit her answering smile, while the glow of the city brightened the broad-paned picture window across the room. She made a pretty profile sitting there, tired and mussed, the Big Apple framing her with its night-piercing incandescence. "Why are you on the couch, Ads?"

The pet name deepened her grin. "Had news. Wanted to tell you in person."

"Grades?"

She scowled. "I hate that you're always one step ahead of me."

"Then let me backtrack." Conor grinned and ruffled her already tangled hair because he knew she hated the maneuver. He cocked her a look of exaggerated surprise. "What kind of news do you have, Ads?"

She laughed and pushed herself up to pull him into a hug he relished. A hug that hadn't existed a few years ago. They'd climbed a lot of hurdles, he and Adelaide, step by step, none of them easy. "My grades are stellar."

"Nice adjective. SAT word. Define stellar."

She yawned, slipped her arm around his waist and pulled him back to the couch where she re-bundled under a hand-knit ivory Irish throw. "Enough so that the registrar sent me a congratulatory e-mail, reminding me to include the professor's accolades on my resume."

"Accolades for...?"

Addie straightened her shoulders, cleared her throat and offered her best imitation of Professor Duane Higgins' graveled voice, "For receiving the highest recorded grade in his Income Tax Law class."

Conor grinned. "Highest, Addie?" He couldn't even begin to pretend that her words didn't tweak his competitive spirit. His shoulders straightened with pride.

She nodded and smirked.

"Beat your old man, did you?"

"Marginally, but a win's a win."

Conor threw back his head and laughed. "Of course, I had a pregnant wife at home, so my attentions were split by necessity."

Addie matched his smile. "I would call that advantageous because I have to maintain myself, my apartment, my meals, my work and my laundry on my own, while dealing with the Washington Metro, or lack thereof. No wife."

"And no worries." Conor wrapped her in a hug, then tilted her chin up. "I'm proud of you, kid."

"And yet, you have no ice cream."

"None?" Conor frowned. Not like he was a big fan, but... "You checked?"

She nodded. "Must have been eating out a lot lately."

He had been, but still...he hated to think there was something she wanted and he couldn't provide it. He reached for the phone. "We'll order some."

"That's so New York." Addie stretched out a hand and slapped the disconnect button. "I can live without ice cream until tomorrow, Dad. Seriously."

He knew she could, but he wanted to celebrate her grades, her time, her inclusion of him in her life at long last. "But this is special."

She grinned. "It'll still be special tomorrow. We can hit Cold Stone as long as we can eat inside. They've got that pumpkin pie concoction I've been dying for."

Conor frowned. "Then why didn't you get one? It's not like D.C. isn't filled with overpriced restaurants, including ice cream parlors."

"Made myself wait. Had to do well. The thought of that ice cream became my reward."

An Alicia trait. Conor smiled, remembering when times were tough and money was tight, how Leash could stretch a dollar to an impossible length, and then reward herself when she stuck to a goal. Worthy attributes.

"Where's the tree?" Addie waved a hand to the big window.

Conor loosened his shirt, tie and whatever else might have constricted his neck for the last eighteen hours as he settled back. "Getting it tomorrow. Kim, Brian, and the Kid are coming over to decorate it."

"Awesome." A quick smile chased more of the sleepy expression from Addie's face. "I'll stay and help, then head out to Mom's on Sunday."

"Was she expecting you today?" Conor kept his voice carefully nonchalant. Talking about Leash at Christmas time always proved a tough go. "Since I wasn't?"

Addie laughed. "I called her and told her about my change in plans. Can't have her worrying about me on top of everything else."

Instant radar spike. "Else?" He gave his youngest daughter an elbow nudge. "Spill it, Ads. What's your mother got to worry about?"

Addie leveled him a considering look slated to do her well in courtrooms and boardrooms in the not too distant future. "To speak or not to speak, that is the question."

"Is she okay?" Conor tried to ebb his rising concern. "She's healthy? Unhurt?"

Addie shot him a look of appraisal, then shrugged. "She wants to leave the library, open her own bookstore and serve coffee and lattés to average Princetonians."

"Average Princetonian? An oxymoron if ever there was one." Conor arched a humorous brow as he weighed this tidbit of information. Leash wanting to start her own business? Broach the world at large? Get out of the library where she'd hidden herself behind towers of shelving for the last eight years? A good thing, all in all. "What's the problem?"

Addie frowned. "A lot of understandable legalese. Red tape. Finding the right location, then getting approval."

Approvals in Princeton were not an easy achievement. Like many old money towns, the locals worked to maintain the sanctity and atmosphere of a cherished lifestyle. Conor understood the advantages and disadvantages of the town's stand. New, fly-by-night businesses were carefully weeded out, keeping commercial and residential property values inflated, but occasionally good, sound enterprise got the wrecking ball as well.

But Alicia was tough, and she had a good lawyer. He'd recommended Bill Pearson himself when their marriage dissolved eight years ago. Funny. It didn't seem like it could possibly be that long, but...

Proof sat before him, in the form of a beautiful young woman who'd managed to nudge his income tax law score into a less notable second place. "I think old Higgins is getting soft," he teased, shifting the subject away from Alicia. "Enamored of a pretty face."

"And I think you got the shellacking you so richly deserved," his daughter shot back. "So. Tomorrow. We'll get ice cream, call it breakfast..."

Conor pushed aside the meteorologist's prediction of twenty-degree temperatures for the weekend.

"Drag the tree up here..."

Then he thanked God for the huge freight elevator that serviced his building from the rear.

"...pull out the decorations..."

"Foster can—"

"It's more fun if we do it ourselves," Addie insisted. "Part of the process."

"I see."

"Then we decorate."

Conor nodded, grinned, stood and reached out a hand. "By that time Kim, Brian and the Kid will be here."

Addie slipped her fingers into his and let him tug her upright before dropping her head to his chest. "I think her name's Grayce."

Conor laughed as he walked Addie toward her room. "She likes it when I call her the Kid."

"I know." Addie shook her head and slanted a gaze up to him. "You've gotten better with kids over the years."

"Taking more time," he admitted, wishing he'd been smart enough to see that option two decades back. Still, he believed things happen for a reason. Acting downright stupid while still considered one of the most informed experts on mergers and acquisitions law was obviously part of some eternal plan. "So." He leaned down and planted a kiss to the top of her head. "You sure that waiting for the ice cream is okay?"

She smiled, "Yes, but I'm glad you understood how much it mattered."

He gave her a crooked smile and a half nod. "You've got a date."

She reached up and gave him another hug. "Love you, Dad. Good night."

His heart swelled. Not too many Christmases ago he'd envisioned a different path for his life. A final path, cold, wet and decidedly uncomfortable. For the short run, anyway, until his options disappeared in a watery grave.

This was definitely a better choice.

As he moved around the corner to his room, he considered Addie's actions and smiled. She'd come here, to New York, to spend time with him. Share her achievements. She could have gone to her mother's in Princeton and called him on the phone, but she didn't. He didn't say 'home' when he referred to Alicia's house. Way too arbitrary. His penthouse was just as much their home as the sprawling salt-box in Princeton.

Funny. He hated that multi-million dollar stone house now as much as he'd admired it twelve years ago. Then it had been a status symbol, an expression of immense wealth, subtle and complete. The gray stone extended Cape Cod screamed success in old money style, not new money crass, and he'd loved that step up.

Why Alicia kept it he had no idea, but her ties to the overpriced piece of real estate must run deep. Deeper than his, anyway.

He refused to think of little Jon in that house. No. He liked to remember his son when he first crawled and toddled around the old brick colonial they'd shared as a family in a less exclusive section of Princeton. Before time ran out for a four-year-old boy and life as Conor knew it came to a sudden, screeching halt while the man who had everything buried his beautiful baby boy.

He sucked in a deep breath and refused to dwell on the loss. He'd done that for years and the downward spiral had nearly killed him. If it hadn't been for a wise, old derelict...

Now Conor put Jon's heart and smile in every task he undertook, every board he chaired, every helpful goal he set. The boy's life took on deepened import through his father's selfless actions. That was good. Solid. Meaningful.

If he'd learned the lesson a few years earlier, he might still have a wife. A place to call home, a recliner that fit his back just right on snowy Sunday afternoons when the Giants played away, and the girls would laugh and squabble and life would be normal. More normal, anyway.

Because he'd still have Alicia.

CHAPTER THREE

"Bill, I know it's almost Christmas. I've got the oh-so-festive lights to prove it," Alicia retorted, irked by the lawyer's offhand manner the following day. "What I don't have is a building for my proposed bookstore. What can we do about this rejection?"

"Not much, I'm afraid," Bill Pearson replied. "Alicia, you've lived here a long time. You know the score. The board doesn't shift right or left and they barely move forward at all."

"Bookstores aren't exactly New Wave." The words came out harsher than she intended. She caught herself, drew a breath and counted to ten, reminding herself this wasn't Bill's fault. "I'm not mad at you, Bill."

His tone stayed deferential, most likely because he occasionally golfed with Conor, weather permitting. "I know that."

"It's just—" She let her voice drift as she gathered her thoughts. "I need to do this," she explained, staring out her back window to the cottage barn that held two splendid horses in their just-right, white-fenced setting, quite prestigious New England. She gripped the phone tighter. "I need to get out of the library. Spread my wings. Try something new."

God bless Bill, he didn't note the irony of 'new' being a bookstore for a burned out librarian. "Let me scout things out, Alicia, but I can't promise much before the holidays. There are no meetings scheduled until after the first of the year."

The intensity of her disappointment surprised Alicia. *Buck up,* she scolded herself. *Get some backbone, for heaven's sake. You buried a child and lost a husband. This is nothing, Cupcake. A walk in the park.*

Only the rejection didn't feel like a walk in the park, and she had no idea why. "All right, Bill. I know you'll do your best. You always do." But Bill's best wouldn't stand a chance against the immovable town board. Maybe that's why the put-off bit so deep. "In the meantime, I'll look for different sites. Sandy McGovern's doing some clandestine checking."

Bill laughed. "Half the deals in this town are done word of mouth. Sandy's a good one to run interference for you. If there's something coming available, Sandy's the go-to girl in Princeton.

"You have a Merry Christmas, Alicia," he continued. "Enjoy those daughters of yours."

Sage advice. She nodded, took a step toward the impeccable kitchen counter and pushed frustration aside. "I will. Thanks, Bill."

"No thanks needed. Just doing my job."

As Alicia moved to put away Christmas groceries, the phone rang again. She glanced at the read-out, smiled and grabbed up the receiver. "Hello, Sandy."

"I'm positively, absolutely, thoroughly ticked off about this message I got from you," spouted the thirty-something Realtor. "If this weren't a professional call, I'd be using language that would make my mama blush to the roots of her expensive dye job, throw things around the office, and spew every bit of dirt I know about each and every member of the Board."

"Really?" Having Sandy's chutzpah on her side felt good. "Anything we can use?"

Sandy sighed, loud and long. "Not a thing. They're all as clean as the driven snow. So Princeton. Just our luck."

"Well at least you're not spouting euphemisms about how it wasn't meant to be and all that other schlock people embrace when the situation gets wrenched out of their hands."

Sandy laughed. "I know better than to pull that with you. You'd toss me out on my ear in a heartbeat. It pays to know your clients, Alicia, then find them the perfect match. There's no big secret in real estate, it's like a pre-schooler playing Memory. Match 'em up, close 'em out, move 'em on. Wanna get coffee?"

Alicia eyed the groceries strewn around the kitchen. "In half an hour? Maybe forty-five minutes?"

"Forty-five's good. We can drown our sorrows in expensive cappuccino with double espresso and caramel drenched froth, plot the demise of the zoning commission and anyone else who stands in our way, then discuss alternative possibilities."

"Are there any? For real?"

Sandy's voice stayed upbeat. "Honey, there are always possibilities. For the right price. An extra zero or two might not affect the global economy, but it bears significant impact in our little neck of the woods."

"Money talks," Alicia translated.

"In every language, Sistah!" Sandy riffled some papers, murmured something to her assistant, then brought her attention back to Alicia. "It's a good thing we're friends and business associates. I can't exactly talk like this to my other clients. They would neither understand nor appreciate my humor."

"Imagine that." Alicia turned, tripped over a bag she'd left in the middle of the floor, stubbed her toe, and shouted something unladylike and massively inappropriate while trying to grab her sore foot and keep hold of the phone.

"Alicia, you okay? Need an ambulance? A really cute stud-muffin doctor? Maybe we can find a McDreamy look-alike in the E.R."

"Not funny. I could be dying here."

"Naw, you're yelling too loud to be terminal. See you in... forty minutes now. Bandage yourself up and head to Small World. I'm buying."

The click of her receiver cut short any comment Alicia might have made if she were quick enough to respond in Sandy's rapid fire manner. That, however, had never been her gift. If it had, she'd have had some wonderful, memorable, snappy one-liners to loft Conor's way when he left their home, their bed, their family and the stupid horses to carouse in New York City with a brilliant young lawyer from an opposing firm. Total conflict of interest. So "Desperate Housewives". Blah, blah, blah...

The toe throb slowed to a steady drub. Alicia gave her foot one last rub and pushed thoughts of Conor aside in favor of organized cupboards. One mattered and one didn't. End of story.

"I love this tree."

Conor grimaced as he and Foster worked to get the over-priced ten-foot blue spruce into the holder. "There are people who do this for money, you know," he noted out loud. "Trained professionals."

"Only in New York can one or should one find a person who designates themselves as a trained professional tree-stander-upper," Addie retorted with a grin.

"I believe the accepted term is "Holiday Organizer", Miss." The gentility of Foster's low tone remained level as his employer worked to settle the tree's trunk into the water basin holder.

"So P.C.," Addie noted, a brow hiked in appreciation. "Well done, Foster."

"I do my best, Miss."

She laughed. "I love coming to visit you guys. You're such... men."

Conor and Foster exchanged puzzled looks. Conor spoke first. "Thank you?"

Addie grinned down at him as she nudged the upper part of the tree a little left, then stepped back to make sure the whole thing stood centered in the sprawling window. "It was definitely a compliment. Guys are fun."

"And you're only just now finding this out?" Kim's voice rang from the foyer. "Ads, you might be book smart, darling, but you're more than a tad slow in gender studies."

Addie met Kim halfway across the room, grabbed her in a hug and spun her about before peeking over her shoulder. "Where are Brian and Grayce?"

"They'll be here in a few minutes," Kim explained as she shrugged off her coat and hat. She tossed them onto the nearest chair and nodded toward the street. "They wanted to play in the park first."

"Is she dressed warm enough?"

Addie and Kim exchanged grins at Conor's concern. Kim nodded. "I do believe she's wearing a delightful coat, hat and scarf set from Saks that mysteriously found its way to Brian's door earlier this week."

Conor winked her way. "Saw it during a whirlwind shopping trip with Sarge. Was the size okay?"

"Perfect. A touch big. Just enough so she'll still be able to wear it on cold days in April."

Kim stepped closer, smooth and serene, not unlike a cat stalking a kill. Conor kept his attention firmly on the tree.

"So." Kim touched the massive and bristly blue spruce and eyed her father. "You and Sarge went shopping? Together?"

"We did."

"For?"

Conor raised his brows in mock-surprise. "You want me to tell you and ruin the surprise?"

"You guys went shopping for me?"

He shrugged. "Not exactly. I'd already done your stuff."

"Hmmm..."

"Kim, you know you'll get nothing out of him," Addie offered from the side. "He stonewalls us like he did Mainichi Global, and nobody does it better."

"Mainichi deserved everything they got," Conor replied, remembering the generous and silent out-of-court settlement. His share and the resultant bonus became the cornerstone for his latest apartment development scheme in Queens. Once refurbishing was complete and the safety and fire inspections done, they'd have new housing for nearly three hundred current homeless, subsidized by grants from both the state and federal governments. In New York City, a little seed money went a long way toward improvement, especially these days. "And then some."

Addie stepped back, eyed the tree, then spun toward the door as Brian and Grayce let themselves in. "Hey, guys! Merry Christmas, Graycie!"

Grayce flew across the room to tackle into Addie, coat and all, her mop of fair curls fighting the constraints of the fringed, blue hat.

Their freedom of expression warmed the corner of Conor's heart that tended toward winter chill on cold, dark nights. The love he'd lost and refound. Some of it, at least. He shoved thoughts of Princeton and Alicia aside, always rougher at Christmas, stepped back from the tree and held open his arms. "Hey. What about me?"

Grayce launched herself at him. Conor swept her up, kissed her, noted that the mingled blues of the hat and coat directly reflected her eyes like he expected they would, and gave her a quizzical look. "So. Where are they, Kid?"

Grayce leaned away and studied his chest, her little mouth twisted in puzzlement, her forehead wrinkled. She seemed to weigh possibilities, then gave a quick nod. "Pants' pocket."

Conner met her gaze. "Right or left?"

She mulled that. "Right. If they were in the left one, I'd be kicking them with my toe."

Too late Conor realized that her right foot was pressed against his left pocket. He laughed into her crinkled-up eyes, withdrew the sack of sugared nuts, and handed them to her with a pleased nod. "Good thinking, Kid. So." He held her high in the air to study the spruce, her sack of peanuts from the nearby street vendor snugged in miniature hands. "What do you think?"

"It's real?" Eyes wide, she reached out a curious finger to the stiff, somewhat unfriendly spruce needles.

"And prickly." Conor gave her a look of dismay. "It was so beautiful that I didn't think about how it would prickle our fingers while we decorate the branches."

"We'll be okay." Grayce made the announcement with such conviction that Conor felt reassured. "We're tough."

"The lights, sir?"

Addie grabbed Kim by one hand and Brian by the other. "You relax a minute, Foster. We'll get them."

Conor watched their retreating backs move down the hall and eyed Grayce. "Did you want to go with them or stay here with an old man?"

She cuddled in. "I like being with you."

Conor's heart turned to mush. He held her closer, his head on hers. "I like being with you, too, Kid." He held her like that, quiet and snug, then raised his head. "You thirsty? Hungry? Want some hot chocolate?"

"Do you have mini-marshmallows?"

Conor had no idea. He raised his gaze to Foster, saw his nod. "I guess we do."

"They're my favorite next to mini-marshmallows and whipped cream."

"Together?"

She nodded. "When we go to Princeton, 'Licia always gives me minis and whipped cream. She says it's what little girls like."

'Licia, huh? Conor smiled, liking the sound of the unintentional nickname. "Well, 'Licia knows a lot about little girls. And other stuff."

Grayce nodded. "She takes me to the library sometimes and shows me where she works." She loosened her coat once Conor set her down and handed the blue and white jacket to Foster with a grave look of understanding. "There are so many books there. 'Licia likes books."

Because she can get lost in them, Conor thought to himself. Great hiding place. Safe. Secure. Silent. Out loud he said, "Licia studied about books in school. About writing books, taking care of books, all the different kinds of books. She's loved them since she was a little girl like you."

"How do you know that?" Grayce eyed him with a look of wonder.

"Because we used to be married," Conor explained, ignoring the stab of pain that still muttered 'Gotcha!' whenever the subject of forever came up. "That's when we had Kim and Addie."

"You lived with 'Licia?" Grayce's expression said she was working to align bits of information in an orderly fashion and came up short.

"I did." He led Grayce into the state-of-the-art kitchen that represented Foster's domain. "There was 'Licia, me, Kim and Addie."

"And Jon." She blindsided Conor with her matter-of-fact tone.

"Who told you about Jon?" He knelt down to her level, wondering how much a six-year-old should hear.

"'Licia and Kim."

Conor heaved a quick breath, uncertain.

Grayce patted his cheek. "I feel really bad sometimes, 'cause my mommy went away too. I wanted her to come back and read to me, to be my mommy forever, but she didn't want to." She lifted tiny shoulders in a way-too-casual shrug belied by the shadowed look in her young eyes. "Sometimes people just go away."

"Oh, baby." Conor lifted her into his arms, feeling her childlike strength and empathy, her honey blonde curls wisping his cheek. "Mommies and daddies don't always do the right thing."

"But they should." Grayce leaned back, her face set in six-year-old sensibilities. "Because they're mommies and daddies."

"I'm afraid there's no argument for that, sir." Foster sent Conor a look tinged with pathos and amusement. "The child understands the rights of hierarchy."

"And probably the demands of a democratic government on a free-enterprise system," Conor shot back. He held Grayce slightly away. "What do you think about the rising price of OPEC oil, Kid?"

"I think alternative fuel sources would benefit all of us in both the long and the short run."

Conor touched his forehead to hers, proud. "You remembered that perfectly. Make sure you say it just that way in front of your father, okay?"

"Actually, Daddy and I talk about the oil crisis," she explained, her brows hiked.

"You do?"

She nodded. "Oh, yes. We think hybrids are the wave of the future."

Conor laughed out loud. "Your father put you up to that, didn't he?"

"Better than owning a parrot, sir," came Brian's voice from the kitchen entry, "and way more cuddly."

Conor clapped him on the back. "You're okay, Brian. For a guy who's dating my daughter."

"About that?"

The look of calm expectation on Brian's face gave Conor a head's up. "Yes?"

"May I have a moment? Alone?"

"Sure." Conor settled Grayce onto one of the spinning stools at the counter and motioned his way down the hall while Foster and Grayce floated a mountain of mini-marshmallows on her mug of hot chocolate. Conor stepped into his office, waved Brian into a chair, then pulled one up alongside him. "I expect I know what this is about."

Brian nodded. "I expect you do, sir. I don't think I hide my feelings for Kim very well."

"You telegraph them like a third-string quarterback, but that's okay." Conor nodded. "Women like to know they're loved."

Brian eyed him, his look not nearly as relaxed as it should have been which meant something was amiss. "I want to marry your daughter. With your blessing, of course."

"Because of my checkbook?"

"Well, there's that." Brian grinned, his face relaxing at the joke. "Okay, sir, mostly that. Who wouldn't want access to your checkbook? The good looking girl with a heart of gold is just frosting on the cake."

"What's troubling you, Brian?" Conor sat back and surveyed the young man's actions, his body language. Nervous and... guilty. So not comforting.

Great.

"Grayce's mother."

Oh, yes. The forbidden subject. Amazing how thoughts of marriage and forever ferreted out the best-kept family secrets. Why did Conor suspect that nothing he was about to hear would be good? He cringed inside but kept his face calm, a maneuver perfected by years of closed-door litigation. "What about her?"

Brian studied his hands, eyes down. "She's a hooker, sir."

That was about the last thing Conor expected the upright young financial analyst to say. "You slept with a hooker? And had Grayce?"

"No." Brian clasped his hands in his lap, worked his jaw and frowned. "Chloe was an aspiring actress and dancer when we met, working for her big break. She did some off-Broadway and waited tables in the theater district, hoping to be discovered. Beautiful girl, and a pretty solid actress, too, from what I saw. I thought she was real good, actually. Then we discovered she was pregnant, and life took a downward spiral for her. She got depressed, didn't want to work, couldn't wait to have the baby and move on with her life. Once Grayce was born, Chloe started back to work. We put Grayce into a good daycare, but Chloe's hours and mine made it nearly impossible to see the baby. We were both always gone. Grayce practically lived at the daycare, with no one but babysitters to read to her, talk to her, see her walk, watch her roll over and crawl."

From the look on Brian's face, Conor knew he didn't have to tell the young man how absolutely, positively stupid he'd been. It was a lot like looking in a two-decades-old mirror. Brian's profession was not unlike his in the early stages. Gone, morning, noon and night, working your way up the corporate ladder of success, hoping for a great resume and an out-of-this-world December bonus. He saw a lot of himself in the young man before him. "And?"

"We fought about it. Chloe wanted her career, I wanted mine because I thought my Harvard degree and my mushrooming financial district income gave us more stability than her waitressing job between two-bit gigs."

Yup. That ideology brought back a memory or two as well. Hadn't he back-burnered Alicia's plans and goals in much the same fashion because of Kim's untimely arrival? He'd had already been recruited by the financial district while in his second year at Georgetown. He forgot to think what might matter to her, that Leash might have had dreams of her own that weren't totally relegated to child rearing and housework. *Good going, Bozo. Mistake number one.* "I can see how that would be a bone of contention."

"And then some." Brian flexed his jaw again, sat back and looked Conor in the eye. "She filed for divorce before Grayce was six months old, got hooked on the party circuit, then addicted to coke, and decided using her body to attract a decent income was a better livelihood than waiting tables. She's part of one of those high-class brothels on the Upper West Side that everyone likes to ignore."

"Does she see Grayce?"

Brian shook his head. "Never. Has never asked to see her, has never expressed interest in seeing her."

"But Grayce misses her." Conor thought of his conversation with the precocious girl in the kitchen. "She told me so."

"Grayce misses the idea of her," Brian corrected. "She has no real memory of Chloe and only wishes for a mother because everyone else in school has one."

"Understandable." Conor sent the younger man a frank look. "They are handy things to have around for special occasions like Mother's Day, mother/daughter banquets, discussions on puberty and sex. You know. The usual."

"Soon she'll have Kim." Brian sounded perfectly content that Grayce's biological mother would remain a non-entity, but Conor had witnessed the resignation in the little girl's earlier statement. Tough to sell a kid on why their mother abandoned them at six months old.

So sad. Conor dropped his head to his hands, thinking. "And you're worried that when she finds out you're engaged to my daughter, Chloe will come crawling out of the woodwork looking for money and connections?"

Brian's sigh of relief told Conor he'd hit the nail on the head. "Yes, sir. Chloe loves money and freedom. We don't communicate because I didn't want Grayce exposed to her mother's lifestyle. Somehow cocaine and stray men aren't the weekend life experience I envision for my daughter."

"I can understand that."

"But Chloe might jump at the chance to make trouble. Blackmail. Coercion."

"Does she have something on you?" Conor studied the young man closely and was relieved by the answer he got.

"No, sir. There's nothing except the embarrassment she could cause me, us," Brian waved a hand toward Conor, then around, indicating the apartment, "by coming out of the closet."

"What last name does she go by?"

Brian sat up straighter. "Chloe Michelle Martin."

"And her address?"

Brian gave it, then leaned forward, his brows furrowed. "Sir?"

"Yes?"

"You aren't going to like..." Brian frowned, his eyes dark, "Kill her or something?"

Conor nearly choked. "What?"

"Well, I—" Brian sputtered, paused, swiped a hand to his forehead, took a breath and straightened his shoulders. "Not that I think you would, sir..."

"I should say not." Conor stood, chin up, shoulders back. "I never do the actual killing myself. Too messy."

Brian paled, then went slightly green. Conor slapped him on the back, then faced him. "Listen, Brian, here's a couple of things you need to know about me. Yeah, I'm rich. Big deal. I'm a rich man who lost his wife by cheating on her after we buried our child, so I'm no father of the year material myself, but I live the straight and narrow now. Clean. Nice. No bodies. None. Zip. Zilch. Nada."

Brian's audible sigh of relief eased his pasty expression. "You had me going there for a moment."

"Meant to. It was fun, actually. As for Chloe, our best defense is a good offense. Instead of letting her crawl out of the closet, we'll invite her out."

"Sir?" Brian's expression said he hoped Conor knew what he was doing. Frankly, so did Conor.

"The firm has contacts who could offer Chloe a hand in a very different direction. Proffer her something other than turning tricks with stupid rich New York businessmen and the occasional foreign dignitary."

"You're familiar with the clientele?"

Conor punched him in the arm. "Son, you live in New York long enough, it pays to be familiar with everything. Familiar doesn't equate with partake."

"I understand, sir."

"I expect you do. As for you and my daughter, you have my blessing. I see you as a necessary accoutrement to gain Graycie as my granddaughter, so you're in."

Brian shook his hand. "If there's anything I can do about the Chloe situation..."

"Be completely honest with my daughter. No surprises."

Brian nodded. "She knows the whole thing, sir. Loves me anyway."

Conor clapped a hand on Brian's shoulder. "No accounting for taste. Let's go see how Foster and the girls have made out with the lights for that tree."

"Addie grabbed the old fashioned ones, said they reminded her of the trees you had when they were little."

A flashback of the quaint brick colonial flooded Conor's brain. The girls in footed pajamas, the tree, full and bright, Jon crawling amidst the wreckage of

Fisher-Price, Playskool, Barbie dolls and wrapping slung every which way.

He couldn't remember what he got Alicia that Christmas. Probably something he ordered over the phone from Tiffany's, picked up wrapped, and never saw until she opened it on Christmas morning.

What a complete, unmitigated scumbag of a husband he'd been. Fawning her off with presents, putting her off with work constraints, conveniently forgetting how deliciously satisfying life had been when money was scarce and pasta loomed like white rice in Asia. Cherry blossom days and wife-filled nights. Afternoons studying at the National zoo, Kim sound asleep in her jungle print stroller, Alicia curled up against him in the grass.

He was a moron, total and unequivocal.

"Sir?"

Conor turned, startled. "Yes?"

Brian eyed him, then shrugged. "I appreciate your help. And your understanding."

"We're too much alike for me to be anything less," Conor told him as they approached the living room. "But you're going to learn your lessons way earlier than I did."

"How's that, sir?"

"'Cause I'll see to it, son." He gave Brian's shoulder a quick squeeze. "And I always keep my promises."

Brian gave him a look that had Mississippi hound dog written all over it. "Sounds wonderful, sir."

CHAPTER FOUR

"Dad!!! Where are you? Pick up the phone, already!"

Kim's voice-mail desperation had Conor hitting his speed dial with awkward fingers on Christmas afternoon. Why had he turned the stupid thing off in the first place?

Okay, he knew why, so he could spend some peaceful time with Sarge. The old guy liked things quiet. Unpretentious. Conor understood that, and the reasoning behind the request, respected it even, but why now? Why this? Not being able to pick up Kim's urgent Christmas morning call put him in the first-class jerk column, big time.

"Dad." Impatience and expectation peppered the single word exclamation when she picked up his call.

"What's up, what's happened? Is the Kid okay? Are you okay? What's wrong?"

"Nothing's wrong, but where were you this morning? It's Christmas!"

Picturing Sarge's request for quiet after the early morning church service, Conor started to answer, but Kim left no leeway.

"Oh, it doesn't matter because you're there now and everything is so, so right! I'm engaged." She stuttered, stopped, laughed and corrected herself. "*We're* engaged. Brian asked me this morning in front of everybody and I said yes. We've got a wedding to plan!"

Conor breathed a huge sigh of relief that Kim's rampant exclamations were of a positive variety, sent Foster a silent 'all's well' look, nodded and peeled off his coat, then handed it to the devoted houseman. "That's wonderful, honey. Congratulations."

"Oh, I know you knew all about it." Kim gushed and Kim never gushed about anything, ever, but at this point in time, gush was the word of the day. "Brian told me he checked with you first because he wanted to stay on the right side of the checkbook."

Conor smiled. "Smart boy. He's going places. Probably with my money."

"And we're ever grateful, sir." Brian's voice came through. "Kim put us on speaker so we could both talk."

"And the Kid?"

"How does the term 'Grandpa' sound?"

"Better than wonderful. Put her on. She's the primary reason I said yes in the first place."

Conor heard some shuffling and murmured voices, then Grayce hailed him from New Jersey. "I get to call you Grandpa. Is that okay? Do you want to be my Grandpa?"

Conor laughed. "It's way okay. And I'll make you hot chocolate just like 'Licia does, and we can go to the park and act silly and pretend we're animals in the zoo trying to get out of our cages."

"I love going to the zoo with you," Grayce exclaimed. "You walk like the best penguin ever, and you make really good monkey sounds."

"My job offers me lots of practice," Conor quipped with humor slightly above the six-year-old's level. He pictured her there, in Alicia's great room, the sprawl of Christmas surrounding the child, the hope and cheer in her voice a blessing of the season. "Hey, listen, I'll let you go back to your new Grandma and Aunt Addie, but I want you to know that I'm real happy to be your Grandpa. Super happy."

"Super Duper happy with sprinkles and nuts and chocolate sauce?"

"Double sprinkles, nuts and chocolate sauce with a cherry on top."

"Triple sprinkles, nuts and chocolate stuff with a cherry on top and lots of whipped cream?"

The joy in Grayce's voice shifted Conor's heart upwards in Grinch-growing fashion, a good thing. "You got it, Kid."

Grayce's voice came through once more. "I love you."

Conor held the phone closer. Tighter. "I love you, too, honey. Merry Christmas."

Kim got back on the line. "So, Dad, we'll be up there tomorrow to celebrate with you, okay?"

Conor eyed the presents beneath the tree, unopened and undisturbed in his quiet, empty, upscale Manhattan apartment and worked to avoid the comparison with Alicia's fun-filled home this Christmas day. "I'm looking forward to it. Love you all. I'll see you tomorrow. And congratulations again."

Her voice went soft and mushy. Total girl. Total not Kim, his quiet, focused, earnest, plan-ahead daughter. "Thank you, Daddy."

Her words made him feel a little mushy himself. Maybe it wasn't a total girl thing. Maybe it was just a love thing. He drew a breath and leaned back in his chair. "You're welcome, Kimber."

"You're up?" Conor glanced at his watch, arched a brow and sent Addie a look of surprise two mornings later. "I didn't figure I'd see you 'til tonight."

Addie stifled a yawn, tugged her robe more snugly around the middle and shook her head. "I wanted to say good-bye before you went to work."

Conor sent her a teasing grin. "While I appreciate the thought, I do manage to get to work on my own most days."

Foster cleared his throat as he filled Addie's favorite mug, the sound mild yet quite deliberate.

"On my own with Foster's help," Conor corrected himself.

"Thank you, sir." Foster noted the exception with his practiced countenance, calm and serene, his dry humor Dickens-friendly. He handed Addie her mug and a small pitcher of vanilla cream before disappearing into the pantry.

"But it's Christmas time so I wanted today to be special." Addie leaned in, breathed deep, smiled and added, "I love my new coat, by the way. Have I mentioned that often enough?"

"Not going to have me arrested or harangued for buying something made of fur-trimmed leather?"

"Are you kidding? The thing is gorgeous and total fun. And it'll keep me warm when I hit the Metro."

"D.C. has cabs," he reminded her, thinking of how open and exposed the Washington Metro could be, then felt ashamed at his snobbishness. Protecting daughters in big city venues was no easy task, nothing to be taken lightly, but from the look on Addie's face, he'd keep that to himself.

"Too surreal, Dad. Please. I like the Metro. Makes me feel normal. And the coat is perfect. It looks great on me, and it is, after all, all about the look, right?" She sparkled up at him, teasing, her grin a reflection of his.

Conor laughed. "I can't disagree, but don't let any of your more liberal professors hear you say that. They'll drop your grade."

"Do you realize how true that is?" Addie wondered out loud.

Foster re-appeared. He nodded to the several small, white boxes he carried. "I've got fresh baked goods from Sweet Things."

"You're serious?" Addie eyed the boxes like an anorexic runway model. "Foster, I love you thiiiis much."

He smiled, slit the string and lifted the lid. "Your father ordered them delivered today with you and your sister in mind."

"Awesome, Dad."

Conor sipped his coffee, thought hard, and decided to dive in with his question of the hour since Addie was awake and cognizant. "So. How was Christmas? How's your mother? Everything okay?"

The look Addie shot him said something to the effect of 'call her yourself and find out', but she kept that fairly obvious opinion quiet with no small amount of effort, probably fearing he'd send the pastries back. "She's good. A little riled over this bookstore thing, but nothing she can't handle."

"Mr. Pearson's overseeing things for her?"

Addie nodded, sent Foster a smile as she wrapped one set of fingers around the handle of her thick, ironstone mug, while the other accepted a flaky French pastry stuffed with cheese and pineapple. Addie waved the sweet into the air, took a deep whiff of the cheesy/buttery essence and smiled. "You spoil me."

"Only because you're smart. If you messed up law school, I'd be serving corn flakes. Generic ones." Conor stepped closer, sat in the chair next to her and cocked a brow once more. "Your mother?"

Addie nodded, back on task. "Ah, yes. Mr. Pearson is helping but he doesn't see much hope because the town board is set in their ways. Sandy McGovern is checking out other possible sites, but Mom really likes this one."

"And where is this one, exactly?"

"Poole Street, just around the corner from Nassau, near the church."

Not far from their first house in Princeton, and their only real home. Teaberry Street had been his very own *Primrose Lane*, with the small park at the end, the peace and quiet of being several blocks removed from the hustle and bustle of the esteemed university and Nassau Street. Close to everything, including the train, but nestled on a quiet road reminiscent of a New England village. Oh, Princeton knew how to do it, all right, and they'd be foolish to allow rampant growth to interfere with the value-enhancing ambiance the town enjoyed.

Despite that, he couldn't imagine why a bookstore on Poole, near Nassau, would pose a problem. He made a note to call Bill Pearson himself and investigate the problem. Between the two of them, they might be able to lawyer Alicia's way into her shop without too much fuss and nonsense.

He noticed Addie's raised awareness, her brain working overtime. Time to change subjects and appear disinterested.

"You should call Mom." Addie advised, her pastry untouched. "Talk to her yourself."

Oops. Too late. Conor stood. "Call me crazy, but I'm willing to bet that wouldn't rank in the top ten list of things Alicia Bradstreet would love to have happen today."

Addie kept her gaze level, firm and trained on him.

Conor twitched his jaw. Shook his head. Despite some major leaps forward in the past eight years, invading Alicia's domain was the one venue he avoided. Guilt? Remorse? Shame?

Descriptive word of choice aside, the idea of allowing his betrayed ex-wife a normal life, unfettered by unwanted contact with him, took precedence over his odd mix of feelings. Some would call the enforced distance childish. Conor preferred to think of it as life-affirming. He left her alone and she didn't try to kill or maim him. Sensible, all around. To Addie, he tilted a look of acceptance. "She likes her life the way it is."

"And you know this because...?"

He grinned, tweaked her hair and grabbed his coat. "Because I'm not afraid to muscle you girls for information."

Addie's look softened. She reached a hand to his arm. "You think we don't know how much you do for her? Unseen? Unheard? Unappreciated?"

While he appreciated Addie's loyalty, Conor saw a very different side of himself where Alicia was concerned. As her husband he'd substituted money for time, stature for presence, and ambition for faith. Not exactly what he'd promised in those wedding vows, spoken in that old Cleveland church where stained glass windows soothed in muted pastel wonder, not a primary color in sight. Pretty. Restful. Peaceful.

Naw. Addie'd been too young to fully understand the trade-offs he made in the name of money and acclaim, but he loved that she'd allowed him a second chance to be the father he should have been all along. "Not enough to make up for what I've done in the past, Sweetheart. And lets just keep those things between us, okay? I'm not even going to ask how you ferret out things you have no business knowing, because I've got a pretty good idea. You've always been a snoop."

Addie stood and wrapped her arms around his waist. "A questioning mind is an invaluable tool in the multi-faceted context of modern law."

"Nice quote. Stay out of my papers."

She laughed. "You don't mind and you know it. So I stumbled on a few references to Bill Pearson along the way. You've been mighty generous, Dad."

"It's just money, Ads." Conor leaned back, raised her chin with a gentle hand and met her gaze. "It means nothing."

"Tell that to the homeless you help along The Bowery. At Penn Station. Grand Central. You can't fool me. I'm just surprised Kimber hasn't figured it out."

Conor thought hard about how closely he guarded his anonymity in some arenas, then came clean. "Kimber has known for years. She um..." he hesitated, shrugged, and blew out a breath, "...works for me."

Addie's expression ran the gamut from surprised to puzzled to knowing. "Homeward Bound." She arched a brow as she named the fast-growing homeless ministry that had won several awards in the last two years. "That's yours?"

Conor hedged, disliking credit. "With a lot of help from my friends. Other companies. Government grants. A combined effort."

Addie hugged his waist tighter, her dark, discordant curls snug against his suit coat. "I saw some of the paperwork in your office. I just assumed they referred to charitable donations in general. A good tax write-off."

Conor acknowledged that with a grin. "It's all of that and more. Nothing wrong with a good tax write off that helps people get a roof over their heads. Food on the table. A decent bed."

"And the medical care from the Mobile Clinic Units." She took a step back, straightened his tie where she'd mussed it, and breathed a sigh of approval. "You're okay for a rich guy."

Conor smiled. "It stays between us, though, okay? I like my life quiet outside the firm."

"The other partners know?"

Conor winked. "Regular contributors."

"Even Whickman?"

Conor laughed out loud. "You do know too much. Yes, even Whickman, because he was afraid he'd look like low man on the totem pole. Certainly not for any altruistic reasons I can glean."

"I'm proud of you, Dad."

He'd waited a long time to hear those words from this particular daughter. They sounded good. Real good. "Feeling's reciprocated. Now I've got to fly and catch a quick ride to the office. Nine o'clock meeting."

She gave him one last hug. "Thanks again for the pastries."

"Save some for your sister," he called back over his shoulder.

Addie's laugh followed him. "You snooze, you lose. Rules of the game."

Would he put it past her to eat all the pastries? Naw. Especially if she hadn't been eating all that well at school, and from the looks of her, she'd been skipping meals in favor of studying, another quality shared.

But he also knew that Foster was man enough to tuck away additional treats to ensure Kim's ongoing happiness. Foster had figured out how to handle his daughters years before Conor had a clue.

He'd have to remember to make sure that thought was reflected in the houseman's bonus.

His cab sat idling at the front entrance of the building. Conor nodded to the morning doorman who ensured Conor's daily trip to the office stayed dry and relatively warm. Curbside service, door to door. Another perk of the rich in New York, one he didn't mind. "Thanks, Juan."

"You're welcome, Mr. Bradstreet. Enjoy your day, sir."

Conor put a hand to the other man's shoulder. "You, too. My best to Alva."

A quickly veiled flash of concern darkened the Latino's gaze. Conor paused, his hand on the cab door. "She's all right?"

Juan looked away as if annoyed with himself before lifting his gaze to Conor's. "The doctors have found a spot on her lung and they say it does not look well. The children are most concerned."

Conor read Juan's tone and knew that the children had nothing on their old man. "I'm sorry to hear that. Who is her doctor?"

"Dr. Johannson with City West."

Conor made note of the name and hospital in his Blackberry. "I'll make some inquiries."

"Mr. Bradstreet, I was not suggesting—" Juan half tripped over his tongue to back peddle. "I was not asking for help, sir. I know your life is busy."

"Not too busy to help a friend." Conor gripped the other man's shoulder, a mark of solidarity. "I'll see what I can find out, what options are available. I know a few people."

The doorman's face lightened at his words. "Thank you, sir."

Conor accepted the thanks with a grave nod as he climbed into his cab.

The health options open to service personnel like Juan were not always the same medical options open to the Conor Bradstreets of the world, a disparate truth that shouldn't exist, but did.

But Conor knew how to iron out disparity. He'd developed a real good hand at the required maneuvers over the years. Whether or not his contacts could help Alva Alvarez was a whole different story, but he'd be wrong not to try, and he'd stopped making those kinds of bad decisions once he walked off that bridge and headed back to his apartment.

His personal pledge had met with some tough challenges. The proximity of the firm's corporate structure to the World Trade Center had put him in the midst of the maelstrom that claimed thousands of innocent lives. He'd dragged people through the doors of their building, pulling them in, off the street, out of the way of billowing ash clouds until the police issued an all clear.

They'd huddled in the lobby, crying, praying, sharing quiet stories, waiting for communication devices to work, or first responders to assure them everything was all right, all the time knowing that nothing would ever really be all right again.

A few of those World Trade Center refugees kept in touch with him after their surreal bonding experience. Most hadn't, probably needing to distance themselves from the horror of the realities they witnessed that fateful morning.

And then there was the Neolithic jerk who broke Addie's heart her senior year at Bryn Mawr. Conor had hated that feeling of helplessness and vulnerability, watching her cry, seeing her fall apart while her back-to-nature boyfriend went back to nature with a Haverford farm girl, citing Addie's ambitions as extreme.

Addie, extreme? The kid shoulda gotten a taste of Addie's old man...

But Addie had toughened up after a while, and Conor had been able to resist the urge to meet up with the young slacker and give him some good, old-fashioned Pennsylvania farm boy discipline. Mostly because the kid's only crime was that he neglected to fall in love with Conor's daughter. Tough lesson, all told, but Ads seemed the stronger for the whole thing. *Now.* Back then?

Rough couple of months.

Weighing things up, he'd had a good run, all told. He'd done what he could, when he could. Except for Alicia. He did okay as long as he didn't think about Alicia. About missing her. Holding her. Touching her. Encroaching on her sacred territory.

But with Addie's information regarding the stalemate in Princeton, Conor couldn't help but think of her now. With no firm directive, he dialed Bill Pearson and was glad when Bill's office assistant put him straight through.

"Conor, how are you? Still dancing in the streets over the out-of-court settlement with our Japanese industrial friends? Saved you no small amount of time while ensuring a beneficent corporate windfall. We're talking some serious yen, my friend."

"With an enviable exchange rate," Conor agreed, amiable. "Bill, without breaking any code of ethics, fill me in on what's going on with Alicia's plans for her bookstore. Addie said your proposal got rejected by the borough's zoning board. Is that the case?"

"Since it's public record, I'm not divulging anything covered under client/counsel privilege," Bill replied. "You know this town, Conor. You know the score. They got a mega deal with a big bookstore to hook up with the University and Alicia got the shaft. End of story."

"But their clientele would vary, right?"

"Absolutely."

"Different market and demographic?"

"For the most part. I think Shipton Books took a burn to the idea of a second bookstore opening in the same quarter and only blocks away—"

"Understandable from their perspective," Conor interrupted.

"Assuredly, but the argument remains that Alicia's proposal should have been heard and assessed for its own merits, the type of place an old world mentality like Princeton craves, but push came to shove and my guess is that Shipton offered to nix their deal if the town okayed two bookstores in that narrow time frame. Off the record, that is."

"Who's heading the board right now?"

"Reggie Preston is the current board chair."

"Of Garlock Aviation?"

"That's him."

Conor filed that information mentally and readdressed Bill. "Bill, for more reasons than I care to enumerate, I want this to go through for Alicia. If I can tweak a reversal, then we're in the clear, right? No more hurdles?"

"Not at this end."

"Okay. I'll see what I can do. And, Bill?"

"Yes?"

"This is on the Q.T. Just between you and me."

"Whatever you say." Conor recognized a touch of curiosity and more than a hint of respect. "You'll get back to me then?"

"Either me or my new best friend Reggie."

Bill's voice held the ease of shared humor. "I'll be waiting."

By late morning Conor had put together a pretty impressive profile of Reggie Preston. A self-made man who married into blue blood, he'd lost two sisters, twins, to childhood cancer, a feeling Conor reflected. Losing Jon so sweet, so young...

Eyeing up an online map of Mercer County, he placed his call to Garlock with a goal in mind and no small number of ways to accomplish his desired end.

Or so he hoped.

"Mr. Preston, my name is Conor Bradstreet, I'm with Wells, Terwilliger, Whickman and Bradstreet in New York."

The CEO's voice reflected a mix of interest and deference. "Mr. Bradstreet, nice to talk to you. I believe our daughters graduated from St. Michael's together, didn't they?"

Good memory. Conor gave him an extra point on that. Obviously he'd been more involved in his child's life at that point than Conor had, but Conor had high speed Internet on his side, and a quest. A quest always put a man one leg up. "They did. The older ones, that is. My younger daughter was two years behind your son Cameron."

"The horseback rider." Preston uttered the phrase with the respect one true horseman shows another. Conor felt himself lucky to know the front of a horse from the back, and that was only because the front had eyes and a nose. He still had a hard time figuring out a person's draw to the smelly creatures, but Addie was a horsewoman, through and through, hence the expensive and always hungry mounts stabled at her mother's house.

"Addie loves her horses," Conor agreed. He sat back in his chair and got right to the point. "Mr. Preston, the reason I'm calling is that you and I might be able to work a deal that's mutually beneficial to both of us and the town of Princeton."

"A deal."

Conor recognized the downturned note and chose to ignore it.

"My former wife is attempting to open a bookstore in town, a double shop front on Poole, just around the corner from Nassau."

"I'm aware of Mrs. Bradstreet's proposal. I believe it was turned down by the board less than two weeks ago."

"Which is why I'm calling."

A hint of displeasure crept into Preston's demeanor. "Mr. Bradstreet, while the board is always willing to hear the many proposals put before it in a timely fashion, there is simply no way—"

"I understand your position, Mr. Preston. I really do. As a property owner in Princeton, I have no innate desire to do anything or see anyone else do anything, including my ambitious ex-wife, which would have a negative effect in any way, shape or form on the local economy. Princeton's small town flavor in an Ivy League setting, a quick train ride out of New York City, makes it an ideal target investment area. Those of us who made that plunge two decades back are currently reaping the long-awaited fruits of that labor, aren't we?"

"I'm always ready to make money, Mr. Bradstreet."

"Conor, please."

"Conor. And I'm Reggie."

Bingo. First connection. Done.

"Reggie, I have a proposal. I want to run it by you because as Board Chair, you have a decided weigh-in on any discussions that come before your core group."

"But just one vote."

"When one's vote is the tie-breaker, it bears significant impact."

"What's your proposal, Conor?" Conor heard the Pling! Pling! Pling! of something on Reggie's end. A paper clip snapping? A rubber band? Reggie doodled. When doodler's thought, their hands needed something to keep them busy, hence the noise. Usually a good sign.

"I understand that several local businessmen and women have been looking into underwriting a camp for kids with cancer and other terminal illnesses on the old Breckinger farm by Longneck Pond."

The plings paused. "How did you hear that?"

"It's not common knowledge?"

A deep sigh that sounded more than a little defensive came through the phone. "Mr. Bradstreet, I'm going to guess you knew that information wasn't common knowledge for very specific reasons. People find out, tongues wag, the price jumps up and the whole thing falls through. Furthermore, I'm going to assume that this phone call is to assure me you won't make our purchase common knowledge as long as the Board rubber stamps your ex-wife's little bookstore scheme. Does that about sum things up?"

"Um. No." Conor cleared his throat as though embarrassed for the other man. He paused one beat, then two, letting the silence stew before saying, "May I continue?" Conor did his level best to maintain a tone of slightly insulted deference without laughing. Not an easy task.

"Go on."

Conor breathed deep and slow. "I think your idea for a local park for kids with serious and terminal illness sounds wonderful. You might not know this, but Alicia and I lost a son to cancer ten years ago."

The indiscriminate pings paused. "I didn't know that."

"Jon was four when he died. He spent over half his young life in and out of hospitals, in treatment programs, being poked, prodded, tested, bled and any other thing they could think of."

"I'm sorry, Conor. I really had no idea."

"Reggie, here's the deal. I'd like to see this cancer camp go through, but the way you guys are working the purchase, it's never going to happen. I don't know who you've got cutting through the layers, but whoever it is isn't earning their pay."

"Because?"

"The clause in Ben Breckinger's will says that the property cannot be sold for recreational purposes."

"But..."

"You're tying his kids' hands with your proposal, especially because they've got split objectives among the second generation. Reword the thing and rework the angle. Go at the purchase from the aspect of a working farm that happens to cater to kids with cancer. Then the ones willing to sell can say yes legally, majority rules, you've got your picturesque piece of property for a very worthy cause, on top of that a sweet donation from me personally and I get..."

"A permit for your wife's bookstore."

"I wouldn't be disappointed."

Reggie breathed out a long sigh. "How did you dig all this up? You must have been working on it for months. Years, even."

Conor didn't dare tell him that wondrous things could be found in a quarter day with the firm's connections. Less time than that, actually, if the

Internet server proved really cooperative. "Let's just say this could be a mutually advantageous phone call."

"But you've already told me what I needed to know," argued Reggie. "From this point on I can ignore your wife's petition, reword the purchase offer for the land and forget this phone call ever happened."

"But you're a gentleman, Reggie, like me, and we don't break those rules. Bend 'em a little, from time to time, but we respect one another. And there is the little matter of my donation."

"Which is?"

Conor named an amount that made the plings start up in quick-fire fashion. "You're serious?"

"Very. Nothing expected in return except that I'd like something in the camp named in honor of my son. Doesn't have to be big, just...nice. Something a little boy would like." The break in Conor's voice wasn't for affect, but its effect proved instantaneous.

"Conor, I understand. Probably more than you know. I lost two sisters to cancer. Twins. It about killed my mother to watch them suffer. It did kill my father. He died of alcohol poisoning less than three years after we buried the girls. They were twelve. I was seventeen. I felt like I should die right along with them. I went through school guilt-ridden that I was strong and healthy while they suffered for almost three years, back and forth. A horrible time."

Conor felt the ache in his heart, imagining another family's pain, the inconsolable loss, the guilt at not being able to protect and nurture your own. "My wife has never really gotten over the loss of our son, Reggie. This bookstore she wants, well..." Conor sighed and blew out a deep breath through a wealth of emotion. "Let's just say it would be really good for her. For all of us. A chance to move on."

"I understand." A short silence ensued, then, "Have her lawyer re-submit the proposal to me before next Thursday's meeting. We'll revisit the situation."

"And Reggie?"

"Yes?"

"My donation stands regardless of the outcome of the board vote on the bookstore. Count me in."

The other man whistled low. "You play hardball, don't you?"

"I do. What I didn't know was how to be a good father before it was too late for my marriage. Let's just say I'm trying to make up for lost time."

"Duly noted. I'll watch for Pearson's resubmission and do my best—"

"No promises needed. It was good talking with you."

"And you."

Conor hung up the phone. He'd done what he could without breaking the law, threatening the other man's person or twisting fate. He'd used wisdom and wit, with no small share of timing. And a little hard cash thrown in.

He slid open his top desk drawer with an easy hand, reached inside and withdrew the five-by-seven photo of a younger Alicia on horseback, Jon straddling the seat in front of her, both grinning. That had been a good day for all of them, just months before Jon took ill. His blond bob framed a toddler face that had Alicia's features and Conor's eyes.

Conor slid the photo back into the desk, braced his hands against the polished cherry top, stood and headed to the two-story workout center installed to keep legal associates in shape when they spent seventy hours a week on the job.

About now he figured an hour or better of punching something might lessen his heart rate, reduce his cholesterol and ease the dredge of pain that gathered whenever he delved into those years of loss and stupidity. How long would it take to forget, to really move on? To make up for mistake upon mistake?

He had no idea, but one thing he did know: He had to keep trying.

CHAPTER FIVE

Alicia pulled out her cell phone, spied Bill Pearson's number, and said hello through gritted teeth, her chin tucked against the bitter Northeast wind as she headed toward her warming car a week later.

Bill's tone sounded uncharacteristically perky. "We've got it."

Alicia frowned and wished she could knot her scarf more snugly against her neck, but that wasn't about to happen with the phone in one hand and her over-stuffed Cole Haan tote clutched in the other. "We've got what?"

"The bookstore," Bill replied.

Alicia's heart rate spiked skyward by more than her struggle against the gusting wind.

"I just heard from Reggie Preston," Bill continued. "The board re-did the vote, approving the location five to four."

"Seriously?"

"Yes."

"But why did they re-vote?" she asked, fumbling her key fob as she reached the side of her big SUV. A woman who wasn't afraid to load hay or straw needed transportation that allowed such well-to-do country idiosyncrasies. The big Land Rover fit the bill. "What inspired them to do that? You?"

Bill paused briefly before replying, "I resubmitted the proposal for a new vote, yes."

"Bill, I am so grateful." Alicia felt like she'd been handed a late Christmas gift, more precious because of its surprise factor. "And humbled by my snarky attitude last week. That's wonderful. I know it's not easy to go against a group that's set in their ways, and I just want you to know how extraordinarily grateful I am."

Whoa.

Quite the speech from her, totally garrulous and gushingly nice, definitely not the norm but appropriate for the moment. Kind of like a baby's first step and a teen's first car. Her own store, her own business, hers, hers, hers. "You went the distance for me. I won't forget that."

Bill's reply sounded almost embarrassed. "It wasn't that big a deal, really. Just part of my job."

Alicia laughed, delighted. "Well I am thrilled you feel that way. Listen to me, will you? I'm not having a hissy fit or kicking anything. And it feels wonderful. Nice turnaround."

Bill laughed, gracious enough not to agree out loud. "Once we get financial concerns set, you should be able to move forward with refurbishing, etc. Can you come in on Monday and we'll go over things?"

Alicia nodded, fumbled her door open and slipped into the front seat, out of the wind. "Yes. I'll call your office and set up a time with Ginny."

"Perfect. And Alicia?"

"Yes?"

"Congratulations."

She beamed into the rear view mirror and decided she really did look better with a smile than a frown. Imagine that. "Thanks, Bill."

Conor heard his phone, frowned, hunted the living room, then finally found the thing under that morning's cast-off newspaper. "Hello, Bill."

"Conor, I've just made your ex-wife very happy."

Conor shoved the newspaper aside, perched his hip on the edge of the table and removed one concern from an elongated list. "They voted yes."

"By the narrowest of margins, but that's academic. She's in."

"Good." Satisfaction flooded him. Alicia would have her chance at long last, as long as she had guts enough to reach out and seize the opportunity. "Very good."

"And I felt like a first class schmuck taking all the credit," Bill continued. "There she was thanking me, over and over, and all I wanted to do was tell her to call you. Thank you."

"But you didn't."

"Not this time. But one of these days I will."

"No, you won't." Conor walked to the window's edge and stood alongside the bright-colored tree slated for takedown in the next few days. "You understand why things have to be done this way. She'd never accept my help knowingly."

"Then you should talk to her. Smooth things over."

Conor laughed outright. "Um, yeah. Good luck on that one, Bill. You've got an ex-wife. How's that whole smoothing things over thing working out for you?"

"Totally different situation, and I'm not still in love with my ex-wife."

"Neither am I." Conor spilled the words so quickly he almost believed them. "But she's the mother of my children and if she suffers, they suffer."

"Do you buy that line you're selling?"

"What line?"

Bill snorted. "The whole 'I'm doing this for the welfare of my children' thing. Conor, anyone that knows you, knows you're still in love with Alicia. What we can't figure out, and I mean anyone who's met the two of you, is why."

"Bill—"

"She's a b—"

Conor cut him off. "Don't say it, Bill."

"What? That she's a beautiful woman?"

"Um..."

"She's all that, Conor, but her attitude about you and men in general is enough to make a sensible man run for the hills and never look back. How come you can't be rational like the rest of us? Pay her off and be done with it?"

"Guilt-stricken, conscience-laden, glutton for punishment." His jocular tone lightened the words, but Conor recognized the false levity. If this were a multiple choice test, he'd be relegated to "D: All of the above." Sure, he'd come a long way from the self-absorbed, ride-'em-high, New York mover and shaker who constantly put work first. For years there'd always been another news-grabbing case bringing cool millions along to sweeten the pot. But he'd abandoned the woman he loved to play his high stakes game. A winner on Wall Street, he became a loser where it counted. He cleared his throat, pushing emotion into a tightly boxed corner of his soul. "Take your pick. For the moment I'm just happy we've got a deal and she can move ahead."

"That we can, my friend. Good talking to you."

Conor nodded, eyeing the lights of New York, the bustle of a city that never sleeps, ever-present, always beckoning, just beyond his door, but while his gaze swept New York, his heart thought of Princeton. "And you."

※

Conor slipped Juan Alvarez a card the next morning. "Give them a call," he advised as he ducked into the waiting cab. "They're expecting to hear from you."

Juan squinted at the card, then raised his chin in question. "This doctor is with..."

Conor waved him off. "Yes. If you need time off to manage all this, we can do that, too."

Juan held the card aloft, his forehead creased. "But how did you do this thing? People wait many months to see this man."

Conor flashed him a look of understanding. "Because your wife deserves the best doctor we can find." He pointed to the card Juan clutched. "I've made arrangements for any costs that might not be covered by your insurance."

Juan swallowed hard. "Mr. Bradstreet—"

Conor glanced to his watch and frowned. "Got to go. You or Alva give them a call today, all right?"

Juan breathed deep and clutched the card as the cab's blinker indicated a move into traffic. "We will do that."

"Mr. Bradstreet?"

Conor answered the assistant's buzz with one eye on his laptop, fingers tapping the keys. "Yes, Colleen?"

"I have Kim on line one."

He smiled, made a short note in the margin of the fact-finder, and leaned back in his chair. "Put her on, please."

Kim's voice bounced through the line. Come to think of it, she'd been bouncing on a regular basis since Christmas. Conor pictured the September wedding date and his calendar turned firmly to January, wondering if all eight months would be conducted at this month's fever pace. Impossible, right?

Thinking back to his wedding, he realized that he had taken no part in the tiniest of preparations, leaving the whole thing in Leash's capable hands, so he had virtually no clue what to expect the next eight months.

Okay, then. He'd learn on this one and be ready for Addie's when the time came.

"Hey, Dad, if you're home tonight, can we talk wedding stuff?"

Conor glanced at his daily calendar and put Kim off a day. "Tomorrow night. I've got that funds coordinating meeting with the mayor's group tonight and it will run late. You know how Alex Krenz is when he's had a glass of wine."

"I think it's the two martinis before the glass of wine that make the difference," Kim noted.

Conor couldn't disagree. "You're astute. And smart. Did your sister get off to Princeton okay?"

"Yes, and I'm heading out there this weekend to go over things with Mom." Kim paused, huffed, took a breath and chastised him. "You guys would make my life a whole lot easier if we could meet together like a normal family, instead of this meet here, meet there, try to sort things out and patch them into some semblance of order from warring camps nonsense."

Conor thought of what an intriguing scene that would make. Probably not the greatest idea Kim ever had. "Awkward, at best, although I'm sorry to put you in the position of go-between."

"Why should now be any different, Dad?"

Kim's reply surprised him. And hurt a little. Maybe more than a little. He didn't have time to answer her complaint before she said, "All right, I've got to go, the van's here. Talk to you later."

She sounded rushed, frustrated and more than a little put out which was somewhat ironic for the daughter of a rich man, wasn't it?

Conor stewed over her reaction most of the day and half the night. By the next morning he left for work ready to calm the waters, from his end, anyway. He hit her number on his speed dial while in the cab. "Kim?"

"Hey, Dad." A flutter of papers and the whir of a machine told him she was already in the office and preparing for her day. "What's up?"

Conor waded in. "I've decided you're absolutely right, your mother and I should be able to sit down with you and Brian and go over things like two mature adults. What time do you want to meet this weekend?"

Silence answered him, just before a low, tight whistle came through the phone. It took him a minute to realize Kim was breathing through clenched teeth. The picture tweaked a half-smile.

"You're sure?"

He wasn't, but he'd fake it. "Gotta do it sometime, right? Why not now? I can't imagine a more important thing than my daughter's wedding to start acting like a family again, even if we live separate lives."

"Well, two of us, anyway," his daughter retorted, her tone dry. "The other fifty percent seem to manage just fine. Is Mom's house okay?"

"As long as it's fine with her," Conor replied. His cab angled to the curb in front of the office high rise. The driver tipped his cap as Conor slid out, cash in one hand, his phone in the other, his laptop satchel tucked beneath his arm. "Let me know when and where."

"And you're really okay with this?" The note of caution in Kim's voice held a tinge of regret at pushing the point the previous day.

Conor acknowledged the doorman with a nod, waved his ID to the guard, sought the private elevator and glanced around the posh building that set the tone for his daily existence. "I'm fine. This is long overdue. Make sure your mother's okay with the whole thing, though. I don't want to blindside her."

On the other hand, maybe he did. Maybe it would do both of them some good.

Or not.

"I will." Now Kim's voice held more than a twinge of regret. On a Richter scale, Conor would hike the degree of discomfort up a full two degrees as Kim pondered the thought of springing him on her mother. Ah, but that's what a girl got for pressing the envelope. Exactly what she thought she wanted.

As Conor moved out of the elevator, he smiled at Colleen, moved through the anteroom to his office, set down his bag and held the phone away, just a touch. "Good luck with that, by the way."

Kim's reply didn't reflect her normal go-with-the-flow attitude. Definitely more along the line of 'what-have-I-gotten-myself-into?' "Yeah. Right. Thanks. I think."

Conor laughed. "You're welcome. And if it's too uncomfortable for her—"

"Translated: if your mother goes ballistic on you..."

"Exactly." Conor eased into his chair, the morning light dimmed with skyscraper shadow, low clouds and city smog. "We can rearrange. But you're right, Kim. It's time to work together. I'll just pre-schedule back-to-back appointments with my local therapist for prep time. Kind of like facing a well-stocked barroom after a decade on the wagon."

"I won't tell Mom you analogized her to a bar," Kim promised. "Until I want something really bad, that is."

"Blackmail's wrong. Sinful. And relatively unnecessary because I never say no."

"I know." She sighed. "You're sure you're okay with this?"

Guilt-laden. Good. Conor considered it a character-building experience, akin to the one she'd laid on him yesterday. Tit for tat. "Positive. Give it your best shot, and call me later. Let me know."

"I will."

The promise didn't sound happy or enthusiastic, but rang as sincere as it could for someone about to face the den of a wronged lioness, hoping to emerge unscathed.

"And Kim?"

"Yes?"

"Just want to wish you luck. You're going to need it."

"Right." She swallowed once, hard, and blew out a sigh. "Don't I know it."

"So." Sandy lifted her mug in a victory toast. "To resilience, persistence, open minds and brilliant lawyers."

"Hear, hear." Alicia clinked her art deco travel mug with Sandy's. "I still have to pinch myself, make sure I'm not dreaming."

"I went by the store earlier," Sandy confessed, "to make sure everything was still secure since the building's been empty for a while."

"And?"

"Everything's fine," Sandy answered. "I can't wait to see what you're going to do inside. That wainscoting alone is a people draw, but the twin bay windows and the pretty view of the churchyard? That screams small town living at its very best."

Alicia ignored the mention of the church. Other than weekly chauffer service for the girls, she had made it a point to avoid the old stone building since Jon's funeral. The blatant church view had been the singular negative issue she'd wrestled with concerning the bookstore's location until she decided to treat the historic house of worship like the non-entity it was. "We actually lived around the corner from the bookstore location when the kids were little," she told Sandy. "On Teaberry."

"Really?" Sandy hiked a brow of interest. "Which one?"

"One-twelve. Along the curve where the yards border the park."

"You're kidding."

"Nope." Alicia sipped her drink and arched a brow in her friend's direction. "That's where we lived before we bought the Miller-Browne estate. One-twelve Teaberry."

"I listed that house this morning."

"No." Alicia stared at her, amazed.

Sandy nodded. "How weird is that? The family called me earlier in the week and said they were leaving the area and would I help them list the house."

"To which you said: 'oh, no, please find another Realtor to do this for you, I have no need for money or financial gain at this point in my life.'"

Sandy made a face at her. "I believe my phrasing was more to the effect of: Yes! Yes! Yes! Another listing to keep me in food and drink. Sign here. Now."

One-twelve Teaberry. A great brick colonial, over thirty-three hundred square feet, set on the slightly sloped east side of a road that featured good-sized lots and neighbors on all sides. Alicia recalled the neighborhood feel of Teaberry, where people were people. Just blocks from Nassau Street, and the hustle and bustle of Princeton University comings and goings, Teaberry had the feel of old colonial grace and time. A nice place, all in all. They'd been happy there. For a while.

"Have you been by lately?" Sandy asked. "Seen what they've done with it?"

Alicia gave a firm shake of her head. "I stay away from there. I've got enough memories to deal with at home. No need to borrow more."

"True enough." Sandy nodded her understanding. "Well, I think they must have called on the Greenwich Village league of *la decorateurs* because the whole inside is done retro chíc."

"No."

Sandy grimaced. "Yes. Who would do that to such a gracious old house?"

"Stupid people."

"No argument from me." Sandy shook her head. "But, because of that, someone's going to get a real nice bargain because the interior looks like a poorly thought combination of fifties' diner and Boston flea market, while the yard is a real handyman's special."

"Ouch." Alicia frowned, remembering the lovely gumwood trim and the beautifully appointed crown moldings. Not to mention her gardens, so sweet and pretty. "Why on earth..."

"Don't ask me." Sandy shook her head. "It's about the only property in Princeton that might have lost value in the last decade."

"How sad." Alicia wasn't sure if she meant the house or herself. One-twelve Teaberry held a lot of nostalgia for her. The girls, growing up, racing around, having fun. Baby Jon, crawling across the glossed hardwood floors, dusting corners with little boy knees. A wave of remorse reminded her why she stayed away from Teaberry Street. She'd have given anything to have had him longer, to have spent more time with the little boy who loved his mommy and adored his dad. She pushed those thoughts aside with effort. "You signed them?"

"Why not?" Sandy puffed a cooling breath over the surface of her latte and sipped with care. "Money's money and if I can find the right buyer I might be able to salvage some investment for these people."

Alicia leaned forward as her phone vibrated in her side pocket. "Do they think it looks good?"

Sandy nodded. "Oddly enough, yes. No accounting for taste."

Alicia smiled, withdrew the phone, saw Kim's name and answered. "Hello, Bride. How are you?"

Kim laughed, but it wasn't the full-bodied laugh she normally sported, a definitive warning sign. "Hi, Mom. What're you up to?"

"Enjoying a cappuccino with Sandy while we discuss the demise of traditional decorating as we know it."

"Great. Can we talk weddings instead?"

"Sure. When?"

"Um." Distinct pause, followed by an equally audible throat-clearing maneuver. "Dad says he can come down either Saturday or Sunday so we can discuss things together."

Alicia held the phone away, eyed it with surprise, gave the device a shake as though clearing static, then brought the high-tech model back to her ear. "Did you say your father wants to discuss wedding plans with me?"

"With all of us, actually. You, me, Brian, Grayce, Dad and Addie. Like old times."

Alicia started to count to ten, realized it was simply of no use whatsoever, and ranted, instead, suddenly unaware that Small World Coffee held people nearby. Normal people, the kind who kept their voices down and conducted family business in private. "We don't do 'old times,' Kim. We don't do walks down Memory Lane and jaunts along the Boardwalk just for kicks, nor strolls along the river. Remember?"

Kim's sigh was probably heard by half the township of Princeton. Mayber Mercer County. "I know, Mom, I know, I just thought that since it's my wedding, we might be able to make an exception in the drama game, but, no. I guess not. At least Dad was willing to try to make my life easier, keep this fun, but I guess it's not meant to be. Never mind. I'll call Dad and reschedule. Brian and I will discuss things with him, then you, then make decisions based on what might suit the opposing teams."

Opposing teams? Is that how they looked and sounded? Like she and Conor were ready to square off at a moment's notice? You'd have to care to be that angry, and Alicia didn't care, not in the least. Not even a smidge.

"Your father agreed to this?" Internal radar flashed a sudden warning. By appearing willing to broach their enforced hiatus, he'd look like the good guy and she'd be the shrew. Well. Why should today be any different? A well-played Conor-move.

"Yes, and pretty gracefully, too. He said there's no better time than a daughter's wedding to put old things aside and start fresh."

She wanted to argue that, but couldn't bring herself to do it because he was right, of course. That made his capitulation into cooperation more maddening.

Blood vessels Alicia didn't know existed swelled within her. She was fairly sure she felt steam puffing from her ears like some crazed cartoon creature, ready to explode.

How dare he take the upper road? Make her look bad? What kind of man did something like that?

"Hey, Mom, listen, it's okay, I'll get back to Dad, tell him you're unavailable, and—"

"I'm available."

Kim paused, hesitant. "You're what?"

"On Saturday, all day. I'm available. What time shall we meet?"

Kim released a long breath, her tone cautious. "One o'clock? At your house?"

Alicia drew herself more upright in the chair and tried to ease the wrinkle-encouraging frown that lay tightly knit between her brows. No way was she about to let Conor push her to botox. No, no, no. "I'll have lunch ready and I'll order dessert from the bakery."

"Mom, you don't have to do all that," Kim protested.

Alicia tut tutted with the finesse of a queen who knew her duty and was determined to do it with grace. Elementary good breeding and all that. "It's just lunch, Kim. No trouble at all. Let your Dad know, okay?"

Kim hesitated once again, then must have decided to leave well enough alone. Smart girl. "Then we'll see you on Saturday. Thanks, Mom."

"You're welcome, honey. See you then."

Sandy leaned back in her seat, her expression wary. "Murder's illegal and offers few perks because state and federal prisons are notably without comforts you've grown accustomed to." She hoisted her mug in example. "Like this."

"Involuntary manslaughter?"

"Doesn't apply if you plan it. Sorry."

"Self defense?"

"Only works if he's packing a weapon and threatening to use it. Not if he's being nice."

"That's just it." Alicia banged her hand on the table and managed to draw additional interest from nearby patrons while bruising her palm. "He's being nice and therefore needs to meet some form of long, slow demise." She stared at her chocolate/hazelnut latte, too angry to fully appreciate the subtle blend of flavors any longer. Definitely Conor's fault. A too-long pause made her shift her gaze back to Sandy. "Why is he doing this?"

Sandy eyed her with more than a little open skepticism. "Because he's matured and moved on? Developed a soul? He's sincerely interested in his daughter's well being and future happiness and is willing to let bygones be bygones?"

"You're romanticizing him. That's like gilding the devil or describing hell as 'tropically warm'. Conor Bradstreet cares about one thing and one thing only. Conor Bradstreet."

Sandy sat silent, studying her mug with rapt attention.

"What?" Alicia demanded, her tone gruff.

Sandy shook her head, maintaining a hands-off attitude but looked like she had plenty to say. Too much, most likely, but wasn't that what girlfriends were for? To thump you upside the head and hold that long-disused mirror to your face? Alicia sighed, scowled, then sighed again. "What are you thinking? That I should be over this by now? That I shouldn't be going off the deep end over something I should have moved beyond years ago?"

Sandy shook her head. "It's not my place to say anything, Alicia. I didn't bury a child or have a husband cheat on me. You've got every right to be mad at the world."

"Except...?" Alicia eyed her friend, certain there was more.

"Except when does it stop? When do you forge ahead? Embrace life again?"

"Now. Here. Today. Starting with my new store, my new venture."

"More books."

"I love books."

"I know." Sandy half smiled, half sighed. "But books are faint comfort when the days are short and the nights are long. When there are no gardens to tend, no children to run after, nothing to clean, polish or prepare. No one should love books that much."

"I do."

Sandy frowned. "Books are where you hide, Alicia. At least with the bookstore you'll be in the open, not working behind the scenes in some antiquated library setting where you conceal yourself from the world and all that's in it."

"Not everyone sees the world like you do, Sandy."

Sandy stood and leaned down. "You used to, Alicia. A long time ago."

Quick tears pricked Alicia's lids. "You don't know what you're talking about."

"Sure I do. And so do you. Maybe it's time to meet with Conor because it's time for you to find yourself again."

"That Alicia is gone. Forgotten."

Sandy shook her head. "Not by me. Or anyone else who remembers you from before Jon died."

"That's enough." Alicia stood, her feelings raw, her heart exposed, her jaw fixed. "I'm not talking about this."

"You never do."

Alicia turned to leave but Sandy put a loving hand to her sleeve. Alicia paused, not trusting herself to words.

"Maybe you should."

Alicia stared straight ahead, her cheeks tight with restrained tears, her throat thick.

"This wedding might be God's way of opening doors for you and your family."

"Then he should have thought of that before he took my son." Alicia stepped away from Sandy's grip and concern. "Goodnight."

She felt Sandy's gaze follow her out of the store, her worry palpable, her voice resigned. "Good night, Alicia."

CHAPTER SIX

Conor. Here. Now.

His profile beyond the door put Alicia's breathing in slow motion and her heart in high gear on Saturday. Still tall and muscular, his wide shoulders filled out his expertly tailored all weather slate-gray trench. As she grabbed the door handle, Conor turned, his eyes meeting hers, his expression unreadable through the faceted crystal entry.

He stood strong and silent as they faced one another, the door now open, but not wide enough to allow him in. Not yet. Maybe if she kept the door like this, half leaned shut, he'd take the hint and go away forever, like she'd planned years ago.

"Alicia."

His voice, warm and low, held command and question. His gaze encompassed the door and her stance. "May I come in?"

No. Not now, not ever. Never again, Conor Bradstreet, with your cinnamon brown eyes and your wavy hair cut all short and legal. A big city looker, even at middle age. How the chicks must dig you with your fancy, cut-so-perfect clothes and your limitless checkbook.

What she said was, "Of course," as she stepped back and broadened the space to allow for his size.

She wished him smaller. Uglier. Definitely less imposing as he unbound his coat and dropped to one knee when Grayce raced across the foyer and jumped into his wide-open arms. The sight of the tow-headed child, and Conor embracing her, clamped a vise around Alicia's heart, taking her back twenty years.

Kim, reading to her daddy, with Addie scrambling for a position on his lap, wanting to keep up with her big sister, both grasping for the scarce time they had with their father. "See, Daddy, I'm teaching Addie about squares and shapes and stuff." Kim held out a red square for her father and little sister to see. "The square has four equal sides."

Conor sent the little girl a slow-smiling look. "And the opposite sides are parallel."

"What's...parallel?" Not to be outdone by anyone or anything, Addie's jaw had tested the word and found the roll of syllables to her liking.

"Parallel means the lines stay the same distance apart, no matter how long you make them. They could go around the entire world, and they'd still be the same distance apart."

"Really, Daddy?" Addie's eyes went round, studying her father. "Around the whole, wide world?"

"The universe, even," promised Conor. "If they're parallel, they'll never touch, never intersect."

"Reminds me of something rather close to home," Alicia had announced with a pointed look in her husband's direction. "The latter, anyway."

Connor had met her gaze, aggrieved, knowing she spoke of them and their lack of time together, the scarcity of intimacy. "I know. I feel the same way. I missed you all this week, but it's hard to get home when the firm's in the middle of something as big as the Westmount Industries takeover." He flashed Alicia a look shaded with fatigue, but she'd ignored the weariness, and him. At least long enough to punish the man for being good at what he did, for being gone.

For a split second now, seeing him with Grayce, she wondered if she'd always carried a vindictive streak and had just begun to see it more clearly.

Conor stood, Grayce in his arms. "Glad to see me, Kid?"

"Yes." Grayce hung back and patted his front pockets. "Empty."

"Guess which one."

She eyed him and studied the lay of his coat. "Inside, right."

"My right or your right?"

She frowned, her lower lip thrust out. "Yours."

"Got it. Good job." Conor slipped his left hand into the folds of his coat and withdrew a sack of sugared nuts. "Barney says hello."

"The dinosaur?" Alicia looked from one to the other, not understanding what a purple dinosaur had to do with peanuts.

"The nut vendor outside my building," Conor explained. "He and Grayce are old friends."

"Not surprising." Alicia turned on her heel and stalked to the back of the house. She'd hemmed and hawed about where to conduct this meeting of the minds, then finally settled on the kitchen. Less formal, more cozy, although the last thing she wanted was for Conor to feel cozy and welcome. Not here, not now. Not ever.

But the girls were her main concern, that and wanting to show she could rise above as well as he, probably better, in fact. Make that absolutely better.

She'd done a buffet along the granite-topped breakfast bar, a selection of soups and sandwich makings, balanced with fruit and salads, just enough variety to say she cared but didn't go to a great deal of fuss and bother, informal yet complete to the last little cup of spicy-hot mustard mixed with horseradish.

Conor sent the spread a look of approval. "Thanks for doing this, Alicia. It's nice."

Like her little spread impressed a guy whose idea of fast food was three-figure take-out? Right. She responded too quickly, always a mistake. "I figured if we were eating, we might not be fighting."

Was it her words or her tone that made him wince? She had no idea, and cared less.

Kim and Brian came into the kitchen, Brian's arm wrapped around her middle, his expression that of a person in love while Kim's darted from her mother to her father as if wondering how to quell the expected exchange of mortar fire.

Grayce shifted her gaze from Alicia to Conor, her knowing look too wise for a six-year-old. "Miss Ellison says that fighting isn't nice, and Jimmy had to sit in the corner for punching Will because Will said Jimmy was a big fatso and eats too many cookies."

"Miss Ellison is right," agreed Conor, palming her head, his voice affable. "When people don't get along, they should try and work things out. Play nice."

"And when that maneuver fails, opportunity allows us to follow up with a good lawyer." Alicia dropped a wink to the little girl, a fake smile pasted on her face.

"Mom." Kim's tone held a hint of warning.

"Mom." Addie's voice chimed in as she entered the kitchen from the far side, eyes wide in exasperation, pocketing her cell phone as she moved. "Really."

Conor handed Grayce's hand to Kim. "Leash, may I see you a minute? In the other room?"

The fact that he called her 'Leash', his old nickname for her, ticked her off. The fact that he wanted to see her away from the kids, out of earshot, only made matters worse, but on top of that, he'd asked in that infuriatingly calm voice of his, the one that drove competitive men and women to drop their cases and pay his firm a bundle of money just so Conor Bradstreet wouldn't show them up in a court of law. "I don't think so," she answered, keeping her gaze averted. "We need to eat so we can talk. Get things settled."

He stepped forward, into her space, forcing her to look up or stare at his broad chest, neither option in her best interest at the moment. "Please?"

She wanted to tear into him because the warm and reasonable sound of his 'please' nicked her armor, gave her a hint of Conor, the man-boy she'd fallen in love with so many years ago.

She didn't ream him. Glancing up, into his eyes, she ignored the swim of emotions there and gave a quick nod. "Probably a good idea."

Conor motioned to the girls. "You guys go ahead and start. Mom and I will be back in a minute." He held the swinging door ajar, waited for her to step through, then followed her to the small sitting room that doubled as her office for...absolutely nothing. A total farce in her life. Why on earth did a town librarian need a home office? Who needs an office if they don't do anything? A whole room to balance a checkbook, write out the few checks that paid bills she couldn't pay online?

Ridiculous.

"We should talk." Conor sat, uninvited, but his action made a glimmer of sense, considering. Alicia sat opposite him, staring at her hands with an occasional glance up. *Yup. Still there. A most unfortunate circumstance.*

"I know this is awkward." Conor studied his hands as well, his jaw shifting right, then left, his cheek offering an occasional twitch. "Kim really wants this." He waved a hand. "You and me to be able to get along, at least for her wedding. And after that..."

"After that," Alicia cut in, her tone sharp with purpose, "we realize we have nothing in common and we're better off at least a train-ride apart for the rest of our days."

Conor continued as if she hadn't spoken. "After that we need to recognize there will most likely be more grandchildren, and Addie's graduation, a wedding in her future and children again." Conor spread his hands. "If we could find a common ground, it would be good for all of us, I think."

Common ground? Where was his concept of common ground when she nursed their sick child? When they traveled that stupid train for doctor's visits, left and right? When her baby boy underwent treatment after treatment, wasting the few months he had.

She hated remembering that Jon's last months were filled with pain because his well-to-do parents couldn't accept the fact that he was dying and had to try every possible procedure to save him.

Selfish, selfish people. Her. Him.

And now Conor wanted a common ground, a respite. Right now she hated this, hated him, hated the person she'd become or maybe always was and didn't realize it until life dealt her cruel blows, back to back. Maybe she'd always been a first class—

"We can do this, Leash." Conor didn't move, but his presence felt closer, his tone low. "If nothing else, then for the girls."

Ah, yes, the girls. Her beautiful, beloved daughters, whose presence kept meaning in her life. Her girls.

And his.

She hated remembering that because thinking of him as their father put him in a whole different light. He cared for them, that was obvious, his affection more evident now than when they were young and missing him.

When she was missing him.

"Leash?" He leaned forward, his voice quiet and thoughtful. "Please?"

A part of her despised him. What he'd done, that he still looked good, that the girls loved him despite the past when she couldn't move two solid feet away from that anger without feeling like she was falling into a bottomless pit, with nothing to catch her, bolster her fall.

He smelled wonderful. A hint of wool and cotton mixed with spicy aftershave, outrageously sexy. Most of all she hated that he still had the power to attract, she knew that the moment she wrenched open the door, seeing him framed there, all power and subtle sex, and all she could imagine were the hordes of successful women in New York, waiting to be loved by the oh-so-wonderful Conor Bradstreet.

She gripped her hands, steeling herself immune to his tone and his proximity. "I'd do anything for Kim and Addie."

He said nothing, but her answer disappointed him. She could tell. Well, what else was new? She'd had more than enough practice doing that while they were married, right? Why should today be any different? She stood, abrupt, and thrust her shoulders back. "That's all I can do, Conor."

He stood as well, but with more thought and caution. "It's a beginning."

It's not, she wanted to shout in "Green Eggs and Ham" fashion, like the guy who gets dogged by Sam-I-Am no matter which route he tries to take. *It's not a beginning, it's not a start, it's not anything.*

She wanted to smack him, and that reaction surprised her, but why should it? He deserved that, and so much more. A beginning? No way, no how. They'd had their beginning, a long time past. Then they had their ending, not quite so noteworthy, with all the aspects of cheesy day-time TV in between. Love, pathos, gratuitous sex. Nope, no way, no how, there'd be no beginnings with Conor Bradstreet, not ever again.

He stepped aside to allow her to pass through the door in front of him. Her toe caught the edge of the braided rug. If he hadn't been there, right there, she'd have fallen, but his arm reached out to brace her.

"Careful," he murmured, his voice soothing and protective. The tone put her in mind of other moments with this man, moments of warmth and romance, passion and peace. She sucked in a breath, wondering if the local doctor had access to anti-memory drugs, and if so, would he prescribe them to a scorned woman possessing a stupid penchant for pain?

"You okay?"

Alicia jerked back, her heart fighting her brain. "Fine."

She strode ahead, wishing he were different, or maybe wishing she was, wishing she could be near him and not want to murder him with her bare hands or possibly fall into his arms and stay there forever. She'd found out the hard way that forever didn't exist in Conor's dictionary of legal terms or moral standings. Just as well. At least she'd discovered the truth early enough to change things.

He stepped into the kitchen directly behind her and placed a hand to her shoulder. She quaked inside at the move, quelling the war of emotions, sealing her expression from the frankly curious eyes of her daughters.

"We've called a truce," Conor stated, his tone easy, but not casual enough to minimize the seriousness of her feelings. Probably a trick he learned in the courtroom. "As in many battle plans, arbitrary lines of disarmament may need to be redrawn from time to time, and truces re-established. I think that's to be expected. But," he gave her shoulder the lightest of pressures before dropping his hand to his side, "we'll try."

"It's a start," approved Kim, her eyes glancing from one to the other. "And my crazy work schedule wants you both to know that I'm grateful. By the way, Mom, this spinach salad is amazing."

Alicia was still trying to shake off the feeling of Conor's hand on her shoulder, his presence behind her, almost...sheltering her. She stepped aside and nodded a brisk thanks to Kim. "Glad you like it. And if your job with the foundation doesn't allow you enough time to get things done, we've got a couple of options." Alicia picked up a plate and moved to the food bar. "You could find a mental health position not quite so labor intensive, even though you love what you're doing. Charitable work is definitely a Morrisey trait."

When she glanced over her shoulder to Kim, she saw Kim exchange an arched-eye glance with both Brian and Conor.

"...or let me know what needs to be done, and I'll take care of it, according to your plans."

Kim smiled. Addie turned Alicia's way. "Even with the bookstore and all?"

Alicia shrugged. "A lot of the initial bookstore work will be hired out so I just have to oversee the process, at least until the opening. It's not like I'm building shelving and constructing walls on my own." She held up Princetonian hands. "I'm okay in a barn, not with a power saw."

Addie flashed her a smile. "You're great in a barn, unlike Dad here, who isn't even sure which building is the barn."

"I was sure enough when I signed the check for it to be built," he retorted.

His words brought Alicia's gaze up. His jaw twitched into the classic Bradstreet smile that got her into so much trouble nearly thirty years before. A little crooked, a little nice and more than a hint naughty.

Addie laughed and gave him a shoulder nudge, her grin a reflection of his.

Alicia pulled her attention back to Kim's wedding and away from crooked grins that took her into dangerous territory. "Anyway, I've got the time and if it doesn't feel like I'm trying to take things over, I'd be glad to help."

"And I've got the checkbook," Conor added. "Well, credit card. Cards. Plural." He handed one to Kim and held the other out to Alicia. "Just put everything on here. Using these ensures cool point rewards. Might even get a power drill out of the deal, or some hip new iPod thing."

Kim frowned, glanced at Brian, and tried to hand the card back. "Dad, this is nice, but—"

Brian chimed in. "Sir, I—"

Alicia took the card without argument. She gave Kim and Brian a strict look and held her card aloft. "Stop being silly. It's our privilege to pay for your wedding. Well..." She shot Conor a glance, then dropped her gaze back to the card in her hand. "His privilege, but it's definitely my privilege to help you spend his money."

"Our money, Leash."

His words paused her sarcastic rant. First a hand to her shoulder, now an inclusive suggestion.

Stop the presses. This little exchange was way too up close and personal for the bickering Bradstreets. She gripped the card but didn't dare chance a glance at Conor, see his face, read those eyes.

Gaze down, she gave a brisk nod. "Our money, then. And I'll be glad to help you spend it, Kim. But not 'til after lunch."

She felt Conor's eyes on her, felt his presence, his attention, even across the room. The knowledge brought heat within her, an increase in temperature despite the January chill.

But at her age it was most likely caused by estrogen imbalance, so she wrote it off as peri-menopause and ate her salad with a heightened degree of attention to chewing, swallowing and breathing.

All because Conor was in the room.

CHAPTER SEVEN

Part of Conor wanted to speed his escape as he directed the Mercedes down Alicia's curving drive toward Route 206. Another part longed to linger, walk with Addie to visit her smelly horses and give the beasts a carrot or an apple, something crunchy, moist and no doubt, saliva-producing.

But he'd refused Addie's offer to go to the barn, sensing that Alicia had reached her limit, probably before he stepped foot in the door.

She looked...

Hardened? A bit. Maybe more than a bit, her hair still dark with hints of red, but her jaw tight, her gaze fierce, the sleek, snazzy woman he'd married hidden somewhere beneath the chilled façade.

Toughened? Most assuredly. He saw that in the flat look of acceptance, her pretty blue eyes dulled by the mottled gray sweater she wore like a suit of armor. He'd felt it in the tension of her shoulders. At one point he was pretty sure she wanted to belt him one, give him a good, old shot to the face, but she'd restrained herself, and didn't appear all that happy by the fact.

Her obvious reaction almost made him smile, but then he probably would have gotten smacked, deservedly so. To keep the peace he'd bottled his reaction in good legal fashion.

With Kim's wedding on the horizon, they needed a new game plan, decent parameters both could respect. No matter what else happened, he wanted the girls to have the shot he'd blown. A chance for a normal, healthy, happy marriage.

And he'd managed to scan the rooms for any visible sign of a man's regular presence, a boyfriend or significant other.

Nothing.

Conor refused to wonder why that made him happy when he should be hoping she'd moved on and kicked him out of her system like a pesky computer virus smacked down by Norton 360.

Turning left, he steered the car away from the municipal buildings, heading toward Nassau Street and the town center, past Palmer Square and its upscale shops, nicely appointed. He paused at Washington Road, the university campus spreading to his right, a good share of the town proper to his left. Moving further, he took the turn onto Poole, remembering years of coming home on the "Dinky", the short train linking Princeton to Princeton Junction, where the mainline shuttled him into the city every Monday, then back on Fridays. Coming home at night...well, that didn't happen as often as it should have. He knew that now. Another wave of remorse sideswiped him as he parked the car, fed the meter and walked up the block to the proposed bookstore's location.

Facing Poole Street, Alicia's new venture would combine the best of small town country and New York upscale. The expansive two-and-a-half story house faced the street with the dignity of old wood and the charm of gingerbread. Eyeing the interior through a thin strip along a front window's edge, Conor noted a curving staircase and a broad-backed room which seemed to taper into some kind of alcove beyond.

A nice layout, the arching staircase a great focal point, its easy proximity inviting customers to lofty second story rooms. Finely tooled display windows balanced both sides of the carved walnut door. The matching bays sported multi-paned panels framing picture windows. Built for display, the lay of the windows allowed for seasonal appointment with their deep-seated shelving beneath.

Studying the gracious old building, Conor nodded his approval, glad he'd intervened. Alicia had picked well, the cozy appearance an instant draw. As he turned toward his car, he paused, eyeing the church across the road with its quaint cemetery beyond.

Unlike his ex-wife, Conor didn't visit Jon's grave often. Now and again, maybe, when he needed a boy to talk to, a son to share secrets with, but the mature Conor understood that his boy didn't lie beneath the burnished stone with the image of a child and a dog chiseled along its eastern face.

Jon's bones might lie there, but not his boy. Not his little son, the kid he'd dubbed Dennis the Menace because of the mischievous brown eyes and Dutch-bobbed hair.

For a long time Conor had shrugged off the existence of a higher being, a celestial power. Right up until he needed to pray for his son, beg for his life, plead for his soul. Somewhere in there, despite losing the boy, he'd gained a seed of faith that lay dormant until that Christmas Eve on the Brooklyn Bridge when he first met Sarge.

He'd almost gone over the edge that night, almost called it a day. Checked out. So close. So ready to die. Who but God could have sent the disheveled old cop his way, had him intervene in such a timely manner?

Jon was gone, yes. Gone from him, from Alicia, from the sisters who loved the funny, scrappy little boy. But Conor believed that his boy lived still, in heaven's embrace, that somehow, someway, God engineered amazing things beyond the ken of mortal man. He had no proof, not an iota, but he didn't need any. He believed, simple as that.

He passed the historic Catholic Church with a wave to the priest who bustled from the rectory toward the arched main doors. The priest waved back, a friendly smile on his ruddy face despite the brisk wind, then disappeared into the recesses behind the tall oak entry.

Conor wove his way between the mix of headstones dotted with angels and saints, sure of his goal. Jon's stone stood out near the back corner, a spark of color in a sea of sun washed gray.

Conor circled the marker and stood before it, then crouched, reaching out to trace the letters, one by one. J-O-N-A...

The headstone showed little wear, unlike its historic counterparts, wearied by decades of wind and rain. The polished look of the marker made Jon's passing seem suddenly more immediate. Conor stood, the past rushing up on him like a tunneled train, thundering, rattling, consuming the ground surrounding its rails like a raging storm of arcing sparks and tempered steel.

"Mr. Bradstreet?"

A hand touched his sleeve. Conor jerked back. The onslaught of emotions hiked his breathing. His fingers quivered with pinpoints of electricity. Turning, he recognized the priest he'd waved to minutes before, and felt the sudden urge to explain his presence. "I'm—"

He was...what? Words eluded him, but the priest made them unnecessary. He nodded, his aging face a compilation of compassion and gentle grace. "No explanation needed. I see Mrs. Bradstreet out here quite often—"

Conor nodded acknowledgement, knowing Alicia's visits outweighed his.

"Maybe too often," the priest continued, his hand warming Conor's arm. "A stone that's well polished is still just a stone."

A weight in Conor's chest eased with the kindness of the words. "I don't see Jon here." He waved a hand in the direction of the russet-flecked grave marker. "What's here isn't my son, isn't what made my son special and wonderful. What lies here is just...bones. Jon was more than bones, more than dust. He was..."

"Special." The priest filled in the blank with a quiet nod of understanding when Conor's throat refused to allow him to form the word. "It's a horrible thing to lose a child." He shook his head, his expression more understanding than sympathetic. "It goes against the order of things, and we mere mortals like our order. Indeed, we do. Then life hands us chaos and we begin to see how little control we actually have."

Conor took a deep breath and released it, easing into the conversation. "I liked control."

The priest nodded. "Most of us do."

"But, now," Conor stepped back and cast a glance to the gravesite then back to the priest, "now I want peace. Joy. Fulfillment."

The priest's face relaxed into an open smile. "I happen to be a reigning expert on that." He waggled five fingers toward the church behind him. "They don't call it amazing grace for nothing, you know."

Conor eyed the back of the familiar church that had been a weekly tradition when the girls were younger. Back then he'd gone because it looked good and fit the part, the focused, hard-working, striving-for-success father coming home to attend church with his picture-perfect family. What a scam artist he'd been. So shallow, so cool. No wonder Alicia...

"Are you living here now?"

The priest's inquiry interrupted Conor's litany of self-degradation. He shook his head. "Planning Kim's wedding."

"Ah, yes. September." The priest nodded. "She called and set the date with us before she booked the reception hall. She scored major points with the rectory staff by doing that, let me tell you."

Conor stared, not understanding.

The priest grinned. "These days a lot of our young people have skewed mindsets." He ticked off his fingers as he recited the list. "Dress, veil, reception site, flowers, cake, girls' dresses, tuxedoes, music, and, oh, yes, we should book a church. Pretty much in that order. Your daughter called us first." He lifted a shoulder in a half-shrug. "We appreciated her priorities."

Conor smiled. "That's Kim. She goes to church with me every week she's in New York, even though it's not exactly convenient for her and I'm sure she's got plenty to do on her short weekend off."

The priest leaned forward, humor gone, his eyes narrowed in understanding. "You've done well, Mr. Bradstreet. No, you can't go back and change what was," he waved a hand to the town in general and the grave beside them, "but you've changed what is, and that's vital. You've helped a lot of people."

Conor drew back. "I don't understand."

The priest offered him a shrewd look as they started walking toward the gate. "I'm neither dumb nor illiterate. With as many parishioners as we have who work in the city, I keep up on things. It's nearly impossible to see your name without a well-disguised charity function nearby."

"Father, I—"

The priest held up a hand. "No, no, you don't have to explain and your secret's safe with me. I respect anonymity in charity. It's a trait employed far too seldom these days, when helping the right cause garners good press and political attention."

Conor nodded, grateful. "I appreciate that, Father."

The priest shrugged off the thanks, raised a humor-filled eyebrow and latched the quaint gate behind them. "I won't pretend to be unaware of the sizable annual donation you make to our parish on behalf of your family. Since Mrs. Bradstreet stopped attending years ago, I'm guessing she's unaware of your quiet support."

"Some things are better left unsaid."

Father Murphy angled his head toward the lovely old home slated to become Alicia's bookstore. "A little too close for comfort, I'd say." He dragged his gaze from the colonial front windows to the far corner of the cemetery beyond, plainly visible from the store's vantage point.

Conor nodded. "I thought the same thing, but maybe it's a good thing."

The priest raised a skeptical brow.

"Confronted with reality, we either cave or grow stronger." Conor eyed the proximity and shrugged. "It's time for Alicia to step out and face the world. I'm hoping this new venture will facilitate that."

"You know her well."

Conor grimaced. "Not as well as I should have, and not soon enough, I'm afraid."

"Are you dead?"

"Am I...?" Conor straightened his shoulders and drew back, surprised. "Am I *what?*"

"Where there's life, there's hope," explained the priest, his voice street tough. "You're single, she's single, you've got time, what's your problem?"

Conor studied the man before him. "You're talking second chances?"

The priest shrugged, matter-of-fact. "God hands them out all the time. Why not you? Why not now?"

Conor could think of at least a hundred reasons why not, but still...

The priest clapped him on the shoulder with a smile. "Just something to think about. Good to see you back in Princeton again. You've been missed."

"Not by everyone," Conor retorted with a look of grim exaggeration. The priest grinned acknowledgement.

"Some things take more time than others," he agreed as he headed back toward the rectory with a quick wave. "Stop by again. Good chatting with you."

"And you. I think."

The priest's deep laugh echoed behind him, like broad wooden wind chimes on a mid-summer's day.

Conor retraced his steps to the car, pulling his coat against the rising wind. At the door he hesitated, one hand out, the other tucked in his side pocket. He turned and eyed the blocks leading toward Teaberry Street, then tugged his collar up against the chill of the January afternoon and headed in that direction.

Minutes later, their old neighborhood stretched to Conor's right. The east-facing homes blocked the west wind. He turned and strode down the winter-bare street, eyeing what changed and what hadn't.

The "For Sale" sign at One-twelve brought Conor to a dead stop. He eyed the sign, then the door to the house, then the sign again, disbelief nudging him forward.

The old house hailed him, as if begging for help, looking for relief from whomever thought pea-green trim looked good with aged Memphis brick. The combination was staggeringly awful, and it wasn't as though Conor had a clue how to put colors together to come out warm and welcoming, a touch he'd taken for granted with Alicia, but he could tell wicked awful when he saw it, and one-twelve Teaberry was all that.

Obviously street appeal was not a skill possessed by the current owners.

The yard lay bereft, Alicia's gently tended flowerbeds long gone, replaced by straggling bushes that appeared as morose as the rest of the setting. The left wing needed a new roof, no, scratch that, the whole place needed a new roof, and Conor could only imagine what that meant to the inside ceilings.

A dog's bark broke the silent winter afternoon, the quiet neighborhood tucked behind closed doors, sheltered from the early January cold and wind. Of course the Giants were slated to play at four, and most self-respecting men were glued to their seats to watch the weekend's playoff games. Conor pushed back the stab of envy accompanying the thought, shoving aside memories of pot roast and little girl chatter, scuffed up baby boy knees and a recliner that sat in just the right spot, not too much sun.

The surrounding homes were much like Conor remembered, sweet and serene, a collection of quaint salt boxes and colonials nestled amid spreading maples, oaks and ash. Teaberry Street was a family neighborhood, despite its upscale price tags, a place where kids played kickball and soccer in the grass, and basketball hoops adorned expensive drives.

Withdrawing his smart phone, Conor jotted pertinent information into the memory, squinted at the house, frowned at the incredibly out-of-place chipped green trim, and headed back the short blocks to his waiting car.

Inside, out of the wind, he dialed an associate in New York. "James?"

"Conor, what's up? You're not working, are you?"

"No, I'm in Princeton, actually, to plan my daughter's wedding. James, I've got a job for you. I want to buy a house."

"Oh?"

"It's here in Princeton, and without going into a lot of detail, I don't want to cut the deal myself. Too much talk and speculation if I do that. Will you ink it for me?"

"Of course. When can we meet?"

"Not necessary. Get me the best price you can, but I'm willing to pay whatever they're asking."

"Must be some house." James' voice paused as Conor heard the tiny tick, tick, tick of a keyboard through the sensitive phone. "Address?"

"One-twelve Teaberry Street, Princeton."

"Realtor?"

"Sandra J. McGovern."

"Listing realty?"

"McGovern and Associates."

"Phone?"

Conor recited the number without resorting to his miniscule computer friend, then turned his car around and headed back toward Teaberry as he talked to James.

"Okay, Conor, I'm on it," his realty associate promised. "I'll call this McGovern woman and set up a showing."

"No showing."

His words inspired a distinct pause at James' end of the phone. "No showing?"

"No."

"You, um..." James hesitated, his voice quiet and curious. "Don't want to see it?"

"I have seen it."

"Oh." James' voice pitched to a more natural tone. "So she knows you're interested."

"No, not at all. I saw it a long time ago. James, listen, it's complicated—"

"Or deceptively easy," James interrupted.

Conor smiled. "That would be my take on it."

"I'll make arrangements and let you know how much you're going to pay for One-twelve Teaberry Street. You're sure about this?"

Conor had never felt so sure of anything in his life. Except maybe that night with Alicia, after the mind-boggling Penn State win in the closing moments of the divisional championship game. Now there was a moment, no, make that a *night* to remember. That was life to the full, right there. How on earth had he ever gotten stupid after that? Taken things for granted?

He had no idea. Eyeing the property that seemed to realize help was on the way, Conor nodded, easy. "I'm sure. Keep in touch, okay?"

"Will do. And, Conor?"

"Yes?"

James paused, quiet, then came back on. "I think this is a good move."

Was it? Conor frowned, unsure, but equally certain he had little choice. The possibility that his old home would be for sale on the very day he took a walk around Princeton? If he were a gambler, he'd have never bet those odds. Too sure to lose, and Conor wasn't a man who liked to lose.

But like the priest said, sometimes life offered a chance to regroup. Change things up. If nothing else, he'd give the old place the love and care it so richly deserved, once the current inhabitants moved out and took their lack of historic sensitivity with them.

He'd be close to Grayce when Kim and Brian headed to Princeton for weekends. He could take the little girl apple picking at Terhune's, or walking in the park, savoring cones from Thomas Sweet's. Maybe even a family trip down to Sesame Place, before she got too big to enjoy the theme park. And he'd be closer to Addie when she came home, making it easier for her to see both parents. So sensible.

Slightly less sensible was that he'd be closer to Alicia. What had Father Murphy asked in that outright manner? Was Conor dead?

Conor shook his head, surprised that the priest read him so well, but to what end? If he hung around Princeton more often, would it help matters or cause Alicia more pain?

The wayward reminiscence of that Penn State game and the life that followed had Conor clenching the wheel with more vigor than necessary for the open streets, traffic scarce because Princeton undergrads were still on Christmas break.

Would it bother Alicia to have him around, to know he lived around the corner from her new venture?

A tiny smile worked the left side of Conor's jaw, remembering her little slip in the office short hours before, the way she listed toward his grip, instead of away. The look in her eyes before anger shoved the spark of compassion aside. For just a moment she'd wavered, a hint of the woman he married, the woman he'd held through life and death, a woman whose recent history had been pretty well buried between towering shelves. The smile grew as he turned the car down Washington Road. Bothering Alicia might be exactly what they both needed.

"Hey, I'm buying a house in Princeton. Would you like to come visit me there? Maybe..." Conor eyed Sarge as they crossed to a communal table... "Live there with me?"

"I'm too old for sleepovers, Sonny." Sarge grimaced as he crossed the floor, gingerly touching his feet to the rug as if each step caused pain. When Conor offered assistance, Sarge waved him off. "Just 'cause you got me gussied up in this place, don't make me old or crippled. Sit."

Conor obeyed, but smiled. "You are old, not crippled, but sick. There's nothing wrong with wanting to help you. You've helped me—"

"Blah, blah, blah." Sarge waved a grumpy hand for silence, a habit whenever anyone tried to offer praise or thanks for his work at the bridge and among the homeless. "Yaddi, yaddi, you're worse than a Jewish mother. How are them girls doing?"

"We're planning Kim's wedding and Addie's raising the bar in law school. She started her new semester and the professors love her."

"Chip off the old block," Sarge reiterated. "I knew that from the first, didn't I?"

Conor nodded, noting the way the old man's hands trembled as he tried to lift his coffee mug. It took concerted effort for Sarge to stop the shaking long enough to sip the hot liquid. Conor's heart ached to see the deterioration, but he'd known the sergeant long enough to understand what an offer to help might get him. Minimal, a good scolding. On a bad day, it might be a backhanded thwack.

"I'll have plenty of room, Sarge, and Princeton has good medical facilities just a few blocks away."

"I've told you before." Sarge chanced another sip before setting the mug down, the gnarled clutch of his hands making simple tasks difficult. "I'm a New Yorker. You tourists come and go. I belong here."

Conor smiled. "Then I'll visit when I'm in the city. Do you need anything, Sarge?"

"I could use a little less attention from these vultures you pay to take care of me."

"But..." Conor cast up a wondering brow in an exaggerated frown. "I, er...um... thought that was the point. I pay big bucks, you get great care. Show me how this is a bad thing."

Sarge leveled him a shrewd look. "Unobtrusive would be the operative word here, Sonny. Make 'em back off or I'll head back to the streets and they'll never find me."

Conor didn't doubt the threat for a minute. He nodded. "I'll take care of it. And you're not heading back to the streets. That was years ago, remember?"

"Nothin' wrong with my memory."

Quite true. Conor acknowledged that with a lift of his shoulders. "I think you've actually gotten used to a bed and a table now. Electricity. Running water."

The old man's face relaxed in a knowing smile. "Hot baths. Now there's a wonderful thing, Sonny, and everyone takes them for granted or doesn't take them at all because a shower's so much quicker, but I'm here to tell you I'm hoping for hot baths in heaven."

"No doubt St. Pete's installing additional plumbing lines as we speak," Conor replied. He stood and handed off a small box. "Don't smoke 'em up here or I'll get in trouble. Use the smoking area downstairs."

Sarge's face crinkled into a Santa Claus smile. "I've got a couple of the night nurses who smoke with me. We talk."

"I bet you do. Do you straighten out their lives like you did mine?"

"If they need it. Some do, some don't. Gotta know your people, read 'em." Sarge pushed to his feet, a little wobbly at first, but steadier after a few seconds. "That was my gift on the force, why they put me on bridge detail in the first place. I read people."

"You do." Conor put a hand to Sarge's elbow as they moved toward his suite of rooms. "Want me to hang out and watch Wheel of Fortune with you?"

"No. You talk too much. Can't figure out the puzzles with you yammering at me."

"Translation: you want Vanna all to yourself," Conor joked.

"Nice girl. Kind of reminds me of..." Sarge's voice tapered off, his forehead knit above his whiskers.

"Of?"

"My wife, when she was young. Tall and pretty. Blonde like Vanna. People always were surprised why she married a guy like me."

Conor slowed his steps. Sarge never talked about his wife or daughter, killed in a car wreck when Sarge pulled overtime duty. The guilt he'd felt for not going home that night, not being there to drive them to the girl's dancing lesson, had driven the man into a life of homelessness and alcoholism. That single decision cost him his family, his job, his home and his self respect for a lot of years. He'd paid a price no man should have to pay, all because he needed the overtime money to afford things like shiny bikes and dancing lessons for his girl. A real catch-22.

Conor waded into this conversation with care. "I thought every woman wanted a good looking cop husband."

Sarge barked a short laugh. "I looked all right, I guess, at least she thought so, but it wasn't so common for a tall woman to marry a shorter guy back then. Now you see it all the time, like it's the next big thing."

"So, you set the stage. Everyone else is a copycat. Was your daughter tall like your wife?"

Sarge shook his head. "Too many Italian genes, I guess. Gina was a peanut. Fragile, almost, like one of them fairy tale princesses. Dark hair from my side, blue eyes from her mom and delicate boning. When she danced, it was like an angel moving, so light and easy. Her body flowed like water. I've never seen anything like it."

She'd been fourteen when she died. After years of Sarge's reticence, Conor had researched him, trying to help, only to realize that Sarge's mission was to help others once he was off the booze. He stayed homeless by choice, mingling, helping, encouraging, protecting. He took on a guardian angel role, and played the part especially well on the bridge, his former stomping grounds as a bridge negotiator for the NYPD.

They reached Sarge's room. He eyed the door, confused for a moment, then flexed his jaw, his whiskers twitching. "You see the Missus?"

Conor nodded. "We're working on Kim's wedding together."

"Good." Again the whiskers twitched back and forth. "Kids don't deserve stupid parents. Remember that."

"An ultimate truism. Got it."

Sarge stuck out a hand. "You've done all right, Sonny."

"I had help."

Sarge shrugged. "Giving help don't always mean people take it. You've changed."

"Aw, Sarge, are you going to give me the 'you're a better person now' talk?"

"Naw." Sarge shook his head and gave a snort. "You don't like the fuss any more than I do. That's why we get along." He waved the pack of cigarettes toward a passing nurse who frowned and pointed to her watch. "That means it's too early for our evening smoke," Sarge told Conor in a quiet aside. "Her break isn't until nine."

"Smoking with the nurses." Conor grinned down at him. "Nice gig if you can get it." He waved a hand to the cigarettes. "Don't you know those things will be the death of you?"

Sarge laughed out loud and gave his tired body a once-over. "Something will, I hope. These bones are wearing out."

Conor clapped a gentle arm around him in a hug. "You need anything, you call me, okay? I'll be back in a few days."

"Get the staff to quit their fussing and I'll die a happy man. They think they've got to fawn over me night and day 'cause I've got a rich benefactor."

"You do?" Conor frowned. "Who?"

"Very funny." Sarge glanced at his watch, squinted, frowned and pushed open his door. "Time for Wheel."

"Good night, Sarge."

The old man waved goodbye. The door swung shut with a swish and a click.

Conor stopped at the nurse's station long enough to have one woman flirt with him openly, one eye him with a bit of curiosity mixed with respect, while the other actually listened to his request to lay off Sarge a bit.

"We do tend to smother patients when it's slow," she agreed, making a note. "And not just the rich ones, despite what Sarge thinks," she added.

Conor laughed. "You've got him pegged. And make a note, too, that if anything happens to him, anything at all, I'm to be called right away. No delays. My numbers should all be in the record."

She nodded. "They are, Mr. Bradstreet. I'll make another note, just to heighten awareness. He's..." she paused, weighing what to say. "He's faltering."

"Going downhill." Conor nodded. Sarge had been fighting cancer for nearly six months, his age and diminished health a deterrent to heavy duty chemo and radiation. His initial therapy bought him some time and comfort. At this stage of the game, that was all they could offer. Conor buttoned his coat as he contemplated the nurse. "I know there's not much to be done, and the hospice staff is aware, but if he can be as comfortable as possible, as happy as possible, without the fussing that's driving him crazy, I'd be most grateful."

She made another note and dropped him a friendly wink. "We'll soften the fuss with a little sarcastic camaraderie and evening smokes. That ought to make him feel at home."

Conor laughed. "You know your patients. Thank you, Miss...?"

"Barnes. Cassie Barnes." She reached out a hand and gave him an 'I'm not looking to get anything from you' smile. Real. Genuine. Conor didn't get nearly as many of those as he would have liked since life handed him an eight-figure salary per annum. Hers felt good.

He grasped her hand and found her grip firm but relaxed, quick and businesslike. No nonsense. He wasn't surprised. "Thank you, Miss Barnes."

Her smile flipped to surprise and chagrin as some sweet old thing began wailing about how Krakatoa Katie wasn't a lady. Nurse Barnes stepped around the pass door quickly. "I'd better get down there. Mrs. Reinschmidt actually knows the dance number that goes with the tune. Creates quite the stir, you know."

Conor frowned, totally lost.

She grinned. "You don't get it? Vintage Mighty Mouse, circa 1940. Great cartoon. Total guy stuff. Check it out."

"I will."

Mighty Mouse, huh? A woman who watched classic cartoons? An oddity, for sure. He didn't know a woman who actually took time to sit back and relax, laugh at nonsense anymore. Of course, the women he knew were as focused and driven as he was, so that narrowed the playing field considerably. And seeing them during work hours was more than enough.

As he hailed a cab outside the facility's door, Conor withdrew his phone and jotted Mighty Mouse onto his Saturday calendar. It wouldn't hurt to take a few minutes, kick back and watch a little TV now and again. The Kid might like a Saturday morning filled with nonsense and goofy mice. He'd have to give Brian a call and see, right after he figured out what to do with Brian's trick-turning ex-wife. Weighing up who had the harder row to hoe, Brian and the hooker or himself with Alicia, he had to give the "win" to Brian. Alicia might shrug her shoulders to the upper echelon of proper Princeton society, but she was every inch a lady, except when he got her good and riled, which he hadn't done in a very long time.

Of course she didn't know that he was buying their old house, planning to spend time in Princeton, her private domain for the past eight years. That would tweak a reaction on par with nuclear disaster in her hallowed corner of the world. A half-smile tugged his jaw as he contemplated her response. Alicia was about to get jerked out of the comfort zone she'd maintained since Jon's death and her husband's betrayal, thrust into fast action mode by those who cared about her. Kim. Addie.

Him.

She might hate him, no, scratch that, hate him *more*, but he was willing to take the risk like Han Solo in his quest to save the irascible Princess Leia in the original Star Wars movies. The princess's appreciation of Han's efforts ran nil through three long movies and multiple solar systems. Conor would be content with one well-mixed, traditions-valued New Jersey town.

He paid the cabbie and strode into his apartment building, whistling the zippy tune he'd heard at the adult care facility.

The night doorman broke into a grin, his white teeth a flash against dark chocolate skin. "Krakatoa Katie."

Conor frowned. "Frankie, am I the only person on the planet who hasn't seen this cartoon?"

The doorman laughed outright. "Believe me, once you've seen her, you'll remember, Mr. Bradstreet. That mouse can dance."

"Ah." Conor pondered that a moment. "I see. Good night, Frankie."

"G'night, sir."

He entered the elevator with a quick nod, his head a montage of images. Sarge, gruff but weakening, his aged body wearing under the weight of years and illness. The crew of nurses, and their divided reactions. Kim, busy with her wedding when she wasn't counseling derelicts on the streets of Manhattan. Addie, shining in school, probably not eating enough, too focused and too driven, her father's child to a "T". Brian, dealing with a past that granted them Grayce, but came fully equipped with a trick-turning, cocaine-addicted ex-wife, and Alicia, nursing her wounds for way too long.

Through them all wove a cartoon mouse, dancing to the upbeat tune running through Conor's head like an advertising jingle on cable, super-hyped.

The sight of Foster's lean frame soothed him as he stepped into the apartment, the houseman's calm countenance a welcome reprieve. "Foster, do you have any deep, dark secrets I need to know?"

Foster never blinked. "Myriads, sir."

"Great." Conor handed off his coat and clapped the other man on the shoulder. "Just wanted to thank you for keeping them to yourself all these years."

"My pleasure, sir." As Foster moved to put away the coat and hat, he arched an eyebrow in Conor's direction. "Would you like a drink, sir?"

"Like, yes, want, no." Conor regarded the employee who'd become so much more than that over the nearly sixteen years they'd been together. "Will you join me in Princeton, Foster?"

The speed with which the older man answered told Conor he'd already contemplated the question. "I think my place is in New York for the most part, but I'm willing to do whatever you'd like, sir."

"I hate that you're always right, Foster. You know that, don't you?"

"Yes, sir, but it gives me great pleasure that you recognize the fact."

Conor grinned. "You're a New Yorker, Foster, despite the British accent. I'm beginning to understand that persona better now."

As Foster moved toward the kitchen, Conor followed, determined to eat, relax and hit the sheets in quick order. "Foster, have you ever heard of a mouse named Krakatoa Katie?"

Foster raised both brows, his glance approving. "As has everyone. World War II, Indonesia. That mouse had legs." Foster's expression smacked of total male appreciation. "And she knew how to use them."

"It's a cartoon, Foster." Feeling suddenly out of the loop and a mite irritated, Conor sank into a kitchen chair, snapped open a napkin and knit his brows into a distinct and uncomfortable furrow.

"When one has seen Katie, one understands the understatement involved in such a cavalier assessment," Foster returned. He served Conor a bowl of steaming, thin soup, stocked with mushroom and barley. The scent alone cried total Fifth Avenue.

Conor sipped the broth, savoring the blend of beef, onion, mushroom and grain. "I could make a meal on this alone, Foster."

The houseman nodded. "A nice blend all in all, but I think I've outdone myself on the steak to follow, sir."

Conor thought of the lunch he missed while he wrangled an extra thirteen-point-five million out of a recalcitrant tech firm that stepped on the wrong toes as they clawed their way to the top. Expensive lesson, but affordable because their stock was on fire at present, ready to split at any time. Next time they'd be more careful, or at least more discreet.

"Have you eaten, Foster?"

"I did, sir."

"You know it's okay to have dinner with me, right? We've trod this ground before."

"Countless times, sir, and even so, it's still aggravating conversation. When you're here, my task is to take care of you. I believe that's why I'm paid, is it not?"

"Doesn't mean we can't eat together." Conor offered the retort with a sardonic look.

Foster shook his head, his expression bland. "All that jumping up and down to wait on you." He patted the general region of his stomach. "Not good for the digestion. Might I suggest a woman friend in my place? Considering Katie the mouse, someone long and leggy might be in order."

Conor choked, coughed and sputtered. "All right, I've got it, I'm now officially dropping the topic of conversation."

"Excellent, sir. How is your steak?"

"Perfect, as always." Conor cast him a glare the manservant ignored. "Any calls this evening?"

Foster shook his head. "None, sir. I believe most people attempt your mobile phone first, knowing your schedule is harried."

Only Foster could use the word harried in his gently imperious tone and sound perfectly normal in Manhattan. Conor chewed his steak slowly, washed some down with a long swallow of coffee he shouldn't have, and eyed his houseman-slash-trusted friend. "Am I doing the right thing, Foster?"

No explanation was necessary. Foster had been around long enough to know Conor, know Alicia, love the girls and miss little Jon. He maintained a firm profile, but nodded. "I believe so, sir. Finally."

Leave it to Foster. "Well, man, if you thought I should do this long ago, why didn't you say something? It's not as if you're generally afraid to speak up on matters that are none of your concern."

"Quite right, sir, but some matters require a need for perfect timing and an air of extreme delicacy. I believe you've achieved those."

Obviously Foster hadn't witnessed Alicia's reaction when he visited Princeton the previous week. Delicate, it wasn't. "You might be wrong on that one, my friend."

"I doubt it, sir."

Conor laughed out loud. Foster joined in with a slight smile that faded with Conor's next words. "I hope you're right. My goal is to not make matters worse."

"Hardly possible, sir, so I sense good things from your full frontal assault."

Conor humphed. "Full frontal would have been to let her know what I was doing. I believe my actions would be better classified as covert and possibly devious."

"Most full frontals begin in the trenches as furtive actions, sir. Then they escalate into full blown war."

"To what end, Foster?"

The houseman grasped Conor's empty plate and steered it toward the sink. "That, sir, remains to be seen."

Conor nodded. "Yes, it does."

CHAPTER EIGHT

Alicia checked her messages as she crossed the library parking lot, then pondered her choices when Conor's name flashed five separate times. Seeing the intermittent *blink, blink, blink* of his name, she curled her lip, then thought of wrinkles and straightened her face with a tired sigh.

If there had been an emergency, he would have called the library direct. Instead, he'd piled her voice mail full of flashing Conor Bradstreet's, not exactly what she had in mind when she agreed to a peaceful and equitable working arrangement for Kim's sake. What was she, his new BFF? Um... No.

She stared at the phone, contemplated her choices, tempted to discard her promise to play nice. She'd behave when absolutely necessary, or when Kim was around to bear witness, but no way was she about to let Conor barge into her work, her barn time with the horses and her peaceful, well-organized existence. End of story.

Conor's name winked like the steady beat of a faithful heart, but Alicia understood the likelihood of that scenario, so the analogy didn't exactly cut it with her.

She weighed her choice quickly, then deleted Conor from the phone's system with somewhat vicious stabs, her toes frosty and her ears stinging with the force of the wind. She pulled her scarf tighter and climbed into her SUV, ruing technology that made her more available than she ever wanted to be for certain people.

The message light on her home phone flashed a hearty welcome as she walked in. Kim's voice bounced into the air when Alicia depressed the play button. "Mom, Dad's been trying to get in touch with you all afternoon about the horse-drawn carriage we wanted to use on the wedding day. He got a line on what seems to be a really nice service just over the border in Pennsylvania, not far from Newtown. He wondered if you wanted to check them out, or should he do it, but when he didn't hear back from you, he went ahead and booked them."

Alicia hit Kim's number on the speed dial. *You will be civil, you will be civil, you will be civil...*

The mantra paced through her brain. After all, it wasn't Kim's fault that her father lived the life of a manipulative powerhouse, ready, willing and able to crook a finger and have things happen on demand. Some people had real lives. Real jobs. Like hers, at the library, cataloguing books. Not earth-shaking like Conor's, but she liked to think she made a difference in her own Dewey Decimal System way. Kim picked up her phone, interrupting Alicia's musings.

"Hey, Mom. Where've you been?"

Kim sounded hurried, but since taking her job with that big foundation in New York, she often sounded that way. Hassled. Harried. Frenzied. So New York.

"Working, honey. Just like you." *Only not as frenetic.*

"I'm glad you called. Dad tried to get through to you earlier, but he never heard back from you, and we were afraid this livery might get booked."

Alicia took a deep breath. "Kim, we're talking a few hours here, nothing major. I was tied up." *You weren't any such thing,* scolded her conscience. *Stubborn: check. Bull-headed? Yes. Still ticked off about things*

long since past? Bingo. Lighten up, why don't ya'?
Seriously. The internal scolding made her clutch the
phone tighter. "What's the scoop?"

"I mentioned to Dad that you were having trouble
finding a horse-drawn carriage service available on
September fifteenth, and he and Colleen managed to
track down a place outside of Newtown, near
Langhorne. They had a cancellation for that day."

"And?"

"And that's why Dad was trying to get a hold of you,
to make sure we booked them."

"Kim it's not like these are the last horses on the
planet, right? I told you I'd take care of it."

Kim's voice tightened. "I know, Mom, and I
appreciate all you've done, but there really are only a
few places that service the Princeton area with horse-
drawn carriages. It seemed prudent to get them locked
in. Teams of horses aren't like limo service these days,
a dime a dozen. Did you know they make Hummer
limos?"

"Can't say I did, nor imagine any reason why they'd
be desirable. So..." Alicia sucked back words of
recrimination. "We're all set then? Dad to the rescue?"

"It wasn't like that."

Alicia paused, realizing she was taking her anger
out on the wrong person, when what she wanted to do
was smack Conor for being so totally efficient,
outrageously self-assured and wretchedly good looking.
She drew a deep breath at her overuse of adverbs and
changed tactics. "You said someone helped your dad?"

"Um, what?"

Obviously Kim's attentions were split. Hearing
Ryan Seacrest's voice in the background, Alicia
understood that the rival for her daughter's attention
was about to ax two initial Idol contestants. Time to
hang up. But, before she did...

"You said your father and someone researched this."

"Colleen helped him," Kim offered. "She's his executive assistant at the firm."

"How nice. So important to have competent help."

"Mom." Kim sighed. The sound meant she really did not want to get into this with her mother. For the life of her, Alicia couldn't figure out why the whole thing took on an air of such importance, but it did. Mr. Perfect strikes again.

"It was no big deal," Kim continued, placating her.

For just a moment Alicia hated that mollifying had become a necessary method for the girls to deal with her on more than occasional rants. What was the matter with her? Didn't she used to be...nice? Kind of? At least a little? Where had that person disappeared to? And if, like Sandy implied, that outgoing person actually had existed, how could she get her back, retrieve a part of her, long gone?

Nothing came to mind. That in itself said too much. Alicia fought the urge to sigh. Or throw something.

Kim's matter-of-fact tone interrupted her examination of conscience. Good thing. She'd found herself in seriously uncharted territory. Dangerous past-time. "Dad found the sites and Colleen placed a few calls. She's cool. You'd actually like her."

Of course she would. Alicia bit back both the grimace and easy retort, took a breath and asked, "We're good to go, then? Mission accomplished?"

"Yes." Kim lowered her voice a notch. "Mom, if this is going to work, I mean, the whole truce thing between you and Dad, you've got to be willing to do your part. Meet him halfway from time to time. He's only trying to help."

Meet him halfway? Like this was her fault that he meddled where he didn't belong, just to look good and come out smelling like a rose?

Halfway my eye. Conor was on a typical Conor-takes-over-the-world ego trip and she'd gotten in the way. How typical.

A twinge of doubt niggled her from within, a tiny voice telling her to be kind, play fair, get over it, already. She hated that voice.

But he'd gotten the horses at least, a task that had befuddled her when no one had any available for mid-September, and Kim seemed happy, her fairy tale wedding coming together.

Now all they needed was a wicked stepmother. If availability became an issue, maybe a peri-menopausal biological mother would suffice. She sighed, glared at the blank TV once she hung up the phone, took a shower and went to bed.

Two days later a letter arrived, addressed in Conor's bold, black script. Fresh from horse chores, Alicia shed her barn coat on the back porch, promised the smelly thing a much-needed washing, kicked off her boots, and stepped into the warmth of her designer kitchen, thankful for central heat and fresh coffee.

Inside the envelope she found a full color brochure labeled *Langhorne Livery and Stables*. Knowing horses, Alicia eyed the photos of the matched Shires and appreciated their stature.

She had to give it to Conor. He'd done well. The sleek black horses with their blaze of white looked tuxedo-ready, a perfect accompaniment for a wedding carriage.

Something slipped from the envelope, landing on the floor. Stooping to retrieve the folded sheet of paper, Alicia found a coffee shop gift card tucked between the folds, bright flowers dotting the front of the card.

'Leash, just wanted to show you a little down time gratitude for all you've done to keep Kimber calm. That in itself is a blessing. Hope the Shires are okay with you. Nice that they already come dressed in formal wear.'

The fact that they shared the same thought about the black and white horses struck her as somewhat endearing and downright frightening. Did they really used to think alike? Of course not. How silly. She frowned, rued the action, straightened her brow, and went back to the note.

I know you like finer-boned horses, but these guys were available so I grabbed them. Got the gift card with flowers, hoping for spring, not because you need money for coffee, but because it's kind of nice to have someone else buy you a cup now and again. Conor.'

Alicia eyed the horses, beautiful specimens of an old, draft breed, knowing exactly what she should do. She should pick up the phone, call Conor's cell and thank him properly. Wavering, indecisive, she opted for the coward's way out, moved to the phone and hit Conor's home number, knowing he'd be at work. *Chicken.*

"Bradstreet residence."

"Foster?"

"Yes, Madam. Good afternoon. How may I help you?"

You had to love Foster. No matter how much of a jerk Conor was and/or is, Alicia would have wished Foster into her half of the divorce settlement. Solid, staid, total perfect deportment and smart as a whip. A good employee and a great friend. "Can you give Conor a message for me?"

The tiny pause that followed meant she should call her ex-husband herself, talk to him, go one-on-one, but she'd gotten so used to using Foster as her go-between that the idea of not using the impeccable houseman put a lump of dread dead center in her belly.

"As you wish, Madam."

One of these days she'd toughen up in proper fashion. Stand her ground. Stop being petty, although it seemed to have become an ingrained social skill. At the moment it seemed like way too much work for a woman about to launch her own business. "Can you tell him the horses are fine and that I appreciate the gift card?"

"I believe Mr. Bradstreet will be home this evening."

Foster launched the words as an invitation to call back, talk to the man in question, do a little tête-à-tête.

Nope. "I'm tied up tonight, Foster. If you'd relay the message, I'd be most grateful."

"As you wish. Anything else, Madam? Any other way I can be of service?"

Alicia hesitated, unsure what to say. *Yes, Foster, I'd actually like to talk to the well-preserved old goat, see if I can hold my own. Have him give me a call when he gets in. I totally lied about being gone tonight, unless you count a trip to Wegman's grocery as a night out. What a life.* "No, Foster, that will be fine."

She hung up, recognizing her cowardice, hating the fact, and totally unsure how to change. Oh, she talked a good game, but talk was cheap. Reality? Facing Conor, dealing with him on a regular basis? Whole other ball game.

Alicia jotted things into a steno-pad the next week, flipping back and forth through pages of notes, then withdrew her cell phone from a side pocket.

Sandy quirked a brow, resigned. "A smart phone would make your life so much easier."

"You're technologically possessed," Alicia retorted. She hit a number and waited, impatient, then got the contractor's machine. Again. Grrrrrrr...

Don't wrinkle your forehead, don't wrinkle your forehead, let the cream do its work, let the cream do its work...

"Harry, this is Alicia Bradstreet. I need confirmation on that carpentry work or our electrician can't continue. Your guy isn't here, it's after ten and the electrician's about to walk and reschedule us in two weeks, which will make me considerably less than happy. At the moment, I'm holding the electrician at bay with coffee and donuts, but my options are dwindling. He eats fast."

Footsteps echoed to her right. Alicia turned and saw the contractor shift his gaze from her to her phone with a look of mock despair. "Mrs. Bradstreet, didn't I promise the work to you?"

"Yes, but—"

"And do you know me to break my promise to anyone in our town?"

"No, but—"

He pointed to the mountain man who lumbered after him, toting a metal box. "Jerome Biltman, Biltman Fine Carpenters. This is Mrs. Bradstreet, our boss."

The younger man stepped around Harry and flashed an easy smile. "Nice to meet you, Mrs. Bradstreet. And?" He arched a brow toward Sandy, his light eyes bright in the shadowed setting.

"Sandy McGovern," she supplied, reaching out a hand. "Of..."

"The Realtor." Jerome nodded as he settled his toolbox on a low worktable before accepting her offered hand. "You handled Mary and Mike Groton's new house on Mercer not too long ago. Well," he paused and shrugged. "New to them, anyway. They liked working with you. Said lots of good things."

Sandy almost preened and in the years that Alicia had known the other woman, Sandy McGovern never preened. Ever. Alicia turned back to the men and tapped her watch. "Who wants to go handle the electrician whose work has been waiting for over an hour?"

"I will." Jerome gave a quick nod and started toward the back room. "We had to finish up a university job for the Human Rights presentation scheduled for tomorrow, and since the President is slated to attend, all work has to be done and approved ahead of time by the Secret Service." He grimaced and ran five fingers through a mop of hair that shrieked misbehavior. "Ran into a problem or I'd have been here on time. I apologize."

Alicia nailed him with her best piercing gaze. "Good thing I like the President, Mr. Biltman, or your excuse wouldn't hold water. As for the university, it's on my persona non grata list right now, so the fact that you did their work first isn't winning you big points from me."

He laughed, showing great teeth and a right side dimple. Sandy clutched the nearby shelving unit for support.

"I'll plug you in before any university work from this point forward," he promised, a hand over his heart. "But right now, I want to go meet with your electrician..."

"Jacob Felding."

The carpenter nodded, his expression appreciative at the name. "Jake's excellent. No wonder he's chomping at the bit. How'd you get him so fast?" He sent her a look of interest as he turned toward the back room. "I heard he was booked solid."

Alicia gave credit where credit was due. "Harry lined him up for me before we even had approval, which is why we get along so well, isn't it, Harry? You let me think I'm in charge and then make sure I'm not."

Harry's look stayed affable. "You are in charge, Mrs. Bradstreet, as long as you sign the checks, and my job is to make sure your job is worry free."

Alicia relaxed into a broad smile. "All right, we'll let you guys get to it, then. So, Harry, you think I'm okay to schedule stocking the shelves by March first?"

"And open in time for St. Patrick's Day." Harry nodded. "That gives us a solid block of time to get things in order, install the shelving units on both levels, label the areas, roll the new carpet and bring the restrooms up to code. We'll be fine."

"Then I'll get out of your way," Alicia told them. As she headed for the door, she angled her head toward the small office area. "There's fresh coffee and donuts and bagels from around the corner. Help yourselves, gentlemen."

"Once we get squared away." Jerome moved toward the back room again, his steps assured.

As the door swung shut behind them, Alicia grabbed Sandy's arm. "You practically swooned at his feet. What's gotten into you?"

"Are ya' blind?"

Alicia sighed. "No, his looks are all right, but he's just a guy, Sandy."

"A to-die-for good looking guy with a great smile, good hands and no ring."

"You scouted his hands? Already?"

"First thing. That's how it's done. Come on, you can't have totally forgotten the rules of engagement?"

"My rules of engagement differ from yours, it seems," Alicia retorted. The mid-February day held a glimmer of spring, but an Arctic cold front was predicted by nightfall, thrusting them back to reality. Alicia could deal with reality, the surety of it. Never mind longing for a season just out of reach. Practicality loomed far too important. "Mine are currently relegated to seeing that wedding plans and wedding deposits get made to keep Kim from knuckling under the demands of her high-pressure job and her upcoming nuptials, and overseeing the progress of my new and exciting venture whose venue we just left."

Making the right onto Witherspoon, Sandy turned into her realty office and swung the door wide to let Alicia precede her. "While mine are currently a quarter-mile down the road on that remarkable hunk of Princeton manhood we just left. Obviously I'm not as immune as you. Where has he been hiding all these years?"

Alicia rolled her eyes. "Once you've been married to Conor, you realize that men can be fairly unnecessary, generally untrustworthy and not all that attractive, despite their initial packaging which may or may not be prime."

"Ouch. There goes civilization as we know it," Sandy lamented. "Me? I'm an old-fashioned kind of girl. Meet Mr. Right, fall in love, get married, have a family, then retire rich."

"Your lack of altruism astounds me. You forgot to save the world someplace in there."

"My biological clock is ticking," Sandy reminded her. "Saving the world takes second place to Mr. Right and procreation."

Alicia couldn't dispute that. "True, unfortunately. So why not call the carpenter, see if he's interested in sperm donation, utilize him as needed to produce the proper end-product, thereby ensuring the kid and or kids, the great job, enough money to guarantee the whole retirement thing and no foolish man to mess up your life."

"That has got to be the worst attitude I've ever encountered, and I've encountered many." Sandy sent her bold look of girlfriend-type assessment. "You've gotten more than a little riled since our friend Conor's come back into the picture. I wonder why that is?"

"The only picture Conor's slated to be in is Kim's wedding picture." Alicia worked to keep her voice mild. "If Kim wants the image of a big, happy family for her wedding, I'm determined to give it to her. Even if it kills me."

Sandy made a face of disbelief.

Alicia ignored it. "Anyway, I'm on at the library this afternoon, once I've got a lock on Garlock Estates for the reception."

"September is beautiful there," agreed Sandy. "And I'm expecting closing papers on a property today, which puts me at my monthly financial goal with fifteen days to go."

"*Cha-ching.*" Alicia smiled. "See? Who needs a man?"

"I'm going to refrain from reminding you that the credit card you've done serious damage to under the guise of this wedding belongs to a man. A very specific man."

"Who's doing what he does best," Alicia noted. "Throwing money around. I'm more than happy to help him spend some of his wad when it comes to my girls. You know that."

"Luckily, they're delightfully normal girls despite their parentage." Sandy arched her brows as she spied an official-looking envelope on her desk. Applying a letter opener, she slit the tape and withdrew the paperwork, eyeing the contents with a knowledgeable expression. As she scanned the pages, she stopped on or about page five, her jaw slack, eyes wide. On a quick intake of air, she called for her assistant.

"Yes?" Brenda Kroder appeared in the door, brows up, hands out.

"Brenda, when did this come in?" She waved the envelope toward the middle-aged woman.

"Minutes ago, next-day delivery. I knew it concerned yesterday's closing, so I logged in the time of delivery and set the envelope there." Brenda pursed her lips and moved forward, her look going from Alicia to Sandy. "If you hadn't come in just then, I was going to call your cell phone and alert you that it arrived."

"Something wrong?" Alicia took a step toward the desk, concerned at Sandy's expression.

"Um...no. Not wrong. Not exactly." Sandy's forehead furrowed. She looked from the sheaf of papers to Alicia, then dropped her gaze back down and tapped a polished finger against the official-looking documents. "These are papers from yesterday's closing, lawyers only, very neat, very quick, no counter-offers, no contingencies, no banks, nothing dickered, not a squabble."

"That's good, right?" Alicia stepped forward again and lifted her shoulders in a light shrug. "Every Realtor's dream. Money, signature, done." She took another step, Sandy's reaction unnerving her. "What property is this, anyway?"

"Your old house," Sandy murmured, her voice uncertain. "One-twelve Teaberry Street."

"Well, maybe the new owner will have better taste than the current one," Alicia quipped, feeling a ping of remorse that her old home had slipped into new hands yet again. Poor old house. What it had been through these past twelve years. They could share stories, no doubt, about love lost and what it feels like to be uncherished and under-appreciated. "It certainly couldn't be worse based on what you said."

"Well, you'd be the best judge of that, my friend."

Alicia frowned, not understanding. She lowered her chin, studying Sandy, and shook her head. "You lost me."

Sandy made a face and tapped her nail against the papers as she chewed the left-hand corner of her lower lip. "The new owner of record is Conor Bradstreet."

Alicia's heart fell out of her chest and landed somewhere in the vicinity of Nassau Street. "You're kidding."

"Oh, honey, I wouldn't kid about something like that. It's here, in the disclosure papers, signed, sealed and delivered with a hefty check besides. Conor Bradstreet became the proud owner of One-twelve Teaberry at two-oh-seven yesterday afternoon."

"How could he do this without your knowing?" Alicia sank into the chair opposite Sandy. "Didn't he have to sign papers, the purchase offer, something to show who was buying the house?"

"He used a representative," Sandy answered, eyeing the papers. "Someone from New York. Very common."

"Of course."

"It's actually a smart move," Sandy told her, her brow still furrowed. "When rich people make it known they want to buy something, the price skyrockets. What Conor did makes perfect business sense."

"What Conor did is underhanded and demoralizing," Alicia snapped. "He bought that house to spite me."

"I don't see how," Sandy began, but Alicia cut her off.

"He's been weaseling his way into the girls' hearts for years now."

"He *is* their father," Sandy reminded her. "These days, with all the deadbeat dads, most mothers would welcome that attention to their children."

"Buying them, you mean."

"They don't act bought, Alicia." Sandy shook her head. "They act like they love their dad and the money is incidental. Neither one of those girls looks for handouts, and they're both hard-working."

"Another Conor trait." Alicia's blood had reached boiling point about ninety seconds before. She stood and shook a finger at the papers on Sandy's desk. "How can we block this?"

Sandy shook her head. "Can't. Deal's done. Signed, sealed, delivered. Conor's bought himself a house."

"Not just a house," Alicia wailed, glad that no one besides Brenda and Sandy were present to witness her total meltdown. "Our house. My old house, where I raised my kids and sat with my neighbors and played T-ball in the park. My house, which sits just around the corner from my new business."

Sandy's look of surprise met Alicia's glare. "I hadn't thought of that."

"He did this on purpose," Alicia declared. "He's like... stalking me. Making me think about him, about us. Turning up around corners, messing with the girls' heads."

Sandy sat back in the chair, musing. "It's a bold move on his part."

"Bold? How about dangerous? Intrusive? Humiliating?"

"Humiliating?" Sandy's expression turned to puzzled. "How?"

"That he'll be here, in town, where I have to see him, run into him, and think about what he did."

"Almost nine years ago, right?"

"Don't do that." Alicia trembled, anger pounding from her temples to her toes. "Don't pretend that time makes everything better, that forgive and forget nonsense. It's not like that with Conor and me."

"No, it's not." Sandy paused a quiet beat before adding, "Maybe it should be."

"I'm leaving." Alicia strode to the door, back rigid, heels tapping a smack-smack rhythm against the polished tile.

"Alicia."

She paused at the door, angry, hurt, and mortified down to the tips of her very cool camel shearling Gucci knock-offs.

"I didn't know about this. You know that, don't you?"

She turned. "And if you had?"

Sandy raised her shoulders in a shrug. "I have to respect client's confidentiality. That's my job. But I'd have had a hard time with this one, girlfriend."

The whole thing proved too much for Alicia to absorb. "I've got to go somewhere where I won't think about this, or about Conor and how nicely he's moved on with his big city lifestyle and his never-ending nights on the town."

"If it's any consolation, he won't find that here."

Alicia worked her jaw and shook her head in agreement. "He never did."

Conor's phone vibrated early that evening. He scanned the display, tried to hide his surprise, then excused himself from the strategically placed dinner table to move to the restaurant corridor, phone in hand. "Alicia? What's up?"

Alicia never called him. Ever. If necessary, she left messages with Foster, or sent terse, tight e-mails with no signature. She didn't text him, because texting was too close to talking. He couldn't remember the last time she used his cell number. "Are you all right?"

"No. I am so far from all right that if I had you in this room I would refuse any internal attempt to restrain myself despite my proper upbringing and cause your demise with my bare hands while taking great joy in ridding myself of your lifeless body, Conor."

Fury. Wrath. Passion. Angst. The combination brought back more than one memory and almost spawned a grin, but Conor had wised up somewhat over the years. He'd need to tread much firmer ground before goading her out of her temper. Still...

"As tempting as that sounds, I have to decline, at least temporarily. I'm at a benefit dinner. Can you murder me later? Give me time to finish this up and catch the late train?"

His attempt at levity was not graciously received. Once she waded through a list of names, some of which Conor felt certain she made up, she got down to business. "You bought our house, Conor. You walked in here, acting all nice and peaceful, Mr. Freakin' Tranquility, then went right out and bought our house without a word to anyone."

Ah, the crux of the matter. She'd found out about One-twelve Teaberry. To say his actions inspired her ire would be a tad short of understatement. Conor drew a deep breath. "I took a walk down the road and the house looked lonely. And somewhat ugly."

His words halted her harangue. "It... what?"

Conor had decided that if they ever got to the point of talking like mature adults again, he'd be upfront and honest, as long as his honesty didn't cause her any more grief. Now seemed as good a time as any to start. "The house. It looked lonely. I stopped over on Poole Street to see your new shop and took a walk down Teaberry. When I saw the 'For Sale' sign, it seemed too good to be true. Except for the ridiculous decorating, of course. By the way, I could use some help getting the place back to its former nice, normal, historic self. You up for the job?"

"Up for the job?" Her tone breathed fire and ice, an interesting combination, very "Lord of the Rings" special effects. "You want me to help you redecorate the house we shared all those years? The house where our children were conceived—"

"Two of them," he interrupted. "I distinctly remember that Kim was—"

"Enough." Alicia's tone smacked down that particular trip into the past. "I don't need a play by play of our sex life. Trust me, toward the end, there wasn't much of note."

"But in the beginning..." Conor drawled the words, part of him wishing he hadn't made her angry, another part glad he'd stirred her enough to place the call, even if it was to ream him out. After all this time, he figured they had to start somewhere. "We had lots of good times there, Alicia. A good life for the most part, except that I was gone too much. Now I just want a place for the girls to come visit me in Princeton, a place Grayce can run to so she can hang out with Grandpa. That's not so awful, is it?"

"Not that house."

Conor disagreed. "Of course that house. Have you

seen what those people did to the place? It's a monstrosity."

"No." Her voice went curt and protective. "I make it a point to stay away from Teaberry Street."

"Just as well or you'd be as angry as I was."

She paused and her breath caught on a half-hitch. "Angry?"

"That they let the place slip like that. Didn't take care of it. That's a great house."

"An investment, you mean."

"I mean a home. So many times I came down Nassau from the Dinky, and couldn't wait to turn that corner, see the lights of the house or the girls playing kickball with the neighbor kids. It was everything a home should be."

Alicia's snort said she wasn't exactly buying the concept. "If you felt that way, you might have considered visiting more often."

Conor didn't disagree. "Stupid then, smarter now. At this point in my life I want to be close to my family as often as possible. That doesn't make me a bad guy."

"You already were a bad guy, Conor. Your actions after we buried our son ascertained that."

He blew out a breath at the direct hit. Funny, he thought he'd moved beyond the point where her arrows could blast dead on, but, no. Guess not. "You're right. I was. I've improved."

"Yeah, to the point where you're making my life miserable yet again. Kindly show me the improvement in that."

"No one's trying to make your life miserable, Alicia."

"You bought our house. Tell me how that's supposed to make me feel?"

Hopeful? Peaceful? That's how he'd felt about the whole thing, but they weren't exactly playing on a level field. Obviously hope and peace weren't feelings she attributed to his projected proximity. But, given time... "My offer still stands. I could use some help with this place and you know that I'm clueless about things like colors and fabric stuff and looks."

"Hire a decorator."

"Too impersonal."

"Ask the girls."

"Too busy."

"Check with one of your girlfriends."

"Fresh out."

"Conor Bradstreet, I am not about to help you put this place back together just so I can work through an entire field of emotions I stowed away a long, long time ago. Leave me out of your equation, leave me out of your life, leave me alone."

"If you change your mind..."

"Hell will grow icicles first."

"Current climate conditions make that unlikely, so I'm going to hope you decide to do it for the girls' sake."

"Don't drag them into this."

He decided not to remind her that she'd suggested using the girls short seconds ago. After all these years, Conor was beginning to understand the moves of the game. Kind of. "I want them to feel at home whichever house they're in. Yours or mine, there or in New York. This move will make their lives more comfortable."

"Kim's getting married, she'll have her own home soon and appears quite comfortable to me. On top of that, Addie's nearly independent."

"Everybody needs a place to come home to, Leash. That's what makes life worth living."

"You can throw those words at me, when for months after Jon died I prayed you'd come home, then prayed you'd stay around a little longer when you did. Talk to me, maybe. Touch me. You were a stone, Conor. Still are."

Harsh words. Harder to hear for their veracity. "I felt like a stone, Leash. Cold and hard. Good analogy. I couldn't seem to fight my way out of it, even for you."

"Or your girls?"

Conor shook his head, contemplating the magnificent city view from the restaurant window. "I hated myself, I hated my life, I hated that I couldn't save Jon no matter how much money I made, and I hated that you hated me."

"Then you shouldn't have made it so easy."

Conor drew a breath, suddenly tired. "You're right. I'll work on that. Right now I have to get back to some really bad chicken concoction that doesn't resemble any chicken dish I've ever had before or care to eat again. Do you still make Chicken Parmesan like you used to, covered with bread crumbs and pan fried in olive oil?"

She hesitated long seconds, then... "Y...yes."

"See if they can serve that at the wedding reception, will you? It's like the best thing in the world. Nothing else I've ever had is as good as that chicken."

"We are not serving Chicken Parmesan at Kim's wedding," she retorted, his request pulling her off the hate-train frenzy for a moment. "Her dinner choices will be point by point delicious and upscale. I have a Garlock Estates menu right here on my desk and I'll go over the options with Kim at her earliest convenience. Then we'll go for a tasting."

"A what?"

She sighed out loud. "A tasting. They prepare the dishes so you can see what each one is, taste it, and decide what you'd like to have served, course by course."

"Count me in," Conor declared.

"Count you in for what?"

"The tasting. Sounds like fun."

Her voice stiffened. "It's not fun for you, it's fun for Kim and me. And Brian, if he wants to be there."

"Brian's one of those involved kind of guys," Conor replied. "He'll want to be there. And since it is my checkbook—"

"Credit card, actually."

"To avoid the squabble, let's just call it a general holder of gross monetary units, hmm? For that alone I should at least get a bite of some frou-frou dish, don't you think?"

"No. I don't think that at all. Isn't your chicken thing getting nasty while you talk?"

"Couldn't get nastier. Trust me on that. When's the tasting?"

She blew out a breath that Conor suspected might be flame-enhanced. Very dragonian. "A week from tomorrow."

"Perfect. I've got that weekend slated to start work on the house, so I'll be in town." He didn't mention that he'd have said the same thing about any date she suggested. Another perk of owning the company, and not a bad one, at that.

"Fine. I'll tell Kim."

"Thanks, Leash. And if you come up with any ideas for how I can fix the house, call me, okay? Good night."

He hung up before she could offer a retort she'd most likely regret by morning and considered himself quite altruistic to save her from herself in such a manner.

Pocketing the phone, he returned to the dining room where his chicken had been removed. For that favor alone, he could bless Alicia's timing. Inadvertently she'd done him a good turn. Foster had made stroganoff the previous day. Conor was sure he remembered leftovers. Foster's stroganoff beat restaurant chicken, any day. Throw in a little crusty bread from the downstairs bakery, and Conor had a meal fit for a king waiting at home.

He spent the next ninety minutes being courted by some of the city's finest schmoozers. He made note of some and dismissed the rest. *Homeward Bound* had become a successful non-profit entity in a city that thrived on non-profit entities. Everyone wanted some good quid pro quo on their resumes as they clawed their way to the top of Big Apple business or politics. Those were the rules of the local game. Charitable credits made people look magnanimous. Caring. Some of them actually were. Those were the ones he made notes on.

Conor had determined years ago that *Homeward Bound* wouldn't move on its own agenda. The foundation's schematic was laid by the men, women and children of the streets, first, last and foremost. With Kim at the helm of the mental health outreach via the mobile van clinics, Conor knew her heart and soul matched his. Success didn't hinge on numbers, but on the opportunity to be a Good Samaritan on the streets of New York, and sometimes beneath the streets of New York, where people scuttled in dark subway and railway tunnels, living like moles in the shaded, moist underworld, trapped by mental frailties and/or addictive behaviors.

Brian had agreed to head up the overall financial picture of the eight-year-old charity, which meant a different direction for the younger man, but one he'd accepted easily.

With acquired real estate to offer decent, clean apartments to hundreds of the formerly homeless, *Homeward Bound* was making a dent in the street population while it made a name for itself among the destitute. His people could be trusted for medical, psychological, and physical care. They took facilities into the streets, seeking the alleys and overhangs, the park rotundas, highway overpasses. Wherever the poor sought shelter from the wind, Conor's vans rolled into place, offering hope and understanding, not recrimination.

And in a few short weeks there would be two hundred and seventy more apartments ready for habitation in a series of buildings they'd nearly completed renovating in Queens.

Not all homeless people wanted to be off the streets. Odd as it seemed, some grew nervous at the idea of being 'boxed' in an apartment.

But many were just down on their luck, waiting for a hand up. His foundation offered that hand, person by person, step by step, earning their trust, and then their friendship, and all because an old man refused to let Conor Bradstreet take the bridge one Christmas Eve, eight years back.

Sarge, bless him, fulfilling his mission to serve those in need.

Conor eyed the gathered assemblage of New York money holed up in a lofty restaurant party room and smiled inside, amazed at the power of one man, a derelict who cared enough to climb a bridge on a cold, wet winter's night under the guise of looking for a match and inspired a man's salvation.

CHAPTER NINE

The mirror refused to cooperate the following Saturday, despite Alicia's intensive efforts. No matter what she rubbed on, wiped off, and re-applied, the face staring back at her remained same-old, same-old when what she wanted was devil-may-care transformation, a sassy good looker, the kind of woman to bring Conor to his knees right before she shrugged him off, cool and crisp.

But fate left her wretchedly normal. Why was that? Would morphing into a leggy, cellulite-free underwear model or a Julia Roberts look-alike spoil some vast eternal plan? She thought not.

Average, it seemed, was the best she could do, except for her hair, still thick, its chestnut color enhanced with pricey monthly help from the local spa girls. Despite the onslaught of magic creams and potions and the inordinate amount of time she'd spent that morning, she looked absolutely normal on a day where she longed to rank above average. Kim's shout interrupted her negative self-appraisal.

"Mom, you almost ready?"

"Be right there." Alicia took one last look in the mirror, spun on her heel, and wished it didn't matter how she looked, but since Conor would be there, appearances mattered. Big time.

Kim smiled up at her as she descended the final steps. "Isn't this exciting?"

Alicia refused to go straight to exciting, not with Conor around. Nerve wracking? Yes. Adrenalin-pumping? Most assuredly. Somewhat brain numbing? Absolutely. But since this was Kim's wedding, an event she'd waited decades for, Alicia smiled and nodded. "Very. Are Brian and Grayce ready?"

"Warming the car. It's wicked cold today."

"I know." Alicia shifted her gaze. The picture window framed a thick, winding slope of old trees edged by an ancient stone fence. The small grove led to the road, highlighted by a dusting of snow. "Almost spring, though."

"And your grand opening." Kim gave her a quick hug. "A lot happening."

Alicia slipped into her coat, pondered a hat, realized it would muss her hair and shelved the idea of warmth in favor of what beauty she could garner. Good hair she had. Might as well make the most of it.

Kim eyed her, puzzled. "No hat?"

"We're just going to the car."

"Or scarf?"

"No."

"The wind chill is below zero," Kim reminded her as she wrapped a great looking, double layer, super long scarf around her head and neck, enough to keep her nice and snug. "You'll freeze. You always bundle up."

"You're starting to sound like a mother." Alicia grabbed her purse, stuffed her lipstick inside just in case she chewed hers off on the drive over, and headed for the door. "I'll be sure to warn Grayce."

"Do you think she'll be okay while we talk with the wedding planner?" Kim angled a slight frown to Alicia as they headed out the door. "She's a great kid, but this could take a while."

"Three adults, one six-year-old. What could go wrong?"

"Four adults," Kim reminded her. "Dad's coming, remember?"

Like she could forget? Please. "I don't generally count him in the adult category."

"Mom."

"Sorry." Alicia paused, sucked in a breath of frigid air that made her nose sting, eyes run, and her throat ache. She hustled to the car as a gust of wind swooped along the eastern edge of the house, swirling tiny ice pellets into her face, notching the pain factor up by a factor of ten, minimum. "I'll behave."

"Good."

Conor's Mercedes sat parked near a side entrance to the main lodge house of Garlock Estates. Esteemed for grace and quiet luxury, the spread of the exclusive facility exuded old money and timeless elegance, from the flawless cedar and mottled brick siding to the cobblestone paved, pillared entrances. The golf club stretched to their far right, while the banquet and conference facilities banked left, nestled in the shelter of sprawling old trees and recurring gardens, dotted with holly and yew, points of green amidst the dull tones of late winter.

The door swung open, and Conor stood like a welcoming committee of one, looking as good, no, make that *better* than he had six weeks before.

The injustice of that reality chipped Alicia's resolve to behave, or was it the way her heart jammed against her ribs that made her want to lash out irrationally?

Suck a calming breath through your nose, breathe deep, and bestow upon him your queenly smile accompanied by a slight nod of acknowledgement. Let him see that his presence has absolutely no effect on you. You've moved above and beyond anything to do with Conor Bradstreet, except where it involves the girls or his bank account. End of story.

Ice-tinged air hit her lungs and stung her cheeks as she stepped from the car. The gale-force wind wrestled the dry wax spray she'd used on her hair. No contest, the wind won, her hair swirling and dancing in her eyes and whipping her face before falling back, catching on her earrings.

Eyes watering, she half-staggered through the door, one hand over her mouth, her purse slipping with a thunk! to the floor, gaping wide, while personal items scattered in a pattern reminiscent of well dropped Pick-up Sticks.

Conor and Grayce swooped to gather her things from the floor while Alicia tried to contain her cough. Grayce held up a pink and white, plastic-wrapped, tube-shaped item to Conor. "Grandpa, what's this?"

Conor never missed a beat. "Something of Grandma's, honey." He tucked the tampon back into its case, shut the inner zipper with sure hands, then piled the rest of Alicia's things on top. "There we go." He smiled at Grayce as he held out the purse to Alicia. "You're a good helper, Kid."

His praise and matter-of-fact attitude satisfied the little girl while Alicia prayed for a do-over, a quick rewind to when Brian first pulled the car into the parking space alongside Conor's, give her just one more chance at her imagined grand entrance.

Conor handed off the purse, the twinkle in those cinnamon eyes his private concession to the embarrassing moment, at least until they started moving down the plush hall toward the offices. Then he leaned over and ran the upper zipper of her bag back and forth across the purse's opening, not once, but twice. "Great invention, zippers. Open, easy access." He slid the zipper shut. "Closed, things stay where they belong. All kinds of things."

Alicia resisted the growing urge to tell him what he could do with zippers. He reached ahead to hold the door for her, his expression amused, as if he knew what she longed to say and trusted she was too much a lady to say it.

He knew her well, too well, and it had been like that since they met, as if there was something about her that fit with him, not unlike the teeth of a zipper, interlocked, bound by fate and clever design.

But the design had faded with time, warped by passing years of his passion for work and her penchant to punish him for his absence. When their lives fell apart in a sea of sorrow and deceit, the ensuing crash seemed anti-climatic, making it easy to blame Conor for everything that had gone wrong.

Seeing him before her, holding the door, his chin tilted down as he angled a brow her way, eyes lit with gentle amusement, she hated that those familiar actions attracted her after all these years.

Worse, she despised that he probably had streams of women at his beck and call, that his good looks had only solidified with time, and that he considered the Big Apple his personal playground while she existed in a four-mile radius of day-to-day life.

Her self-assessment had "Loser" printed all over it.

When had she gotten this way? More to the point, why had she stayed this way, stodgy and stubborn?

Conor's voice interrupted her escalating train of thought. "Has Kim decided on this place?"

Alicia turned and tuned into the purpose of the day, determined to focus on the wedding and not on the scent of his leather jacket, or the dark umber turtleneck beneath. She wondered if he knew how well the shirt went with his eyes, then remembered this was Conor...of course he did.

She answered his question without looking up. "As far as I know, yes."

"Because?"

"It's pretty, gracious, well-appointed and outrageously expensive."

"Convincing points, all around," Conor noted, his voice easy. "How's the food?"

"I'm sure it's amazing. That's why we're here, right?"

Conor nodded as Kim and Brian stepped into a well-presented office at the end of the hall. "Did you ask about the Chicken Parm?"

What was it with this guy and the stupid chicken? Hello? They were not about to serve breaded Chicken Parmesan at Kim's wedding reception. Talk about prosaic. "I'm sure they'll have several good selections, but I'm equally sure that won't be one of them."

Conor shrugged as if disappointed. "It wouldn't be as good as yours, anyway."

Alicia's heart paused at his words, right before she gave herself another internal scolding, remembering who he was and why he lived in New York while she lived in Princeton. The small matter of cheating on his wife with a leggy lawyer and the resultant divorce. No doubt they'd been the talk of the cocktail party circuit for months on end. It had taken time and effort to regain a sense of control, to feel like she had the reins firmly in hand, her daily existence calm and unquestioned.

Until he bought their old house so he could rub her nose in his presence.

Conor slid back a chair for her. She sank into the tufted leather seat without a whisper of acknowledgement, refusing to chance a look his way, bemused by how quickly he slid under her guard, beneath her radar. Looking straight ahead, she focused her attention on the wedding planner's elitist presentation.

A soft knock at the door drew their attention. The wedding planner surged to her feet. "Mr. Preston. Good morning."

"Good morning, Rachel." He smiled and nodded at the woman as if his presence hadn't flustered her. His eyes scanned the room, landed on Conor. "Mr. Bradstreet." He took a couple of steps and held out his hand as Conor rose. "We had the pleasure of talking not too long ago."

"We did." Conor took the other man's hand in a steady grip, his manner a tad uncomfortable. "Nice to meet you in person."

"And you."

The wedding planner appeared to rediscover her purpose for living. "Mr. Bradstreet, you obviously know Mr. Preston."

Conor gave a quick nod. "We've done business together."

"Mrs. Bradstreet." The young woman nodded to Alicia. "This is Mr. Preston, the CEO of Garlock Aviation and the co-owner of Garlock Estates."

Alicia offered her hand. "And chairman of the Princeton Zoning Commission."

"Guilty, on all counts. How are your plans for the bookstore coming?"

Conor stiffened beside her, but Alicia ignored the action. "Fine, thank you. We're looking forward to a St. Patrick's Day opening."

He smiled and made a really bad attempt at an Irish brogue. "Earnin' your first bit o' green on the wearin' o' the green."

Conor winced. "You might need to work on the accent, Reggie." He waved a hand, indicating the rest of the family. "My daughter Kim, her fiancé Brian, and his daughter Grayce, aka The Flower Girl."

Grayce wiggled at the mention of her name, offering a smile that lacked two top teeth.

Reggie shook hands all around, then turned back to Conor. "When you're done here, may I have a minute?"

Conor's gaze flicked to his family, then back to Reggie. "Now is fine. I believe my primary objective here is food-tasting, and we're not to that point yet, so I'm okay to step out as long as they promise to save me a bite or two."

"We can probably manage that," Kim promised.

Conor stepped forward, then turned back. "Oh, and, Kim?"

Kim met his look. "Yes?"

"See if they make Chicken Parm, would you?"

Alicia bit back a groan and a laugh, miffed that she even considered the latter.

Kim flashed him a smile. "If not, I'll make it for you soon."

Conor copped an abject look of fear. Kim laughed out loud. "Okay, maybe I'll take you out for it instead."

Conor gave her a wink and laid his big, broad hand along her cheek, smiling. "Much better idea."

The planner acknowledged his humor with a well practiced smile beneath an immovable brow, botoxed, no doubt. "We'll move down the hall for the tasting, Mr. Bradstreet. I'll be sure you're back with us before we do, and of course our chef can create a perfectly elegant *Pollo Parmigiano Italiano* for your wedding guests if you'd like."

Kim's brow arched up when Conor turned his gaze Alicia's way. "Not quite the same, I'm afraid."

Points of heat bit Alicia's cheeks, caused by Conor or an upsurge in estrogen. Maybe Conor's presence spurred an upsurge in estrogen? Conor and hormones seemed to go hand in hand.

Conor laid a light hand on Alicia's shoulder and bent down, his mouth near her ear. "I'll be right back."

His breath feathered wisps of hair along the edge of her neck, his words tickling the sensitive skin, while the pressure of his hand felt warm and comforting, like a well-washed quilt.

Red alert! Red alert! Red alert!

Instantly she waxed into zone mode, the calm, cool, detached persona she donned when emotions spun out of control. "Of course."

Her words were prim and proper, but her heart rate rose by a factor of five, maybe six, she might have to give him the extra multiple depending on whether or not she survived the imminent heart attack. A growing flush crept up from her lower neck, her breath coming in butterfly puffs, light and ethereal.

He squeezed her shoulder, gentle but definitive, his touch as sure and composed as the man himself.

Shivers spiraled down her back, her arms. She crossed her arms in self-defense and Kim leaned her way.

"Cold?"

"Um, no. No. I'm fine."

She put effort into listening to Rachel's spiel on the harmony of a well-planned wedding day, and couldn't help but think back to her own wedding, somewhat hurriedly planned due to Kim's impending arrival.

They'd been married in the church of her youth, an ancient, ivory-stoned affair in Cleveland, whose parish numbers dwindled with the rise of suburban home building. The old church now faced the danger of closing. The remaining parishioners would be shuffled to a neighboring parish whose priest served both communities. The news saddened Alicia, dimming the memories of the old city church, the comfort she'd known there, a staple of her early life, but the thoughts of her wedding day stood out, bright and clear, a young couple with big dreams, bright futures, and all the hope and promise of young love. Funny how life could beat a good thing into the ground, given enough time and lack of effort on the part of the participants.

Footsteps sounded outside the door. Conor stepped back in, his look assessing. "I didn't miss the food, did I?"

Rachel laughed. "I just got a message from our chef that everything's ready in the Dubonnet room. Your timing is perfect."

Conor flashed her the grin that melted female hearts. "Where food is concerned, anyway."

Kim stood and glanced at her watch, then whistled softly. "Mom, can Dad drive you and Grayce home when we're done here? Brian and I have some things that need to get done today, and it would help the cause greatly if we can head south while you guys head west. Is that okay with you, Dad?"

Conor hiked a brow to Alicia, his expression unreadable. "I'm fine with it." He raised his chin slightly. "Alicia?"

Caught between Kim's time constraints and the lovely Rachel's obvious admiration of:

A. Conor's money

B. Conor's looks

C. Conor's humor

Alicia took the high road. She nodded to Kim. "That's fine, honey," then swung her gaze up to Conor. "You're sure you've got time?"

He shrugged. "Nothing but time. The weekend's totally free. Why don't we swing around the old place and you can fill me in on what needs to be done?"

Trapped. Foiled. Ensnared in a Conor-web. How did he manage to do that so well? Alicia hemmed and hawed, then gave in, unwilling to make Kim fret or tweak Rachel's attraction further. "We'll have Grayce with us."

Conor tugged the little girl's hair, then swooped her up into broad, sturdy arms. "In that case, I think a trip to Thomas Sweet's for ice cream would be in order, don't you, Grandma? Like we used to do when Kim and Addie were small."

The thought of swinging into the popular local ice cream parlor like any old family out for a Saturday treat seemed way too normal an event to share with Conor, but once again she acquiesced due to her surroundings, a fact, no doubt, Conor read and understood. "I'm sure Grayce would enjoy that."

"I love ice cream thiiiiiiiiis much." Grayce extended her arms from side to side, stretching to make her point.

"That's significant," Conor noted. He winked at Alicia, the action transporting her back thirty years, to the very moment she felt her heart tumble and fall into his. He'd winked then, too, from the tennis court where he'd just completed a set against a Supreme Court nominee. Beat him, too, despite the fact that the sitting Federal Court judge might preside over a Bradstreet case at a later time.

Conor didn't care. Even then he recognized that he was good enough and strong enough to make his case when necessary.

His actions showed that Conor was no ordinary man. That fact alone should have made her run for the hills in search of average and every day, but the thrill of Conor's ambition drew her, his quest to conquer the world of New York finance an idealist's dream in a lion's mindset, patient, pacing, ready to pounce at the most opportune moment.

She'd been drawn to both sides of him, until the reality of the lion meant long weeks alone while Conor wheeled and dealed his way around New York.

She'd discovered that single parenthood wasn't her cup of tea, and let Conor know it with increasing regularity. Someplace along the way she'd turned into a bona fide fishwife, nagging and haranguing, wanting more of him, but unwilling to spend time in the city to achieve that goal. In the end she ended up the very thing she didn't want to be: a single parent. She'd lost on all fronts, her son, her husband and a good share of her self-respect.

Would things have been different if she'd been different?

An internal slap to the head junked that train of thought. Conor did her wrong, and at the worst possible time. No normal woman could forget that, and hadn't she ascertained her status just that morning? Alicia Bradstreet was, is and ever would be, nothing more than normal.

Conor pulled into the driveway of his newly acquired old home and waited for Alicia's reaction. She didn't disappoint him.

"Oh." Her mouth dropped open, eyes narrowed, forehead knit in disbelief. Her jaw worked to one side, then back, while she shifted her gaze from the disaster of a paint job to the condition of the roof, and the yard. "How bad is the inside?"

Conor shook his head. "Don't know. Haven't seen it yet."

When his words registered, she shifted the look of disbelief his way. "Haven't seen it?"

"No."

"You bought the house unseen?"

Conor shrugged. "We lived here, Leash, it's not like I'm unfamiliar with the place."

"That was a long time ago," she protested, eyes wide, brows drawn up. "Conor, they could have totally trashed the inside."

He pushed open his door, moved to the back seat, and withdrew Grayce. "Let's go see."

Alicia's face shadowed as they swung the pea-green door wide and stepped into the entry. "This is... awful."

Conor tried to look at the bright side. "But, other than the roof, I think it's structurally sound. I'm having the roof inspected this week, then we'll take care of replacing that and fixing any hidden damage beneath the shingles. In the meantime, the first floor can be taken care of. I figured I'd wait on the second story and the attic until the roofing was complete."

Alicia had moved forward, her gaze sweeping multiple directions. "How could anyone be this stupid?"

"Stupid's not a nice word, Grandma."

Alicia's wince said she realized the same thing the moment Grayce opened her mouth. She turned back. "Sorry, honey, Grandma should have said careless."

"Or clueless, foolish, dense, inane, or idiotic," Conor supplied, ever helpful.

Alicia crossed a nutmeg shaded rug to study the hand-carved mantel above the bricked fireplace, soot-stained and drab in the afternoon light, then frowned, glanced down at her light-toned pants and growled, one hand slapping her pants as she ran back to Conor. He reached out his free arm to catch her. "What's wrong?"

Alicia bent and batted, her hands moving in furious fashion. "Fleas."

"No." Conor glared at the rug, then reached down to slap two more hoppy little fellows from Alicia's leg.

"Oh, yes." Alicia scooted for the door. "Conor Bradstreet, if you've infested me with fleas on top of everything else you've ever done, I'll..."

"You'll what?"

When she swung back he stood right behind her, inches away, clutching Grayce, searching her gaze for something to hang onto, come home to.

Her breath caught when she met his eyes. For a split second she leaned forward instead of back, he was sure of it, her body language betraying her words. "You'll pay, big time."

He laughed down at her and was relieved to see her relax into a smile. He reached out a hand to her hair, palming her cheek, amazed that she could still feel so right after all these years. "I already pay, big time. You'll have to do better than that, woman."

He thought she turned her cheek into his hand for just a moment, but then she headed back to the car, out of the wind, and away from the fleas, and he wasn't sure if he'd invented her reaction or witnessed it.

Once he had Grayce belted into her booster seat, he slid into the front, huffed and puffed cold air, and started the engine. Grayce's voice hailed him from behind.

"Grandpa, I think it's too cold for ice cream today. Can we go to Grandma 'Licia's and drink hot chocolate? She knows how to make it the special way."

Disappointment speared Conor. No way was Alicia about to offer Grayce's special recipe hot chocolate to him, loaded with marshmallows and whipped cream, but he couldn't deny the little girl's request. The bitter wind did make ice cream less noteworthy for the moment. He put his emotions on hold and nodded, keeping his expression easy. "Whatever you want, Kid."

She preened at him through the rear-view mirror. Alicia visibly relaxed by his side, any nuance of attraction gone with the backlash of winter cold. As he wound through the town and curved onto Route 206, he wished the day could go on, spend a little more time with her, make her laugh. She didn't laugh like she used to, not nearly as often, or nearly as well, and he took full responsibility for that.

She'd laughed a lot when she liked him, and more when she loved him, and it would be good to hear her laugh again, see her unwind. Did she know how beautiful she was? How desirable? How cute her expressions were? Well...

Some of them, anyway. She had developed a few un-enticing ones as well. Watching her that morning, sensing her unease, he was pretty sure their break up did a serious number on her self-esteem.

Kids don't deserve stupid parents.

Sarge's words flooded back to him as he contemplated the woman at his side. If Alicia was a big case with major components, he'd break them down one by one, stretching time and effort to piece a mosaic that provided a full and accurate picture.

Part of him wanted to beg her forgiveness, ask for the second chance he didn't deserve, but the slightly smarter lawyer side of him promised that actions spoke louder than words.

Prepare ye the way...

St. John's words soothed him, their simple message a light at the end of a decade-long tunnel.

He hadn't won Alicia's heart overnight, nor lost it in a day. Romancing a woman took time and heart, qualities he'd developed in his more recent past.

Pulling the car into her driveway, he angled the Mercedes around the curves and pulled up to the garage door. Getting out, he unbuckled Grayce while Alicia messed with the door lock, her hands awkward. Did the cold make her fingers fumble, or was it his presence?

Once the door swung open, she reached for Grayce. "Thanks for bringing us home, Conor. And for the fleas."

No invitation in. Not like he expected one, but a guy could hope. He nodded. "I'm at the Nassau Inn if you need anything. You know. Like bug spray. Anti-itch cream."

She tried hard not to smile.

A tiny corner of his heart relaxed. "Or have any ideas about the house."

"An exterminator?"

"I was aiming for post-extermination ideas."

"Burn it and start again?"

He tilted his head, his gaze on hers. "Leash."

She sighed, dropped her cheek to Grayce's knit hat and nodded. "If I think of anything, I'll let you know."

"Thank you." He wanted to touch her, just once more, raise his hand to her cheek, so fair, so soft, a hint of ruddiness from the day's cold, but she stepped into the doorway and the chance was gone.

"Goodbye, Conor."

Grayce suddenly realized he was leaving. "Grandpa, can't you stay and have hot chocolate with us? Please? I'll play Memory with you."

He wanted to. Longed to.

Sensing Alicia's withdrawal, he shook his head. *Prepare ye the way...* "Not this time, Kid. Grandpa's got to figure out how to fix up the old house so your Grandma doesn't get attacked by fleas when she visits."

Alicia's eyes darted to his, as if the idea of visiting him was totally alien. He met the gaze head on and smiled, keeping his voice low. "We can't have bugs bothering Grandma 'Licia, now, can we?"

"Oh, no." Grayce gave an emphatic shake to her head as though protecting Alicia was the goal of the day. "We love her."

"That's right, Kid." Conor flicked his gaze from the girl to the woman and let his eyes say more, then stepped back, raising his hand in a quick salute. "You girls have a good day."

He refused to turn back to check Alicia's reaction, despite how much he wanted to. Good or bad, he needed to let her find her own balance, her own way, without undue pressure. Besides, the idea of romancing her took hold in his brain, a seed working toward fruition. His only concern was that if he messed this up, Kim and Addie stood in line to be hurt again. He didn't want that.

Then don't mess up.

A stab of doubt needled him as he remembered Alicia's jabs and thrusts. She'd been hurt and angered by his choices. Re-establishing a trust relationship wouldn't be easy, but he'd faced plenty of difficult situations over the years. He understood the framework, the importance of laying groundwork before building a case. And being in Princeton on weekends meant he'd have the opportunity to run into her on a more regular basis.

Patience. Groundwork. Framework...
But first things, first.
Fleas.

CHAPTER TEN

Conor lifted his office handset as he scanned the latest figures for *Homeward Bound* on his laptop screen, a half-eaten sandwich spilling crumbs across his executive desk. Why didn't they ever pack enough napkins? "Conor Bradstreet."

"Mr. Bradstreet, Frank Antori here, from Princeton. I just wanted you to know that the rather delicate matter you brought to our attention has been eradicated."

Delicate matter? Fleas? Conor pinched the bridge of his nose and sighed. Only in Princeton. "You're certain about this, Mr. Antori? The women in my life have a strict 'no flea' policy. Go figure."

The other man laughed, discreetly, of course. "You have not only the reputation of our company, PPC, but my own as well and my personal guarantee, Mr. Bradstreet. We zapped the little creatures with our most strident measures."

Conor envisioned a team of masked, armed men storming his beleagured house, opening fire on the unsuspecting bugs in "Caddyshack" fashion. "I'll be there this weekend, Mr. Antori. Did your inspection show any other problems?"

"A small mouse or two. Nothing of import. A basement window was improperly closed, allowing possible entry along the gap. I closed the window personally and set the lock. I also put out residual poison in the attic, which I'll remove on Friday. With no other food source, we should be in the clear by the middle of the week. If a strange, musty odor should occur..."

Oh, Alicia would love that. What woman wouldn't be attracted to strange, musty odors? "Yes?"

The exterminator cleared his throat. "Dead mice emit such an odor, and are sometimes trapped between walls. A few days of olfactory suffering and then they're history. Probably a better solution than removing the wall to reach the remains."

Conor choked back a laugh. "Mr. Antori, I appreciate your concern, but I live in New York. Do you really think I've never smelled decaying rodents?"

"Of course you have, sir. I mean, why wouldn't you?" The Italian man backpedaled with nowhere to go. Finally he paused, took a breath, and asked, "If there is anything else you need, please call us."

Conor's lips twitched. He kept his voice easy. "I'm hoping I won't be in need of your services again, but I'll keep your card, just in case. Because you never know. Even in Princeton."

Antori's voice dropped a level. "Yes, sir. Even in Princeton."

Conor laughed out loud as he hung up the phone, the exterminator's attitude a reminder of why he liked the city. New York attitudes were tough because they had to be, no ifs, ands, or buts. If Mr. Antori worked in Brooklyn, he'd be shouting his number of kills from the rooftops, and the people would respect him. Probably throw him a party.

In Princeton such matters were handled with arched brows and quiet dignity, rarely spoken aloud, even when sloppy student housing encouraged the proliferation of wee beasties. Grinning, Conor recalled his undergrad housing at Penn State, prior to swearing off weekend parties and before he met Alicia.

He and his friends had given up naming the mice when they got to number seventeen. Prolific little creatures. A few actually met their demise by drowning in leftover beers, an effective method of pest control by Conor's early standards. You couldn't exactly recycle the bottle, then, but that was okay.

"What's so funny?" George Bleu stepped into Conor's office, a folder in one hand, an envelope in the other.

"Mice. Rats. Fleas."

"Positively hysterical." George's look said he didn't get it and was singularly okay with that.

Conor sat more upright. "The difference in how they're perceived between New York and Princeton."

"Or Venus and Mars." George nodded, his expression grim. "Same difference. We have a problem." He voiced the words in a tone that meant they really had a problem.

"Oh?" Conor reached out a hand, scanned the folder, left brow up, jaw working. "When did we hear about this?"

"Now."

Conor growled, flipped through a few pages, then shook his head. "This is big trouble for Ehrmentraut. Who did the audit?"

"Schlueter and Schuth."

Conor whistled through his teeth at the mention of the top-notch firm. "I'll need a team."

George nodded. His shoulders lightened, as if relieved. Conor flicked his gaze upwards. "You didn't think I'd take this?"

"You're busy," George explained. He shrugged, his hands out, palms up. "You just wiped up that Asian catastrophe and I know *Homeward Bound* has you tied up—"

Conor refuted that. "The art of finding the right people for the right jobs has me untied, other than benefits and schmoozing New York's elite."

George nodded toward the folder marked **CONFIDENTIAL**. "This will bill a lot of hours."

"At some mighty impressive bucks," Conor agreed, "on top of a hefty percentage." He shook his head, eyeing the report. "What on earth were they thinking?"

"CFO and Comptroller got greedy. If you're good enough with figures, and have collusion, you can make a lot of funds disappear in a relatively short space of time when dealing with a billion dollar industry."

Conor sent him a look of disgust. "These guys are already rich. What makes a man like that reassign funds to offshore accounts?"

George tapped a finger to the CFO's name. "Gambling. Women. Likes the big life at the casinos. Amazing how many millions a man can go through in one weekend."

His words sickened Conor. The lack of respect for hard-earned funds ran epidemic among some of the privileged. Too many forgot where they'd been, what they'd done before and developed a 'never enough' mindset. "And the Comptroller?"

"Drugs. Blackmailed by his suppliers. A real interesting network. Liked to frequent the high priced girls on the Westside as well."

"Great." Conor already had one problem to deal with in that venue. Why not two? "Are the police aware of this?"

"If not, they will be. Once the e-trail began to open up, the CEO got us on board to protect their interests."

"He might have thought a little harder about who he employed, in that case." Conor knew the CEO of Ehrmentraut Consulting, a huge firm with international ties. The corporate leader was well respected, but obviously not attentive to business. Ehrmentraut was the company other businesses called when they needed to polish the workplace, tidy things up, let people go, cut spending and payroll. Pity they didn't bother to do the same thing internally. "We haven't had a case like this since MacMillan and MacMillan."

"No. And that one rocked the nation. Who do you want on the team?"

Conor listed a handful of names, then paused. "Addie's going to be here as a summer associate in May."

George nodded.

"Slot her with me when the time comes. It's rare that an early associate gets a peek at what happens when a big company like this plays dirty. The snowball effect will fascinate her."

"And other associates?"

Conor stood and stretched. "I'll hand pick them, with a nice cross-group of people to avoid any appearance of favoritism toward conservative males."

George laughed. "If that girl of yours is any example, I think the company profile may be changing in the coming decade."

"A lot of smart women out there," Conor agreed. He tapped the envelope in George's hand. "And this is?"

"Your bonus."

"Hand delivered?"

"Actually just the receipt as requested. The bonus itself was electronically deposited in your account at twelve-oh-one this morning."

"To the tune of..." Conor slit the envelope, smiled, whistled and nodded. "...an incredibly significant figure."

"Earned and deserved," declared George, no doubt making himself feel better for a similar deposit.

Conor shook his head. "No one deserves this, George. It's ridiculous. But I've got plenty of places slated for this baby, to keep it on task for the future."

"Your homeless project..."

Conor nodded. "And there's a church in Cleveland struggling to stay open while they keep their school up and running. It's in a disadvantaged area, the kids' test scores are wonderful comparatively, so this little school has a big effect on a minority group, but they'll need to close without an influx of funds."

"Which you feel pressed to provide." George shook his head. "Make sure you keep enough for a sandwich. Or a Venti Machiato."

Conor laughed as they crossed through the door. "You'd be surprised to know how much you can keep once you start giving things away. Trusts? Scholarship funds? Compound interest on bulk sums with multi-year guarantees? Seed money is the wonderful cornerstone of an ongoing American economy."

"The hand up theory."

Conor waited.

George cleared his throat. "My grandmother used to say that when they were young, older siblings reached a hand out to younger ones, to help with education, or their first house, the down payment on a farm. Nothing was expected, it was just how things were done. They gave them a hand up."

"So." Conor hiked a brow as they walked through the quiet corridor leading to the elevators. "Who have you given a hand to, George?"

George's expression was enough of an admission. Conor clapped him on the back. "Still time. Plenty of stuff out there that could use a little spare change. How's your grandson doing? The one with autism?"

George straightened his shoulders. "Between the government and university funding grants, hordes of money goes into medical research."

Conor shrugged. "What about the private sector centers that teach kids like Wyatt? Autistic kids, kids with disabilities. There are a lot of them that could use help, and it's something that hits close to home. Or the Special Olympics."

George twitched as if uneasy. "It's hard for me to be around that many kids with problems."

Conor longed to smack some sense into his partner, but swayed in favor of logical argument. He leaned closer. "I'm not suggesting actually seeing them, George, visually." Conor made a 'V' with his pointer and middle finger, indicating George's vision. "Write the check. Start a foundation. Share the wealth."

"You make it sound easy." George expelled a lungful of air on a huff. "I thought my job was to make the big bucks and employ the trickle down theory."

"By the time our funds trickle down, people are dead," Conor reminded him. "Hire a secretary to set things in motion, and oversee them. Fund him or her with your own money, thereby insuring a happy taxman with good write-offs and an overseer of the fund. Designate specific uses or general use, sign the transfer, and done. Piece of cake."

George eyed him. "You've changed over the years. It's either revolting or positively refreshing."

"Thank God for that." Conor glanced at his watch and paused by Colleen's desk. "Have we heard back from Chloe Martin?"

Colleen shook her head as she tapped her keyboard with nails that should have made the task impossible. "Not as yet."

"Then I'll try her again this afternoon." Conor flexed his jaw, made a face of dismay at the slow progress of the corporate elevator, and headed left. "I'm taking the stairs." He quirked a brow at George and tapped the folder one more time. "Stupid."

"Very."

"But in terms of billable hours..."

"Magnificent."

"Fleas?" Sandy stood stock-still and stared at Alicia. "You're kidding."

"Millions of the little suckers, hopping about, trying to eat me alive. Great fun."

"I don't believe it."

"Believe it." Alicia eyed the perfect planes of the ivoried oak trim in contrast to the cranberry upper wall of the centered, second floor bedroom, perfect for displaying New England folk art. "He's just lucky none of them hitchhiked home with me."

"They had a dog, but I never realized..." Sandy's voice died off. "Conor must hate me."

That comment drew Alicia's attention. "Why?"

"He paid some pretty big bucks for a flea-ridden piece of property."

"He can afford it."

Sandy shook her head. "That's not the point. I'm going to offer to take care of the exterminator."

Alicia's jaw dropped open as Sandy withdrew her cell phone. "You'll do no such thing. Conor's made of money."

"Doesn't matter. I presented the house to him in good faith, and the deal didn't include fleas. It's the right thing to do. What's his number?"

Alicia sighed, huffed, then recited Conor's cell phone from memory.

Sandy met her gaze, one brow elevated just the tiniest little bit. "Memorized, huh? I thought you never called him."

"Not calling doesn't mean it isn't important to know how to call him in case of emergency."

"Hmmm..." Sandy's eyes narrowed slightly, listening, before she spoke. "Mr. Bradstreet, Sandra McGovern of McGovern and Associates in Princeton. I just found out from Alicia that your new home is flea-infested. I'm so sorry. Since that wasn't how I presented the sale, I would feel much better about things if you would allow McGovern and Associates to pay any extermination costs you might incur to fix the problem. My number here is 555-SALE, and I should be available for the next several hours."

Once Sandra disconnected, Alicia shook her head. "You're being silly. Conor's a big boy. He can take care of himself. And didn't you say the people jumped at his first offer, no counters?"

"His first offer was generous and I made that point abundantly clear to them," Sandy replied. She tucked a lock of hair behind her ear as the downstairs door opened and closed.

"Ladies. What a nice surprise." Jerome Biltman flashed his great smile from below as he moved toward the winding stair. Once at the top, he turned toward Alicia and waved toward the bedroom. "What do you think?"

Not prone to gushing over anything, ever, Alicia wanted to wax poetic over the room.. "It's perfect, and totally goes against what I'd pictured."

He grinned. "I'm glad you're pleased. Harmony between the plaster and wood is important for the overall feel of the space."

"Men rarely understand that," Sandy noted, her voice carefully flat. "Where'd you get a head for decorating?" Judging from Sandy's too bland expression, Alicia knew she hoped for a definitive masculine answer.

"My mother." Jerome reached across, picked up a magazine from the workbench, and held up the center page, a pictorial layout of a Seattle home that made misted ocean breezes a reality by just viewing the pictures. "Lucille O'Leary. She has a head for seeing things, not as they are, but as they should be. Passed it on to me."

"Lucille O'Leary is your mother?" Alicia cocked a brow his way.

He nodded. "Yeah. She's pretty amazing, too. Managed to raise all three of us between here and New York, totally encouraged my ambitions into carpentry and fine finishing work, which is somewhat unusual for a New York or Princeton mom."

His easy words tweaked Alicia's guilt factor. She fought it down.

"She got a kick out of me being me, but then she's about the most secure, self-composed woman I've ever met." Jerome shifted his gaze toward Sandy. "Kind of like our Realtor, here."

Sandy stepped back, surprised. "Me?"

Jerome regarded her, his eyes narrowed. "Yes. Focused but not foolish, ambitious, not driven, self-possessed, not steered by someone else's timeline."

Sandy's expression was a dead giveaway. Alicia intervened, determined to save her from herself. "We should probably let you get back to work, Jerome. You're doing a wonderful job."

He shifted his gaze from Sandy to Alicia, but not before winking at Sandy. "Thanks. With the preliminary work complete up here, I'm on to the third bedroom today."

"Teal."

He nodded. "Let's see if you like that as well once we're done."

Alicia shook her head, hands up. "You've convinced me. Totally. And since it's historically accurate, I-"

Sandy's cell phone picked that moment to ring. She stepped away, but the bare rooms of the old house made her voice bounce from wall to wall. "Mr. Bradstreet, thank you for returning my call."

Alicia drew her shoulders back and her chin up, listening because it was impossible not to.

"First, I want to apologize for not recognizing the infestation initially..."

Sandy paused and laughed at something Conor said, her eyes bright. "Well, that would have been an indicator, I guess. I knew they had a dog, but I was caught unaware by the flea invasion."

Alicia tried to read her friend's face. Was Conor teasing her or righteously insulted by her offer to pay?

Was he playing out his hand, liking the sound of Sandy's voice, jousting with humor?

"No, I insist, Mr. Bradstreet. All right, then, Conor. No, seriously, I feel bad, the least you can do is allow me to cover the costs you incurred for extermination."

A moment of silence ensued, then Sandy raised her eyes to Alicia's. "Right here, actually. Would you like to talk to her?"

The thump of Alicia's heart most likely audiated throughout the room. Drat and double drat. Conor was asking about her. Why?

Sandy laughed. "I'll ask her." She covered the sensitive mouthpiece and met Alicia's look. "He wants to know if you have any advice for him yet as far as home refurbishing."

Alicia shifted her gaze from Sandy to Jerome, then back. "Sure. Tell him to hire Jerome."

Sandy arched a brow and obeyed. She sent Alicia a look of question at Conor's response. "He wants to know who Jerome is and will you approve his work?"

Alicia reached out a hand. "Give me the phone."

Sandy handed it off with a grin and stepped back to Jerome's side.

"You have to ask my friends to question me? You can't call me yourself?"

"Will you pick up when I do?"

Ah, that melted butter voice. Why did she always get soft and squishy when she heard it? She hesitated, considering her response, then..."Yes."

"You haven't always."

"We're playing nice now. Wedding, remember?"

"I do. Great concept, weddings. The fleas are gone."

"Fleas lay eggs that resist death at all costs," she informed him, her voice tart. "Did they really kill them or just their parents, grandparents, great-grandparents and assorted aunts, uncles and cousins, leaving future hatchlings to latch onto my unsuspecting legs?"

"You have great legs and your flea knowledge astounds me, but I have it on the authority of Mr. Frank Antori of Princeton Pest Control that our house is safe for habitation."

"Your house."

"Sorry. Old habits die hard. So. Who's Jerome?"

Alicia thought she detected a heightened note in Conor's tone, almost as if he was...jealous. The impossibility of that made it easy to rule out. "He's the fine carpenter I hired to do the finishing work on the bookstore. He's remarkable, Conor. Everything he touches is perfect."

"Really?"

"He's got a great eye for balance and color and his trim is precision cut. Amazing."

"Gay, huh?"

Alicia sized up the way Jerome was leaning toward Sandy, his attention obvious. "Um...no."

"Is there a reason you sound so sure?"

"Conor, I'm not having this conversation."

"And yet, you told me to call you."

"About normal things, yes," she hissed into the phone. "Not things like that. Sandy's right here. And Jerome, too."

"You're right. Discussing his personal life would be awkward with him in the room. Want to talk about it this weekend, say...over dinner on Saturday?"

"Does Kim want to meet about something?"

"Not to my knowledge."

Alicia's heart tha-wumped again, a cool but disconcerting maneuver against her breastbone. "You mean dinner just...you and me?"

"Yes. Are you feeling daring this week, Leash?"

"Conor, I don't consider it daring to eat with you. More like...stupid."

"Bad word, remember?"

"Grayce isn't here."

"Bad habit, then. She'll catch you every time. Might as well clean up the language now." He paused for three long seconds. "So. Dinner. You. Me. Food. Quiet time."

She shouldn't. She knew that, knew he was danger to the 'nth' degree, but wasn't that part of what drew her years ago? "Your girlfriends all out of town?"

"No girlfriend. Told you that a few weeks back. Fresh out."

"Perfect time to ask the "ex" out, then."

Conor's voice softened. "I've had other perfect times, but I was pretty sure she'd give me a flat-out 'no'."

"So what makes you think she won't this time?"

He paused, then exhaled. "Because she's trying to play nice. Me, too. I think dinner should be our reward. It's been nearly two months of nice. Gotta be some kind of record."

Alicia clutched the phone a little closer, remembering a time when playing nice was the norm, but that was a long, long time ago. "All right. Dinner. Where and when?"

"None of your business. We're doing this the old-fashioned way. I pick you up at the house, take you out, and then bring you back home. None of that meet you stuff. Too easy to duck out, then."

He'd read her mind. She hesitated.

"It'll be fine, Leash. Promise."

It seemed nice, but crazy, too, seriously crazy to go out on a date with Conor when she could be...watching the Saturday six o'clock movie alone. "Okay."

She almost thought she heard him relax. "And tell your friend I'd be honored to have her foot the bill for the exterminator if it means that much to her."

Alicia considered his use of words, then nodded. "I'll tell her. And Conor?"

"Yes?"

"The kitchen should be done in antiqued cabinetry, maybe with an ivory wash or a light stain. Since it faces north, the kitchen tended to be dark with the cherry tones of the old cabinets. Something lighter would brighten things up appreciably."

"Tell Jerome."

She smiled and held the phone with a little more ease. "I will. Goodbye."

CHAPTER ELEVEN

"Mr. Bradstreet?"

Conor's executive assistant keyed him through the inter-office phone later that day.

"Yes, Colleen?"

"Chloe Martin is here to see you."

Brian's ex-wife. Conor breathed deep, stood, straightened his tie and nodded. "I'll be right out."

He strode through the door, unpretentious. Executive offices could intimidate, and his goal was to coax this young woman to their side, not frighten her off. He appraised her as he approached. Tall, lithe, eyes a touch glassy, pupils too wide, focus forced. *Still using.* Conor tucked aside the wave of disappointment. Rich guy disapproval would win him no points with this woman, he was certain of that.

"Ms. Martin, nice to meet you." Conor presented his hand. She took it, her grip uncertain. "Thanks for coming in to meet with me. Would you like coffee? A soda? Water?" He sent a glance to his assistant. "What else is available, Colleen?"

She stood and gave them an easy smile. "There's a Starbucks downstairs, so the list is extensive."

Colleen's comfortable air seemed to relax Chloe. "I'd kill for a white chocolate mocha."

"I recognize that emotion," Colleen replied with a nod. "Venti or Grande?"

Chloe smiled. "The tall is just way too short, isn't it? What a misnomer." She glanced from Colleen to Conor. "Grande is fine."

"Mr. Bradstreet, the usual?"

Conor nodded appreciation. "You can bring them in when they arrive, Colleen."

"They arrive?" Chloe sent him a look that said his words impressed her. "Starbucks sends them up?"

Conor leaned forward. "Over a thousand employees captured within our floors of this building, seventy hour work weeks for many of them. Starbucks is very okay with delivering to us."

"I'll bet."

Conor stepped back and indicated the short, carpeted corridor to his office. "After you."

She surveyed the wall as she went, an eyebrow arched occasionally as she scanned the artwork. Stepping into his office, she looked around, appreciative. "Beautiful, Mr. Bradstreet."

"Thank you." He waved toward the plush leather seating area against the far wall. "Have a seat."

She sat on the couch and studied the table between them, one hand smoothing across the pieced wood surface. "Great effect. Intricate. A hint of cowboy beneath the suit and tie, perhaps?"

"Southwestern." Conor pointed to a couple of Navajo prints on the wall and the woven blanket suspended below them. "I like Southwestern with leather. It fits."

"What doesn't fit with leather?" She sat back and offered him a more sensuous expression, fingers trailing the mellow surface of the couch back. "I find leather... enticing."

Her tone and look alerted Conor to the fact that she thought she was here under different circumstances. *Great.* He leaned forward, his gaze frank. "Ms. Martin, I didn't ask you here for professional purposes."

"Oh?" She curved a smile as though she heard that line fairly often. And she probably did. That way men could deny the pre-meditation, fool themselves into believing a relationship with a high-priced hooker just happened. For a moment he understood his ex-wife's disdain of his gender a little better. He tucked that thought aside for later examination. "Your ex-husband is engaged to my daughter Kim."

"Oh." The carefully sculpted face flattened, making Chloe look older than her twenty-seven years. "I see."

"Probably not," Conor disagreed, keeping his tone comfortable. "The reason I called you here—"

"Was to shut me up or buy me off."

He frowned. "None of the above, but I forgive you for jumping to those conclusions. Totally understandable, under the circumstances. Ms. Martin," Conor shifted forward, then raised his eyes and smiled his thanks as Colleen stepped in with their drinks. "Thanks, Colleen."

He handed Chloe her sweet-smelling concoction and set down his machiato. He turned toward Brian's ex-wife once again. "Do you like what you do, Ms. Martin?"

The look she gave him hardened. "Depends who I'm doing it with."

Conor nodded. "Good answer, geared to throw me off guard, but I'm pretty inured to drama. Been there, done that, not a big fan. Here's what I'm wondering." Conor slipped her a recent photo of Grayce, prayed he was doing the right thing, and steepled his hands. "Brian said you loved to act and that you were good. I think his actual words were 'really good'. He was impressed."

"Nothing I did impressed Brian." The rose-tipped fingers gripping the Starbucks cup whitened as she stared at the child's photo. "In or out of the apartment."

"You're wrong." Conor gentled his voice, sensing delicate ground. Alicia would have been proud because sensitivity hadn't exactly been his strong suit back in the day. "Being divorced myself, I can see how easily opinions get skewed to the last available option. It's hard to see there are other choices out there. Here's what I'm wondering." He considered how to phrase his offer to heighten its appeal, then shrugged. "If I could help you get into another line of work and off the drugs, would you like to be part of Grayce's life again?"

Her eyes darted to his. "You think you can muscle me through her? Silence me? Keep me on the outside by dangling my daughter in front of me?"

"Absolutely not." Conor met her angry gaze head on. "What I'd like is to see you clean up your act and become part of the family. You're Grayce's mother. She misses you and doesn't understand why everyone else's mommy likes them and hers went away. I'd like to see her have the best possible shot at growing up normal."

"Define normal. Her father's about to marry your daughter. I'm a drug user and a high-end hooker, disease-free last time we checked. No way does Brian want his strung-out, trick-turning ex-wife to be anywhere around his precious little girl."

Conor lifted his cup of coffee and studied her through hooded eyes. "Or is it that you don't want to be around for her to see the choices you made over her?"

Chloe Martin surged to her feet. "Listen, you know nothing, got it? Nothing. I gave up my life for that kid, turned my back on an acting career that was this close," she held two fingers together to show the narrow margin of fate, "then ended up pregnant and out of the line-up."

"You kept the baby," Conor told her, keeping his seat. "That shows character."

"Or fear."

Conor acknowledged that with a nod. "Understandable. Ms. Martin, I won't coerce you. That's not my style."

"Tell that to Mainichi Global."

Conor shrugged. "You cheat, you pay. Simple justice. Some pay more than others. I think you've already paid enough, Ms. Martin."

"You don't know the half of it."

Conor stood. He thought of the file he'd had run on the young woman before him, but kept that information to himself. "If you want things to get better, I can help."

"Afraid of appearances, Mr. Bradstreet?" She rolled one shoulder, an effective runway move, the loose drape of her silk shirt outlining delightful feminine curves.

"No. Just figured it's nice to get a second chance. Sometimes that extra chance makes all the difference."

She took a step forward.

Conor took a distinct step back. "Think about things. Please. You've got choices, including the stage, if that's what you truly want, but the drugs have to go and the high-paying job that funds them has to go with them. For Grayce's sake."

She stared at him, jaw slack, eyes wide and scared. Haunted, almost, but for a brief moment, Conor thought he discerned a glimmer of hope.

"Call me," Conor told her, handing her his card. "Let me know what you decide. It's a big step, I know." The look he gave her was meant to reassure. "But a friend once said to me, 'kids don't deserve stupid parents'"

"And you bought into that?" She hiked up her chin, her face stiff, her tone slightly insolent and a touch... encouraged? Conor thought so.

"I figured he was right." Conor offered his hand. "Thank you for coming to see me, taking the time. I appreciate it, Ms. Martin."

She eyed the hand as though intimidated, then accepted the handshake with caution. Conor gave her a firm, direct grip and some fatherly advice. "Call me. Let me help. There's a world of things out there for a beautiful young woman like yourself. Don't be afraid to reach for them."

Expectation blossomed in her dark blue eyes, but its light dimmed as she contemplated the magnitude of her options. "I'll think about it."

"That's all I ask." Conor saw her to the door and wondered if there was a specific saint or angel for ladies of the night. If so, he could use him/her/them right about now, en masse. "Nice to meet you, Ms. Martin."

She eyed him as though weighing the sincerity of his words and life in general, her brow furrowed, her eyes narrow. "Goodbye."

Conor re-entered his office, sank into the chair he'd just vacated, folded his hands and prayed he did the right thing by asking her in, offering his help, encouraging her by using Grayce. Brian would most likely have his head on a platter for that move, but Conor had seen the sadness in Grayce's eyes, her equanimity about being dumped by her mother. What kid feels good about being left by their mother, the one person in all the world who should love and cherish you no matter what?

He'd square things up with Brian that night, fill him in, then take the blows as they came. Better to be upfront than uptight, and Brian had asked his help, although Conor was fairly certain the younger man didn't expect this approach.

Still, if he was any judge of character, Chloe Martin seemed disgusted with herself and her current lifestyle. Good actress that she was, or had been before coke messed up her mindset, she'd been able to pull off the show of bravado with little mis-step, but Conor sensed the nicks in her armor. Maybe, just maybe, with divine intervention, some time and some money, Chloe could regain the life she'd sought eight years before.

The timeline didn't surprise Conor. Not at all. About the same time he contemplated ending his life, Chloe Martin jumped into a way of life she didn't want and made decisions that brought their paths together at a critical intersection.

Some things in life were coincidental. Sometimes stuff just happens, he believed that. If you roll for snake eyes fifty times, you have an equal shot of getting them with each roll, despite the rolls that went before.

People didn't equate so easily though, and Conor sensed a path for Chloe Martin that could make all the difference, if only she saw her way clear to tough out the beginning. Starting anew might be harsh, he understood that reality, but the young woman had spunk. She could do it if she wanted to, and that would be the crux of the matter. Did she want it badly enough?

Time would tell.

Conor stepped through the front door of Alicia's new venture on Saturday morning and was fairly certain he'd interrupted a significant clinch between a shaggy-haired guy wearing casual clothing and a tall woman in what he thought was a Kaspar suit, light-toned stockings and really nice strappy heels. He cleared his throat and glanced away, trying to hide his amusement.

Alicia appeared on the landing above, her hair a mess, a hole in the knee of ancient, well-washed blue jeans. Her black sweatshirt read: *WARRIORS TAKE NO PRISONERS* in flaked gold print across the front, a leftover from the girls' high school years at St. Michael's Academy. Minimum age of the ratty shirt was five years, and that was if Addie wore the thing her senior year. In actuality, it looked older than dirt, so he'd guess Kim, circa freshman. The fact that Alicia not only kept the ragged thing, but wore it, said more than he could possibly figure out in one lifetime.

Alicia flicked a glance at her watch. "What are you doing here?"

He held her gaze, ignoring her look of surprise and chagrin, wondering what bothered her more, his presence, or him seeing her looking like a bedraggled waif. He'd bet the latter. "I wanted to see the progress you've made, view Jerome's work first-hand, and meet the artisan in person."

Disregarding her frown, Conor shifted his gaze to the couple, now significantly separated, to his right. "Jerome?"

"Yes." The carpenter stepped forward, his movements fluid and easy, no visible trace of embarrassment. "Jerome Biltman." He offered Conor a strong, self-assured handshake. A guy's guy, thought Conor, and judging from what Conor had witnessed, Alicia's assessment of Jerome's gender preference was spot on.

Conor exchanged a brief look of understanding with him, then turned toward the woman as Alicia descended the stairs, appearing annoyed, disheveled and possibly murderous.

The tall woman with great shoes moved his way. "I'm Sandra McGovern, Mr. Bradstreet. We spoke earlier this week."

"Conor, remember?"

A hint sheepish, over the bugs or the clinch, he wasn't quite sure, she extended her hand. "Conor."

He nodded, grinned, shook her hand, winked at the two of them, then turned toward Alicia. "I hope I'm not interrupting anything."

"You know you are. I don't know why you bother saying things like that."

"To annoy you."

"Done."

"Excellent." Conor shifted his gaze to include Jerome and Sandra. "I just came from the house and I was hoping you were still impressed with Mr. Biltman's endeavors."

That topic loosened her up. She bobbed her head and smiled at Jerome who, in turn, tried to look humble and failed. "Jerome's excellent."

Conor shifted his attention to Sandra. "And you agree, Ms. McGovern?"

She blushed clear to the roots of well done highlighted hair and nodded. "Amazing."

"Hmm." Conor didn't dare meet the laughing eyes of the craftsman. They'd never keep things under control then. He switched his interest back to Alicia. "Have you talked with him about the house?"

Jerome glanced from Alicia to Conor and back, an eyebrow up.

Alicia shook her head. "Not yet. I figured he'd want to see it and you'd be down this weekend."

"I see." Without moving, Conor met Jerome's look of interest. "We have a house—"

"You have a house."

Chin down, Conor ignored Alicia's declaration. "That's in need of some major renovations. It's on Teaberry, just a few minutes from here. My wife, excuse me, former wife," Conor tipped his gaze her way as if to salute her sovereignty, "recommends you highly. If you're interested, I'm here this weekend. I'd be glad to have you look the place over."

"The electric's on?"

Conor nodded.

"And the fleas are gone?" queried Alicia, her voice way too helpful.

Sandra groaned and glared up at her. "You don't have to keep bringing them up, do you?"

Heightened awareness brightened Jerome's gaze. He arched a Buzz Lightyear-type brow. "You... bought a house with fleas?"

Conor met his interest with equanimity. "Sandra sold me a house believed to be uninhabited. The non-contractual fleas came as an added bonus."

"I see." Jerome hiked a brow in Sandra's direction. "Fiendishly clever."

The flush of her cheeks deepened. "A totally unintentional bonus whose extermination I'm underwriting."

Conor flashed her a grin. "And unnecessary though it is, Alicia and I thank you."

"Alicia's got nothing to do with this," said Alicia from her perch on the third winding step. "This is your boondoggle, not mine."

"You offered your help."

"I didn't."

"Kitchen cabinets, ivory washed or light stained?" Conor quoted, holding her gaze, pretending not to notice the hint of interest she worked so hard to hide.

Her expression said he got her, and the fact that he did delighted him. Tweaking her was an art he'd laid to rest a long time ago. He'd forgotten how much fun it was, and the delightful task that fell to him in soothing ruffled feathers afterwards.

Jerome gave him a look of approval, stepped closer, chin down, and muttered. "Nicely done."

Conor matched his low tone, chin tucked. "Years of practice."

"Still..." The look Jerome offered was pure appreciation. "Impressive."

Alicia came down the last three steps and looked suddenly smaller without the artificial height bolstering her. "Let's show him Jerome's work or we'll never get rid of him."

Conor nodded, affable. "And since I have a lot to do before our date tonight, I need to hustle." The word 'date' brought Sandra's head around, another half-smile from Jerome and a glare from Alicia.

"I hardly think that getting together to talk about our girls is a date."

"For dinner?"

"People have to eat."

Conor took a step closer, holding her gaze, taking far too much pleasure in watching her smolder. "Benedetti's."

Her eyes widened at the name of the upscale restaurant, but she held her ground. "Conor, it's not like price is a factor for you."

He acknowledged that with a slow nod and edged closer. "Don't they have that dark chocolate/caramel/nut dessert you find intriguing?"

Her cheeks pinked, no doubt remembering another night when they shared desserts from Benedetti's. They'd done take out that night, for dessert, anyway. Most interesting evening. Conor let a few seconds slide by before he smiled. "Great stuff," he noted before turning back to Jerome. "So. Care to give me a tour?"

Jerome nodded and headed for the stairs. "The upstairs is done, that's why Alicia's cleaning up here. They'll start installing the bookshelves on Tuesday as long as everything's ready."

Conor sent Alicia a look over his shoulder. "Can't wait to see it."

The look she flashed him mixed frustration with grudging admiration, enough so that he paused and smiled down at her, openly flirting with the wife he'd turned his back on, the wife who lost her son and husband in one fell swoop because he wasn't faithful enough or man enough to cling to her in his sorrow.

Moron.

But the smile he gave inspired one in return, albeit smaller and a little more hesitant. Another part of his heart opened full size. Over the years Conor had come to realize that heart expansion was a slow and somewhat tedious process unless you were a fictional Christmas character like Scrooge or The Grinch. Mere mortals grew bigger and better hearts step by step, day by day, laying a base that proved sometimes painful and often gut-wrenching.

But today, seeing Alicia smile up at him, her eyes bright and a hint wistful, the heart expansion was virtually pain-free.

CHAPTER TWELVE

Jerome's countenance stayed unreadable as he walked through the vintage two-and-a-half story brick home that afternoon. To Conor, the lack of emotion translated to extra zeroes in the upcoming estimate. With every thoughtful hand Jerome raised to his chin, Conor saw dollar signs. As Jerome finished his inspection in the nearly hundred-year-old basement, he pointed to the six-inch wide beams suspended above their heads, eyes wide, tone reverent. "Masterfully done."

Conor eyed the dark wooden supports, arched a brow and nodded. "Yes."

Jerome flashed him a grin, the first emotion he'd shown since Conor pushed through the front door. "Stick to finance, I'll do wood."

Conor acquiesced with little provocation. "That's why I brought you here. You've got the knowledge, I've got the funds."

As they moved back upstairs, Jerome withdrew a small notebook from his back pocket and scribbled a number across the page, then handed the entire notebook to Conor, who whistled and stopped. "You've ascertained this from one look and no measurements?"

Jerome hiked a brow. "When you're good, you're good."

Conor mulled the number. "Alicia loves your work."

"And you want her happy."

"I wouldn't go straight to happy," Conor deadpanned. "Less than confrontational would be a good start." He waved a hand, indicating the house around them. "I want Alicia comfortable when she's here, that's all."

Jerome gave him a skeptical glance and drawled a question. "Christmas together?"

Little hairs rose along the nape of Conor's neck. "Something like that."

"Right." Jerome reached out and regained control of the notebook. He slashed out the first estimate and wrote a new one beneath. "Price just went up."

Conor stared at him, then the paper, then back at Jerome. "You can't do that."

"Can. Did. I like Alicia. More so, Sandy loves your ex-wife. If you in any way, shape or form do her dirt and I'm working for you, I stand to lose." Jerome shook his head. "I don't lose well."

Conor stood his ground, arms folded, jaw tight. "Neither do I."

"I figured that." Jerome nodded. "Which is the only reason I agreed to come over here, but I work on my terms."

"Pricey because I'm rich."

"I prefer to think it's because I'm the best," Jerome shot back. "And because if you're going to pretend that this isn't all about getting your wife back, then I'm going to charge more to deal with levels of stupid insincerity a gifted artist like me finds to be a pain in the—"

"I get the drift." Conor swept the kitchen a look. "I want this done to suit Alicia. She's got a good eye for detail and appeal—"

"Ever tell her that?"

Conor worked his jaw, his emotions rising. "Not often enough. Anway, she did say she'd lend advice on how to restore things, so for details, you'll need to work with her as she's available."

"She's not available," came a stressed-out woman's voice from behind them. "She's so not available as to be a non-entity. Conor, I've already explained that."

Conor turned her way, but not before exchanging a quick look with Jerome. The other man's expression said he had no idea how long she'd been standing there either. "We'll work around your schedule, Leash."

She cast him a frenzied look, but her appearance softened as she gazed around, then down to check her pants. "No bugs."

"No." Conor smiled at her. "I had them especially killed for you, dear."

"My hero." Walking forward, she gave Jerome a poke in the chest. "My store comes first."

He nodded. "Absolutely."

She jerked a thumb in Conor's direction. "No matter how much he offers you. Got it?"

Jerome put up his hands in surrender. "I can't be bought. Got it."

Alicia seemed to evaluate their combined sincerity, then gave up altogether. "I'm done at the library this week. That'll give me more time."

Conor gave her a brisk nod. "Perfect. Jerome, am I bumping work you've already contracted?"

Jerome shook his head. "No, there's enough of us to go around. My younger brother runs the construction side of the business as a general contractor, dealing with subcontractors, coordinating the work, and using only the best people. I do the artsy side of the wood, the finished product that tricks out an old place into an even better edition of itself. My sister handles the books and plays the fiddle. A real Dixie Chick, complete with attitude. Imagine that."

Conor leveled a gaze to his ex-wife. "You in?"

She frowned and hesitated, one hand gripping the other. "Yes, but I'm not sure why."

He softened his expression and held her gaze until she shifted away, arms folded.

"Price is good. How absolute is it?" he asked Jerome, shoving the small notebook into his inner jacket pocket so Jerome couldn't hike the final tally again.

Jerome shook his head. "I'll work up price estimates on a room-by-room basis, but that's the top end for the moment." He raised his chin and stared Conor in the eye. "Unless we run into a problem, of course." His look drifted to Alicia, rife with meaning.

Conor acknowledged the silent interchange with a brief nod. "So noted."

As they moved outside, Jerome waved toward the former carriage house near the back corner of the southern property line. "Does that need work?"

Conor patted the notebook in his pocket. "Isn't this more than enough to feed you for the rest of your natural life?"

Jerome shoved his hands into his pockets and headed for the brick and cedar building. "It's shoddy to redo the house and ignore the outbuildings. The Conor Bradstreets of this world don't do shoddy."

"We could start." Conor shot him a bemused look, applied a key, and slid open the first bay of the old carriage barn.

A sub-human noise stopped them in their tracks. Conor looked at Alicia. She shrugged, eyes wide then narrow as she peered into the dark recesses of the three-car garage. Reaching to her right, she flicked the light switch between the bays.

Nothing switched on.

The noise came again, from the back right corner. Jerome touched Conor's arm. "I've got a flashlight in the car." He headed down the drive at a trot and was back by the time Conor lifted the second and third bay doors.

"Aaarrrrrrmmmmmmmmmmmmmm." The mournful plea weakened toward the end, then faded completely.

"There." Alicia grabbed Conor's arm as the flashlight beam caught the silhouette of a dark, prone form in the farthest corner.

The sound came again, smaller this time, while the thin beam of light penetrated the shadows. "Conor, it's a dog."

Conor's sensibilities didn't want her to be right, because if this was, indeed, a dog tied to the eye-hook on the back stud, that could only mean one thing. The poor creature had been there for weeks. He grabbed Alicia's arm as she started forward. She tried to jerk free, but he held tight. "I'll go. We don't know if he's hurt or diseased on top of being starved and neglected."

When she wrested her arm free with a glare, Conor dipped his chin, concern edging his voice. "Just let me check him first."

Her lips thinned, but she gave a quick nod. "All right."

The wretched animal moved. The action created a stench of unwashed dog, urine and feces. While a well-used dirtied area to Conor's left showed the dog tried to move away for bathroom facilities, the fouled area around him meant he'd probably lost the energy to extend that far. An old bag of dog food lay empty and out of reach. A scarred Dutch-oven kettle, not unlike those Conor's mother used, stood off to the side, long since empty of water. As Conor approached, the dog tried to stand, his tail making a concerted effort to wag a greeting.

The wag was all Alicia needed. She moved forward, cooing warm, maternal sounds that took Conor back to another place and time. For that reason alone his tone came out harsher than originally intended. "I told you to stay back. Let me check him."

"Conor, anything that wags a tail like that has got to be perfectly harmless, aren't you boy?" Alicia sank to her knees, ignoring the fetid smell. With gentle hands, she worked her fingers into the scruff of the dog's neck, kneading carefully. "There, fella, that feels good, doesn't it? Of course it does."

Jerome had disappeared again, but now he trotted into the garage, a large blanket splayed between his hands. Conor circled the dog's neck with care, looking for the clasped hook to unchain him, found the latch and refused to think what might be matted in the animal's fur. As he unclasped the chain, he held tight to the dog's collar while Jerome handed him the blanket.

No need. The neglected animal could barely stand, much less run. Conor wrapped the chilled beast in the nappy spread and hoisted him with surprising ease. He sent Alicia and Jerome a no nonsense look. "Nearest vet?"

"On Witherspoon, near the hospital." Alicia moved ahead of him, her footsteps brisk. "We'll take my car." Hurrying to the back door of the SUV, she wrenched it open. With help from Jerome, Conor climbed up, still clutching the dog, ignoring the horrific smell.

"In?" Alicia sent him a look through the rear view mirror once she'd climbed into the driver's seat.

"In. Drive."

"I'm on it," she muttered, her forehead etched in concern. She didn't once pinch her nose or whine about her Range Rover's upholstery. She took the turn onto Nassau with more speed than normal, flicked a glance to Conor and made a face of apology. "Sorry. Had to jump out. Saturday afternoon traffic."

He nodded, keeping a grip on the near lifeless animal in his arms. "We're okay."

Within minutes they arrived at the vet clinic. A tech swung open the door, eyed them with surprise, then winced at the odor emanating from the blanketed figure in Conor's arms. "We need help, fast."

She nodded, swung the door shut behind them, climbed a short flight of stairs and grabbed up a phone. A few minutes later a man strode in, buttoning a scrub coat over Saturday dress that looked golf club friendly. "What've we got?"

Conor shook his head, one hand atop the dog's matted head. "Some kind of dog. Abandoned. We found him tethered in the garage of a piece of property we bought two weeks ago."

"Not yours, then?"

Conor met Alicia's look of concern over the top of the prone figure. "No. Former owner, I would guess."

The vet eased the blanket away, his eyes watering at the rank odor.

Conor bent low and stroked the dog's head. "It's okay, old boy. We're okay." His tone, deep and low, seemed to soothe the animal's anxiety. Sighing, the dog dropped his snout to his front paws, as though grateful for help at last.

"Our best bet would be to put him down," counseled the vet, his expression saying he found the decision more repugnant than the odor. "He's malnourished, bug-infested, with body sores from laying in his own waste. His name is..." the vet bent and peered at the oval metal disk attached to the dog's collar. "Sarge. He's deserted and homeless, possibly untrustworthy—"

The name jabbed Conor's heart. Why hadn't he examined the carriage shed last week? His carelessness caused this poor animal six extra days of suffering. "He's not homeless anymore." Conor straightened, keeping a gentle hand to the ruff of the dog's neck. "He's mine."

Alicia stared at him. "Conor Bradstreet, since when did you grow a heart?"

"It's taken a while," he responded, keeping his voice soft, eyes down. "A long process, all told."

"Where do you expect to keep him in New York?" she demanded, coming around the table. "You think Foster will babysit him?"

Conor flashed her a look. "You'd be amazed what Foster can do, but no. I'm not sure where we'll house him, but that's moot for the time being. He needs veterinary care and convalescent time, right, Doc?"

The doctor gave him a careful once-over. "Mr. Bradstreet..."

Ah, yes. He'd caught the name and knew who he was dealing with. Conor mentally saw the cash register add in every possible extra a sick dog could need, right down to a puppy pedicure...

"I know you can afford this dog's treatment." The vet gave Conor a look that showed more concern for the dog and less for harnessing Conor's money than Conor had given him credit for. "In Princeton, that's rarely an issue. But, given his condition, and the probable treatment he's undergone, this dog—"

"Sarge," Conor supplied. At the word, the dog's head rose slightly and the tail thumped three times before he sighed and dropped his head again.

The vet nodded. "Sarge. He may not be the best choice for co-habitation. What I'm saying is, he may have been mistreated to the point of not being reliable any more. If he ever was."

Conor gazed into the animal's amber eyes and saw no choice. "We need to take a chance."

The vet's gaze traveled from Conor to Alicia and back. He nodded. "All right. Serena?"

The young woman who met them at the door re-entered the room. The vet nodded her way and gave orders in an easy but authoritative tone. The dog lay submissive, eyes half-closed, his breathing more relaxed as if recognizing help.

"Do you think he'll make it?" Alicia chanced a look into Conor's eyes as they climbed into her smelly SUV, and was taken aback by the mix of emotions she saw there. Compassion, mercy, a hint of fear. The realization took her aback.

She'd steeled herself long since to see Conor as the callous, legalistic, financial guru, respected by all and hated by a choice few. She'd made the short list in that respect years before.

Funny how the man who showed up in her living room a few months ago wasn't the cold-hearted monster she'd created in her head. Maybe he never was. Maybe monsters grew in proportion to broken hearts. If so, it was no wonder her demons were combo-meal super-sized, minus the refreshing cold drink.

Conor gave a firm nod. "He has to."

He had to? Because...? Alicia sensed a puzzle behind his words, but didn't pursue it because of his next statement.

"Let's stop by Jon's grave."

Her heart stutter-stepped in her chest. They hadn't gone to Jon's grave together since the funeral, and that was a day she didn't care to relive. Not now, not ever. So many people, strangers, really, business acquaintances of Conor's, or those wishing to score points by showing up in Princeton to pay their respects, uninvited and unwelcome, in her sphere, anyway.

She'd kept herself aside, hating those people and their polished New York lives, their hustle and bustle, the every day busyness they would return to while she'd wake up to a house bereft of a little boy's footsteps. His laughter. His voice, once full of life, expectant, now silenced in the grave.

Alicia gripped the wheel, emotions spinning, then caught hold of herself. Jaw tight, she gave a quick nod. "Sure."

"Thanks."

Conor's staid profile hid the depths of his feelings, but then it always had. She'd known that, had twitted him about the fact when they were younger, back when they laughed together and teasing was an integral part of their relationship, in and out of the bedroom.

A spot of heat worked its way to her cheeks, recalling their interchange in the bookstore that morning. For just a moment it had been the old Conor and Alicia, trading quips and barbs, his wry humor spurring her smiles.

She pushed a mountain of emotions aside as she parked the car at the lower end of the cemetery. They walked the shallow slope side by side, Conor's gaze dipped, his footfall steady. He held the gate open for her. She stepped through, then turned. "Thank you."

His right hand stole to her cheek, his touch a caress, his expression almost...tender. The look and the touch made her want to press her cheek into his palm, feel the thickness of his fingers, the warmth of his hand against her skin.

He shifted his attention and dropped his hand, her cheek suddenly cool in the afternoon chill. Moving right, he headed for their son's grave, his steps silent against late winter grass. Alicia followed, awkward, feeling out of place, which was ridiculous because wasn't she the one who polished the stone on a regular basis, who tended the flowers, who scrubbed the lower right-hand surface with a mild bleach solution to discourage the mold that longed to grow along the narrow, northern face?

Yet Conor seemed quite at home, despite his years away.

He turned to face her at that moment. Held out his hand in a gesture she'd longed for in the weeks and months following Jon's death. She'd prayed that he would reach for her then, come to her, just be with her, anything to ease the horrible pain and emptiness that wrenched her each and every morning.

He hadn't. He'd stayed away as often and as long as possible, leaving her to struggle through her grief while raising two teenage girls whose schedules refused to allow time to wallow in emotion. She wasn't sure if that was good or bad, didn't care, not really, she only knew that Conor's extended hand was about eight years too late. She dropped her chin, stubborn, anger clenching her heart, strangling what soul she had left, and it wasn't all that much.

"Alicia." His voice, still and deep, sent a blanket of warmth around her, a remembered feeling she needed to resist. Too much had happened during those lost years, too much pain and heartache. Anger. But what did he know of that with his all-so-important New York lifestyle? Nothing, not a darned thing. She set her jaw and shifted her gaze, rock solid stubborn.

"Leash." His voice stayed husky low. She chanced a glance his way, saw his face, his eyes, the anguish reflected there. His offered hand reached for her. "Come here."

Why did she move forward? Why, after all this time, all this drama, all this anger, did the simple sound of his voice and the touch of his hand bring her to his side in this hallowed ground?

His arm stole around her, drawing her in. She felt the smoothness of his lambskin jacket, the strong grip of the arm sheltering her shoulders, the scent of unwashed dog and pricey after-shave. Conor raised his free hand to his face, two fingers pinching the bridge of his nose, staving...

She looked, saddened and mesmerized by the dampness and grief on Conor's face, his cheeks wet, despite the effort to still the tears.

He dropped his chin to her hair, his gaze on the ruddy stone, his grip warm and embracing. "I think it's time we grieved our son together, Leash."

She knew exactly what he meant. They'd gone their separate ways following Jon's death, bitter, angry, sorrowful, and more than a little guilty that a rich family couldn't save the life of one little tow-haired boy.

Conor's second arm wrapped around her, pulling her close, hugging her, spurring a feeling both ancient and new. His voice cracked on his next words. "I'm so sorry, Alicia."

For once her mind didn't leap to the wealth of things he should be sorry for. Not this time. She burrowed her head further into his coat, not caring that he smelled less than fresh after cradling a tormented dog in his arms. "I know. Me, too."

His grip shifted at her words. She felt his cheek on her hair, his arms snug around her, cradling her, his heartbeat soft beneath the layers of clothes. "Well, then."

She had no idea how long they stood like that, tears flowing. The squeak of the gate pulled them apart some time later. She glanced up, wiping her eyes with fingers that smelled of antiseptic soap from the vet clinic, wishing for a tissue or a hanky.

The approaching priest held a thick wad of tissues in his hand. "Thought these might be of use."

Alicia accepted them, self-conscious.

Conor didn't appear embarrassed at all. "Thank you, Father."

The priest offered the full benefit of a gentle Celtic smile. "Laughter and tears. The best medicine, and the price is often right."

Conor sighed deep, looked down at the grave, then up at the priest. "Therapeutic?"

"Exponentially when coupled with prayer," the old priest announced, his voice warm with hope.

Alicia stepped back. "And when God doesn't answer your prayers, Father?"

The look he bestowed on her held the wisdom of ages and the warmth of gathered angels. The combination thoroughly pissed her off. "Oh, he answers, right enough. We just don't always like his decisions."

"I can't argue that." Shattered walls re-established themselves within her. Feeling boxed by the two men, she took another step back, then another. "I'll be in the car."

She turned and strode toward the gate, her movements swift and sure, anger punctuating every step.

Conor sighed, swiped a hand across his face, then sighed again.

"You're not quitting, are you?"

He met the priest's gaze, puzzled. "Quitting?"

"The campaign."

"For?"

"Her."

"Ah." Conor shifted his look to Alicia's swiftly departing back. "It's not exactly a campaign, Father."

"No?"

"More like an effort to right old wrongs. Bring us both some peace."

The priest nodded, his look disbelieving. He clapped Conor on the back with a grip belied by his passing years. "You keep telling yourself that, my son. See if it works."

"Father, I—"

The old priest's eyes crinkled with amusement and male understanding that shouldn't be possible in a celibate man. "I'm praying for you. Both of you. In fact," he leaned forward, his gaze measured, eyes merry. "I'll make you a deal. If you can get her into church, other than Kim's wedding, before year's end, I'll take the dunking booth at the summer festival. Half of Princeton's been waiting for a chance to drop me into that tub of water." His eyes gleamed. "Great fund raiser. Are you a betting man?"

Conor shook his head, but took the pastor's offered hand. "No, but this is one I won't pass up. And if we get you onto that dunking stool, Father, I'll match the festival's take, dollar for dollar. See if we can help you stay in the black."

The priest offered a quick nod of agreement. "You do your job. I'll do mine."

A hint of peace flowed through Conor, easing a still ragged section of his worn heart. "It's a deal, Father."

CHAPTER THIRTEEN

Conor stared at the empty parking spot that used to hold Alicia's 4X4 and sighed, wishing his returning headache away. The morning pills must have worn off and he felt the beat of his heart against his temple in a steady thrump, thrump, thrump. He zipped his smelly jacket a bit higher and walked the short blocks to Teaberry Street, determined to ignore the pain.

Her SUV wasn't there, either, nor was it parked near the bookstore. She'd gone home, most likely, back to her pale and pristine existence, away from prying priests and smelly ex-husbands.

Once back in his hotel suite, he shed his clothing, called for laundry service, showered hot and long, then did it again, just in case he missed a spot. He scanned his cell phone as he re-dressed. Two missed calls. One from the vet, one from Alicia. Weighing his options, he called the vet first.

"Sarge is resting comfortably right now, Mr. Bradstreet," the vet assured him. "We've got him on IV fluids, I don't see any internal injuries, although we can't rule out organ damage caused by lack of food and water."

A stab of guilt renewed itself in Conor's chest. If he'd checked the carriage house last weekend, the dog's suffering wouldn't be nearly so bad. The thought of six long days without food or water, suffered in silence, chained in filth, made Conor's head swim. He sat down on the edge of the bed, feeling tired and a touch woozy. "Will he make it?"

The vet hesitated. "Let's give him a little time to re-acclimate. He's had a rough go and dogs in this condition often survive, but some don't. His age is in his favor."

"It is?" Conor had supposed the dog to be well on in years.

"He's not more than three I would guess. And Shepherds are renowned for their resilience, so I'm not counting our friend out for the count."

A Shepherd, huh? Envisioning the regal stance of Shepherds paraded around Central Park, Conor wouldn't have guessed that lineage a few hours back. Relieved, he gripped the phone tighter. "Thank you, Doctor."

"I'll keep in touch. We have staff on duty at all times, so if Sarge runs into any kind of difficulty, he's not alone."

His declaration eased another burden from Conor. Mulling the dog's deteriorated condition, he was determined that Sarge would never be left alone again.

A knock sounded. Frowning, he crossed the room and swung open the door. Alicia stood in the tastefully decorated hall, definitely fresher than she'd been two hours before. She stepped in, chin up, nose wrinkling. "Where are they?"

"They...?" Conor deepened his frown, leaned down, took a deep breath of her hair, fruity soap-and-water clean, eased back and smiled his appreciation. "Much better. They what?"

"Your disgusting clothes," she told him, sniffing the air like a well-trained hound. "No way are you sending dog poop clothes to the hotel laundry."

"Oops." Conor met her gaze, feigning chagrin while he fought a smile. "I figured the sooner I got them out of here, the better."

"I don't believe this." She sank onto the edge of the couch, her lower lip thrust out, her face mulish. "Why would you do that? You're letting perfect strangers wash poopy clothing."

"I tipped them quite well."

"Conor."

"Ummm..." Conor crossed the short space between them and took the chair opposite her. "How's this for an answer? Because I never in my wildest dreams thought you'd show up here after eight years of hating me and offer to wash dog poop clothes. My bad."

A tiny smile worked the right side of her mouth. Conor touched one finger to the smile, tracing the curve, remembering a time when he could make love to those lips, that mouth and all the delightful things that came with the package at no extra cost.

Her lips parted and he knew if he pressed forward, just a little, he could taste what he'd missed all these years. For that reason alone he moved back, wanting her to be sure, knowing she wasn't.

He tweaked her nose, smiled and stood, reaching out a hand. "Will you still have dinner with me?"

The look in her eyes said she knew what she'd just missed, and didn't like the realization.

But she understood his actions, just like he did. Their daughters had gone through a lot during their divorce. Steps toward anything resembling reconciliation involved a whole lot more than a middle-aged, used-to-be-married couple with really great memories of early life between the sheets. Or on the rug. And there was that delightful tryst in their old kitchen, when his late-night supper became a non-entity because she looked way too good in hot pink shorts and some kind of orange and pink flowered bathing suit top, her hair thick and damp from the pool.

She sighed, pouted, glared, then stood, shrugging her purse up on her shoulder. "I don't think so."

He moved closer, feeling her breath against his chest, wondering if her heart fared better than his, knowing a down-soft bed with great pillows lay just a few feet due south. "Please?"

"No."

He smiled and leaned in, crowding her space. "Pretty please?"

"Umm...No."

"Pretty please with sprinkles and nuts and chocolate sauce?"

"Umm..." The 'umm' sounded less definitive, but she held her ground like a trooper. Almost. "No. I think."

Conor grinned and nuzzled her cheek, her hair, her ear. "With sprinkles and nuts and chocolate sauce and whipped cream?" he whispered.

She groaned, batted his chest with her right hand and took a step back. "You don't play fair."

"I know." He smiled down at her. "Have supper with me, just the two of us, Leash. No expectations, no rules, just two people who shared a lot of life, the good and the bad. No pressure."

She waved a hand toward her clothing. "I came here for dirty laundry, not a date." Her mouth pursed right before she sent him a rueful look. "I'm not exactly dressed for Benedetti's."

He gave her a once-over that made her draw a deep breath. Her chest rose and fell with the action, the fit of the silk turtleneck taking him back in time. This time it was Conor who sucked a breath. "You look wonderful." He tilted his chin down and arched a brow. "Supper with an old guy? Whaddya think?"

Her smile told him enough, but her answer frosted the cake. "Yes."

Princeton's streets glowed amber in the late-winter twilight, the mellow radiance softening the smudge of salted pavement and leftover snow. Alicia's hair bounced the light, casting a hint of copper into the night. He longed to touch those curls, weave his hands into the tumble of hair he'd first noticed thirty years before as she stepped into a D.C. coffee shop with a friend.

Despite his best efforts, which were pretty well practiced at the time, she held him at bay for weeks back then. Their banter became a game, one with high stakes. He knew she recognized the inherent danger of falling in love with him. Citing his former relationships in alphabetical order, she made herself perfectly clear.

But Conor was born persistent and something about Alicia's manner magnetized him. Were they a perfect match? In some ways, yes. While many stood in awe of his brains, Alicia stood her ground, never cowed, toe-to-toe, step by step. Unafraid to challenge his committed beliefs, she nudged open the door to a reality check that Conor sorely needed at that point in his life.

Then again about twenty years later.

Dear God, he missed her.

He longed to swing an arm around her, draw her close as they walked, grip her shoulder through the layers of jacket and shirt.

Would she slip her arm around his waist? Allow the freedom? Or punch him?

Uncertainty made him hesitate and smile. She'd kept him uncertain back in the day, too. He'd forgotten how delightfully frustrating time with her could be.

He reached ahead to pull open the restaurant door. She turned, her face near his, her mouth way too close. Without allowing time to consider the action, he dipped his mouth to hers. Warmth seeped through him at the sweet taste, the scent of his wife, her skin on his. Her mouth softened with his kiss and he found it difficult to pull back, but since there was little choice, he did. "Thanks for coming out with me."

She sent him a long, slow look that made him cave on the spot. "How fast can we eat?"

Conor gawked, then grinned, still holding the door. "We could skip dinner altogether."

She pretended to mull his offer, then shook her head as she stepped inside. "I'm hungry."

"Then we can order food to go," Conor negotiated, glancing at his watch to underscore his thoughts. Negotiations were, after all, his forte. "We could be back to my suite within twenty minutes."

She tapped a finger to her mouth, musing. "But then they might hurry my steak, and you know I like things..." The finger at her lips lost speed, the movement deliberate, nerve wracking and delightfully Alicia. "Done slow."

Conor jumped in to play a game he'd missed for too long. "Sometimes."

She glanced away, her smile teasing. "Well..."

Conor laughed and gave her a half-hug. "I've missed you, woman."

She met his gaze, her expression bemused. "Me, too. And just so you know, feeling that way almost makes me want to take the bridge because I've spent a lot of years wishing you gone. I mean, really gone."

Conor thought of how she almost got her wish one Christmas Eve, how close he came... "And now?"

"Déjà vu, Memory Lane, however you'd like to analogize this—"

"Love? Affection?"

Alicia rolled her eyes. "Mid-life crisis, most likely."

"Ouch. You still know how to quash a mood."

"Wealth of experience."

Conor leaned in, his mouth to her ear. "Still, I do recall an innate ability to overcome objections in a timely fashion."

She blushed and stayed unusually quiet as they were seated. Once he slid her chair in, he let his hands linger on her shoulders a few beats longer than just friends.

She arched him a brow as he took the seat next to her. "You're still smooth."

"Yet unpracticed."

"Right." The look she sent him told him she didn't buy that for a minute.

"Believe what you will, Mrs. Bradstreet, I'm not the guy you think I am."

"Rich, spoiled, headstrong, obnoxious?"

"Flattery will get you no where." Conor frowned and rubbed his temple. "Do you have aspirin with you?"

Alicia reached a hand to his face. "Are you okay?"

He nodded, then shrugged. "Headache. Started yesterday, off and on. Now it's most definitely on."

Alicia rummaged through the purse that Conor knew held at least a small drugstore of interesting items. "Here."

He eyed the bottle. "That's not aspirin."

"Ibuprofen. It's stronger."

He grinned. "Right. About that: I recognize ibuprofen, honey. Slattery Pharmaceuticals, remember? I think that's how I bought your house, actually."

She nodded. "How could I forget? You slept with the opposing lawyer."

"Not until after the case," Conor pointed out as he moved toward her. Might as well have this out now. "And it was the stupidest thing I've ever done, Alicia. I have no excuses but plenty of regrets." He palmed her cheek with his hand, the feel of silk-soft skin stirring a pot of swimming emotions. "Forgive me. Please."

She contemplated throwing the stupid pills into his face before storming out the door, thoughts of that time beating against her brain.

But other thoughts invaded as well, the times she shut him out for working hard, turned away because he wasn't home more.

She never once went to meet him in the city without whining and complaining about the traffic, the noise, the smells, the people. And here were both her daughters, beautiful, bright, Princeton-raised girls, eagerly embracing careers in the city, time with their father, life in the fast lane while she sat stuck in second gear, about to become a prosaic owner of, of all things neutral, a bookstore.

Conor eyed her, waiting, his brow lightly etched in concern or pain, she wasn't sure. Reaching over, she handed him the ibuprofen and a small confession. "I wasn't exactly a perfect wife, Conor."

When he started to protest, she pressed three fingers to his mouth, silencing him. "I know that now. I've had lots of time to consider the situation. And maybe we would have made it if Jon hadn't gotten sick. Maybe we'd have turned things around because I don't think we ever stopped loving each other. I think we just got sidetracked." She drew her lower lip between her teeth, thoughtful. "Then we got blindsided and the rest is history."

"Then let's leave it history. We've come a long way, Leash. The girls are grown, they're amazing young women. You did a great job with them."

"Oh, Conor." She rubbed a finger across the condensation filming her water glass, then gave him a wry smile. "We did a great job, Conor, once you put your foot down and became 'Dad' again. The girls adore you."

"And rightfully so." He rubbed his forearm against hers, the feel of his sport coat smooth and rough, all male. He was close enough that she could count the mixed weave of the wool. One gold, one gray, one sage, one slate. Repeat. One gold, one gray...

The dark gray turtleneck he wore beneath the jacket kept him deceptively casual and distinctly urbane. Total Conor. He encroached on her space just a little bit more. "How about their mom? Think she can start to like me again? A little?"

"A little?" His eyes had her heart somersaulting in her chest, his scent had her wishing him closer, his touch made her think of things quite impossible in a restaurant unless you were Julia Roberts with Richard Gere, in which case...

She paused, took a breath and ordered her emotions into pause mode. "Maybe a little."

He smiled as if reading her thoughts. "A good start."

He downed the pain relievers, then opened his menu, eyes crinkled in merriment. "Pick whatever you'd like, honey. It's on me."

"You're such a dork."

"I know." He rubbed her calf with the inside edge of his foot, watching for a reaction, smiling more when she gave none. "But lovable."

"That remains to be seen."

His expression changed. Moving back, he withdrew his cell phone and scanned the display before answering. "Yes?"

His professional voice. Of course. She should have known that dinner with her didn't rank high enough to turn his phone off. She pushed back the urge to grab the intrusive instrument and launch it into the nearest sewer, with Conor right behind. What kind of man conducted business on a... well... not a date, exactly, but what could have been a really nice evening with an ex-wife. Despite the contradiction of terms.

"Yes, absolutely. Thanks for keeping me informed. I'll tell my... Mrs. Bradstreet."

Tell her what? Alicia cocked a brow his way.

"Sarge is doing fine so far," he reported as he set the phone aside. "They're re-hydrating him with warm IV fluids, administering antibiotics, and they have warming blankets on him, but he seems to be responding to treatment."

"Already?" Alicia didn't know a lot about dogs. Judging from the animal's condition earlier that day, Conor's report bordered on miraculous, but that was quite impossible. She'd stopped believing in miracles a long time ago.

"Amazing, isn't it?" Conor swiped his hand to his forehead, his expression less than comfortable. "Leash is it hot in here?"

She reached out a hand to his forehead. "You've got a fever."

"No."

"Yes."

He shook his head. "I don't get fevers."

"Uh huh." She rose and held out a hand. "We'll do dinner another time. Let's get you back to the hotel."

"Alicia." The look of regret on his face said the rest. She took his arm and headed for the door.

"You can seduce me another night. Maybe. Right now, you need to lie down and let the ibuprofen work some magic. You're not having chest pains or anything, are you?"

He shook his head. "Probably flu."

She sent him a look of unfeigned irritation. "Great. Keep it to yourself. I've got a bookstore to open and a wedding to organize. No time for flu."

"Did you have your shot?"

"Yes."

"Then you should be fine. Except..."

"Except what?"

"I had mine, too, and I still got it."

"If this is the flu."

"Does the flu make you feel like death all of a sudden, like a freight train just ran over your body and every major organ is screaming resistance?"

"Accurate description."

"Then I'm going with my first guess and the anomaly of getting the flu despite the shot. What else could make someone feel this bad, this fast?" His foot caught the edge of the doorway as he spoke, almost tripping him.

Alicia held tight. "Conor, you're scaring me. Can you make it back to the hotel? Shall I go get my car? Call an ambulance?"

"The car... might be... nice... but then... I'd have to wait... alone..."

He half-shuffled along, his shoulders curved in, his chin down. From the look on his face, it was all he could do to put one foot in front of the other.

"I'm calling an ambulance."

"Nonsense." Conor took a deep breath, turned a shade of green formerly unknown to civilization, straightened his shoulders and pushed on. "I just need to lie down."

Long minutes later she got him into his hotel room and out of his jacket. He sprawled on the bed, the gratitude in his eyes showing the difficulty of the two-block walk back to Palmer Square. "I'll be fine, Leash. Just need some..."

He closed his eyes and was gone.

Alicia contemplated the man before her, and her choices. Should she hang around in case he needed her, or leave him to sleep his way through?

Having raised two girls, she knew how quick a nasty virus could take hold of the body. Conor's timing on this went way beyond awful, but maybe that was for the best. Flirting with fire, the way they'd done tonight, might not be a great scenario for all concerned, although she'd have a hard time explaining her logic to an over-anxious libido whose hopes had risen throughout the day.

Torn, she eyed Conor. Sound asleep, feverish, but resting, and the ibuprofen should take care of the fever in short order. Just in case he had none, she drew a glass of water and left it and her bottle of pills on his bedside table. Breathing deep with decision, she turned and walked out the door.

CHAPTER FOURTEEN

The choking cough pushed Conor to fight for air, his chest heavy with the pressure of... something. Working his eyes open, the room swam before him like crazed mirrors at a theme park, wavy and distorted.

Silence greeted him. No Alicia. A part of his memory saw her, felt her presence beside the bed, but his eyes took in the empty room, the still, night air.

Chills racked his body, but the weight of the blankets seemed too painful a compromise. Still...

He reached for the covers he'd cast aside. Another coughing spasm shook him to the core, leaving him breathless and pain-filled.

He needed help. Whatever was wrong with him was not simple or easily tackled by a few doses of ibuprofen. He understood that now, in the darkness of his hotel room, his body on fire, his brain half-addled.

He reached for his cell phone but only managed to knock the skinny thing to the floor and the floor seemed too far away. Conor sank back into the pillow, exhausted and frustrated. He'd rest a bit, then tackle the distance to the phone in a few minutes.

Huddled under the covers, long, violent shivers quaked his body. His head pounded with the fierceness of an African drum, his hands arched, numb and useless, his spine sore and his chest crushed like his lungs supported the weight of the world, only twice as heavy.

Alicia.

He needed her. He needed help. She'd get it for him, if only she were here.

Alicia.

Dry, parched lips couldn't say her name. The syllables blurred, his tongue thick, his mouth uncooperative. There was no way she could hear him, no way she'd know he was in trouble, calling her name.

A sense of panic seized him. What if this was it? The big one? The final chapter in the oh-so-notable life of Conor Bradstreet?

Could he die without saying what he should, telling her how he felt? Could he leave her thinking he hadn't spent the last years thinking of her, wanting her, wishing they could recreate the life they foolishly wasted?

Words jumbled in his brain, the heat inside him scorching his skin, his mouth. Tiredness stole over him, a welcome reprieve. He'd give in to the blanket of weariness, let it drift him away, at least for a while. Then he'd tell her.

Alicia woke just after three A.M., certain something was wrong.

Conor.

His name flooded her senses. She slapped back the feeling, sleep-riddled and still half-drunk with how she felt in his presence hours before. The guy was a total self-absorbed jerk. Wasn't he?

But sick. Remembering that, she climbed out of bed and grabbed up her phone to call his cell number.

Nothing.

She tried again.

Same thing.

Conor always answered his cell. A guy like him never knew what might be going down in Tokyo or

Beijing or London. Random hands on clocks meant nothing to the Conor Bradstreets of the world. He used to ask her to tag along on business jaunts, quick trips to fanciful places scattered in various hemispheres.

She refused while she was raising the girls, citing all sorts of reasons, but mostly to make him think twice about being away from home.

She tried his cell one more time, jabbing the tiny numbers as if force at her end would produce an answer on his.

Nothing.

A stab of worry pushed her to the pile of clothes she'd shed the night before. Throwing them on, she didn't bother warming the SUV, just hopped in and drove the short distance to Nassau Street, realizing that the last time she'd worried this much about Conor was that ill-fated September morning in 2001, when terrorists attacked the twin towers nearly adjacent to Conor's workplace. She'd stared at the television, her heart in her throat, hands clasped, praying despite herself, studying the screen to discern the shape of Conor's building in the varied shots of the financial district, knowing that a number of Princeton families earned their living in those esteemed towers. Despite their rough history, her thoughts went to Conor. His safety. His well-being.

Had he survived? Was he out of harm's way?

Horrible images crashed through her brain as the world tumbled down around a man she thought she hated. More than a small spark of thanksgiving lit her soul when Addie called with news that Conor was alive and holed up in a building not far from the toppled World Trade Centers.

She'd felt almost guilty that he'd lived while others died, that she'd celebrated his escape in her heart when she didn't even like him all that much. But her girls did, and that was reason enough. Wasn't it?

Rushing toward his hotel now, she wondered why she never realized how hard it must have been for those who lived to return to the financial centers day after day, watching the ever-present rise of dust, seeing the workers move like well-orchestrated ants, clearing debris. Had she ever put herself in Conor's shoes, fully considering the effect such a thing might have on him? No. Because he was Conor, the invincible. She felt her stupid-o-meter rise notably with the realization. What a dolt.

Once she pulled up in front of the first-rate hotel, she parked the car, pushed through the front doors, and had the surprised and somewhat suspicious desk clerk call Conor's room. The room phone sat near the bed. Surely its intrusive ring would wake him.

No answer, still.

Citing Conor's illness, she talked the clerk into accompanying her upstairs with a key.

Dread filled her when Conor didn't answer the knock on the door. The clerk's expression showed mixed feelings, but he applied the slide key and swung the door open at her insistence, a quality Conor had never found endearing. If he were conscious, no, slash that, *alive*, he might be a little bit grateful for her persistence tonight.

Conor's strained breathing spurred their instant action once inside. "Call an ambulance," Alicia ordered the clerk, motioning to the phone. "Tell them to hurry."

She moved to Conor's side, hands gentle, heart racing. His gray pallor and raging temperature told her he was beyond any influenza she'd ever seen.

The next hours passed in a flurry of activity followed by more than enough time to beat herself up over her choices. Why hadn't she stayed with him? She saw how sick he was, how he collapsed onto that bed, so unlike Conor. If she'd stayed she could have gotten help sooner, had him in professional care in a more timely fashion, but no. She'd gone home to her perfect house on her perfect street, curled up and gone to sleep while both Conor and the poor dog fought for their lives. What kind of woman was she?

By the time Kim arrived at the hospital, Alicia had thrashed herself fairly well.

"How is he?" Kim asked, hurrying toward her mother, her coat draped over one arm, her scarf trailing unnoticed along the floor.

Alicia waved a hand and shook her head. "Not good. On top of that, they won't let me see him."

Kim stared at her, her expression blank. "Because?"

"I'm not family."

"And?" Kim's look said she still didn't quite get the drift.

Alicia glared. "And they should, that's all. He's got pneumonia."

Kim gave her a look of disbelief. "Pneumonia? And he's this sick?"

"I know." Alicia slapped a hand to the back of a vinyl chair. "It doesn't make any sense. Your father's got the constitution of an iron horse, there's no way something like pneumonia would get him down."

"Pneumonia." Kim rolled the word like a well-played tune, then stood. "Where's his doctor?"

"In the room. Why?"

"This way?" She pointed through the locked double doors of the ICU.

"Yes."

"What's his name?"

"Montoya. Why, Kim?" Alicia stood, concerned by the expression on Kim's face. Kim took two strides and hit the intercom button with singular force.

"Yes?"

"This is Kimberly Bradstreet. I need to speak with Dr. Montoya, STAT."

"Are you a relative of the patient?"

Alicia watched Kim's eyes narrow in a look she recognized from her own mirror. It made her proud.

"I'm his daughter and next of kin and I need to talk to the doctor now."

"Kim, I..."

"Mom." Kim turned away from the intercom and held up a hand. "One of Dad's workers got diagnosed with Legionnaire's disease on Friday, then another one was hospitalized last night with similar symptoms. Dad was at their worksite on Tuesday, and had lunch with them."

Alicia heard Kim's words but made no sense of them. "Worksite? He had lunch with the workers? Kim, what are you talking about?"

The doctor banged through the door, looking short on sleep. He glared at Alicia as if she were personally responsible for Conor's condition and medicine's inability to lessen the 106.2 fever wracking Conor's body. His look shifted from her to Kim. "What is this about?"

Kim stepped forward and extended her hand. "I'm Conor Bradstreet's daughter, Kim. I work for him. On one of his current projects we've had two workers hospitalized this week with similar life-threatening symptoms. The first patient was positively diagnosed with Legionnaire's late yesterday."

The doctor's expression went from angry to empowered in the space of her words. "Was your father exposed?"

Kim nodded. "He visited the site and had lunch with the workers on Tuesday. On Friday afternoon he complained to me of a headache and tiredness. If you knew my father, Doctor, you'd know that he rarely complains and he never gets tired."

Doctor Montoya gave a grim nod. "This news is good and bad. Good because erythromycin is quite effective against Legionnaire's. Bad because the mortality rate for this particular pneumonia is not good. Which hospitals are these other patients in?"

"Forest Hills in Queens and Suny Downstate in Brooklyn. No other cases that I'm aware of at this time."

"And your father has no underlying illness or condition I should be aware of?"

Kim shook her head. "Healthy as a horse. Until now."

"Then that is in our favor." The doctor gave a quick nod before pushing back through the interlocking access doors, his footfall hurried.

Alicia eyed her oldest daughter. "Have a seat, Kim."

Kim arched a brow, pressed her lips into a thin line and sat. "I want to see Dad."

"They'll call us in when they're ready," Alicia advised her. "Right now they're trying everything they can to bring his fever down."

"How high?"

"Over one hundred and six."

"Dear Lord." Kim bowed her head, hands clasped, lips moving. Addie showed up right then.

"Mom. Kim. How is he? How's Dad?"

Kim stood, flashed Alicia a look, then took a step back.

Alicia hugged Addie, then snaked an arm around Kim's waist. "He's very sick, honey. High fever, pneumonia, dehydration and possible organ shut down."

Addie stepped back, her face, Conor's face, washed pale. "He could die?"

Kim opened her mouth to answer but Alicia arched an eyebrow. "Somehow I don't think heaven's ready for the likes of your father yet. Kim, just what kind of worksite was your father visiting on Tuesday and since when do you work for him?"

Addie made an 'oh, no' face while Kim's look went suddenly thoughtful. "You know I work for *Homeward Bound*."

Alicia nodded, one eye on the door, wondering when they'd be updated on Conor's condition. Soon, she hoped. "Yes."

"What you don't know is that Dad started *Homeward Bound* about eight years ago."

Kim's words took a moment to register. "He what?"

Kim nodded. Addie stepped closer to her sister's side. "He devised a program that encompassed mobile meals, medical care, toiletry needs, and eventually housing for those homeless that want it. One of the new worksites is in Queens. They've been finishing up the work there to open enough space in eight different apartment high-rises to accommodate nearly three hundred homeless people."

Alicia stared at Kim, then shifted her look to Addie. "You were aware of this as well?"

Addie nodded. "It wasn't a secret, Mom, it's just that you kind of freak every time we talk about Dad so we..."

"Didn't." Kim finished the sentence for her sister. "What would have been the point of upsetting you?"

Dismay smacked Alicia with the weight of an oversized I-beam. "Your father heads up this homeless project in addition to his partnership and active practice at Wells, Terwilliger, Whickman and Bradstreet?"

"Dad's good at managing things." Kim shrugged, unapologetic. "Pretty incredible, actually."

She'd known that all along, Alicia realized, her heart heavy with this newsflash. Obviously, somewhere along the way, Conor had done some big league changing, unbeknownst to her. Of course that could be because she'd treated him like a poisonous snake for nearly a decade.

She moved toward the exit door, the pressure in her chest tight and raw.

"Mom? Where are you going?" Addie stepped forward, a hand out. "Won't you stay?"

Alicia heard the hurt and surprise in Addie's tone. She turned. Nodded. "But I need a little time to think, Ads. Really think. Your father—"

Addie held up a hand of dismissal. "I know, I know. It's just—"

Alicia stepped back and grasped Addie's upper arms. "You don't know. Your father and I, well..." She thought of the way he'd looked at her yesterday, of the man who strode forward carrying a smelly, neglected dog, who cradled the dying animal just like he cradled Jon all those years ago. Dear God, how could she have forgotten that, the time and effort Conor put forth to save their son, his disappointment that no matter how hard he tried, nothing worked? Seeing Addie's worried gaze, Alicia tried to soften her expression. "I need to go see the vet about your father's dog. He'll want a report as soon as he wakes up."

"His...what?" Kim eyed her as though she, too, might be fevered.

"Dad has a dog?" Addie's face said that the day couldn't get much stranger.

Alicia stepped back toward the door, her mind racing, her heart beating a zigzag rhythm. "Yes, but the dog's sick. I need to see if he's okay."

The girls' expressions said they thought her delusional, but she'd explain later. Right now she needed a little time, a little space and some sort of magic Alice pill that made her suddenly mixed up world right again.

Quiet, she stole through the side door of the gray-stoned church across from her bookstore a few minutes later. The lustrous interior smelled of lemon wax and incense. Nice. Catholic. Comforting.

Alicia slid into a west-side pew and knelt, angled sunlight flooding dawn-facing stained glass scenes, their colors a rainbow of promise and light. She stared at the altar, hands clasped, her eyes registering the empty church, her heart seeing the last time she'd knelt on the drop down kneelers.

That day Conor had been by her side, his breathing tight, his face tormented. She'd leaned against him, grateful for his bulk, his muscle.

How foolish she'd been, expecting him to be the strong one. Expecting him to handle her grief on top of his own. Assuming he'd make everything right, same as always. This was Conor, the man, the myth, the legend. How on earth had things gone so terribly wrong?

On that day he was just another poor guy burying a child.

"Mrs. Bradstreet?"

Alicia turned, startled. Fr. Murphy stood at the end of her pew, his hands extended in comfort.

"I just got a call from the hospital, asking for an anointing."

She nodded, lips dry, heart aching. *Oh, Conor, not this. Not now.* "My husband is very ill."

If the old priest noted her word of choice, he ignored it. Or maybe he just accepted the use, believing marriage should be forever. Alicia tried not to think of what Conor must have faced, going in to work, day after day, pretending to be strong because she needed someone to be strong and he got elected by default. She dropped her chin, embarrassed.

The aging rector moved into the pew, his voice gentle. "I never expected he'd go to these extremes when we talked yesterday, but this is Conor we're dealing with."

Alicia frowned her confusion.

He settled onto the pew alongside her. "Your husband. We had a bet. I never thought he'd pull it off, but he's a sly one, he is. Commendably speaking, of course."

Alicia sat back, eyeing him. "You bet with Conor, Father? Isn't that against the rules?"

The priest grinned. "Naw. Catholics like the odd game of chance now and again. Keeps life interesting. But I never thought he'd stoop to this."

"This?" Alicia frowned, puzzled.

He dipped his chin as though sharing a confidence. "I bet him that if he could get you back into church, I'd take a turn in the dunking booth during the June festival. I knew full well that nothing short of catastrophic illness would send you through these doors, and Conor appeared quite hale and healthy yesterday afternoon, so I figured I was a sure bet to stay dry this summer." He shook his head, his face creased in smiles. "The man plays to win."

"Always." Alicia regarded the rector, an eyebrow arched, a slow boil simmering within her chest. "You bet on me?"

The priest nodded and stood. "For your own good, of course."

For a brief moment, Alicia wondered what the penalty was for pummeling a man of God. Father Murphy must have sensed her train of thought because he moved toward the aisle, his gaze compassionate but alert. "Stay as long as you like. I'm going to join the girls and do some praying at the bedside. It's the least I can do for a man who's been so generous to our parish. I expect I'll see you there?"

She stared up into the rugged, aged face, knowing he was sending her a message, and not as surprised as she would have thought. "I'll be there shortly."

Tiny lights swam in her field of vision. She blinked back tears, wishing the old priest had thought to bring along his handy box of tissues.

No such luck. Swiping her sleeve to her eyes as the priest's footsteps moved to the door, her gaze centered on the dancing points, her vision clearing. Candlelight flickered in cranberry-glass votive holders, their glow spreading rose-hued light, the color of a mid-summer sunrise.

She'd never lit a candle for Jon, figuring the custom old and archaic, but today she felt the need to bring more light into the world. Anything to pretend she wasn't totally helpless again and somewhat foolish still. Would she ever learn?

She moved forward and withdrew the long taper from its resting spot, then dropped to her knees, the feeling both familiar and comforting. Igniting the used end, she reached out and lit the first candle on her left, the petite flare shedding a glimmer of warmth. On impulse she lit the next, then the next, then each one after it, until the entire bank of candles waved bright bits of flame.

Reaching into her purse she withdrew a wad of cash and stuffed the entire amount into the offertory box, then stood, her knees tight. At the side door she paused and looked back, the twinkle of tiny lights sending a fleeting pattern across the deep-grained wood of the suspended cross. With a half sigh at how much time she'd already wasted, Alicia pushed out the door, the cool air and bright sun less welcoming than the gloaming corners of the sweet-smelling church.

She called the veterinary office as she headed back to Conor, her head dipped against a cool wind. The news was less than good. Sarge had relapsed since his minor improvements the night before.

"This is not abnormal for a recovery of this sort." The vet's voice held an edge of reassurance. "His body took weeks to deteriorate into this condition. We need to be patient and allow him time to recuperate."

Alicia swallowed her disappointment. "Of course. I understand. Please call me at this number if there's any news."

"As well as Mr. Bradstreet?"

What to tell him? Alicia sucked in a breath. "Mr. Bradstreet's been taken ill, but I'll keep him apprised of any changes in Sarge's condition."

A moment of silence followed before the vet spoke. "I'll keep you informed personally, Mrs. Bradstreet."

So formal. Prescribed. Feeling like she needed to break loose of her surrounding cage, she told him, "Alicia, please, and my husband is Conor."Another short span elapsed as the vet addressed someone in the clinic before saying, "Alicia, then. I'll call you later today."

"Thank you."

What a dweeb she was, standing here, feeling all good and holier than thou because she'd just asked the veterinarian to call her by her first name, like that was some big thrill for him.

But that little step forward made her feel a million times better, so who cared if the vet thought her silly or goofy or pretentious. She hurried into the hospital, anxious to see Conor, wanting to let him know that Sarge was holding his own and expected no less from his master.

CHAPTER FIFTEEN

Lead anchors hung from Conor's legs, no doubt some form of Princetonian ex-husband torture. Odd images flashed before his eyes in chaotic fashion, sporadic, disconnected, making little sense.

He saw himself coming home to their old house, the curtains hung fresh and crisp the way Alicia liked them, the sweet-spiced scent of candle wax enveloping him as he pushed through the oak and glass door.

Fleas attacked from all sides, hopping to and fro, rhythmic and cadenced, a scene straight out of Disney, the bugs tap-dancing their way across the room before him. Then a sorry looking dog ran through, trailed by a sarong-wearing mouse who danced with the fleas like Ginger Rogers leading a Broadway chorus line. Then Jon stepped in, their boy, their son, strong and healthy and years older than he'd been when they laid his tired body in the ground. Hale and hearty the boy looked, laughing at the dog, dodging the mouse and fleas, throwing a ball, then accepting the soggy mess back from the dog's jowls without a word of discouragement as they moved into a leaf-strewn field.

Conor hurried toward his son, calling his name, his heart filled with unspeakable joy. Wait until he told Alicia! She'd be so happy to know Jon wasn't really dead, that he'd grown into a fine, strong young man, a little gangly, but perfectly understandable for an adolescent.

Conor moved into the back field, his lungs screaming at the exertion, his chest on fire as the boy and dog outdistanced him.

The anchors on his legs slowed his progress. No matter how hard he tried, he couldn't get his lower limbs to cooperate, the leaden weight holding him back, pressing him down.

He called Jon's name, not once, but twice, hoping the boy could hear, longing for a chance to feast his eyes one more time.

But now Conor's eyes felt as heavy as his legs, encumbered by some unseen force, weighty and powerful, pushing him away.

Sinking back, the bright day ebbed, leaving him in the dark, surrounded by strange noises and odd voices bearing an air of urgency he knew he disliked, but was too tired to fight now. Way too tired.

He slept.

Alicia found Addie pacing outside the double doors to the ICU. "How's he doing?"

Addie's jaw quivered. She shook her head. "Not good."

"Is Kim with him?"

Addie nodded. "With Father Murphy. He's... he's..."

She couldn't mouth the words. Alicia gathered her in, this daughter who'd been her staunch defender as a teen, who'd made hating her father a practiced art, mostly at Alicia's behest. Somehow, Addie managed to grow into a delightful and knowledgeable young woman in spite of her mother's sheltering arrogance. And she'd grown to love her dad. Go figure. "Ads, you've got to believe he's going to be all right. This is Dad we're talking about. No stupid little bacteria can do him in. I promise."

"But—"

"Trust me on this." Alicia pulled back and gave Addie the look she reserved for discussions on STD's and best brands of chocolate. "Your father will be fine."

For some reason her assurance bolstered Addie, but when Alicia was allowed in to Conor's bedside an hour later, doubts plagued her. Equipment hummed or beeped around his lax form, his color ashen. A ventilator pumped air into his chest, a precaution Dr. Montoya said, to allow him time to rest, but Alicia knew vents weren't employed casually.

She stood beside the bed, studying the strong man felled by a microscopic organism, praying they'd gotten to him in time. Someone slid a chair alongside her. Grateful, she sat and reached for his hand.

He jerked at her touch, but she refused to let go, his skin slightly cooler than it had been hours before. Addie sat on the opposite side, worried and distraught, clasping his other hand.

Alicia brought Conor's fingers to her mouth in a quiet kiss, then laid his palm against her cheek like he'd done the day before. The touch was different now, flat and lifeless, the skin tepid and loose. She leaned forward, her lips to his ear. "Don't even think of dying on me now, Conor Bradstreet. We have things to discuss, remember?" Memories of their restaurant banter should have made her blush, but no. Thinking of how often Conor had teased her in the past, goading her into bed, their playful talk seemed as normal as breathing and way more invigorating. "Get strong, Conor. Come on, you can do this. It's crazy annoying that you can't talk back to me. Fight with me." *Make love to me*, she added silently, Addie's presence a deterrent to total verbal honesty. She laid her head against his shoulder, letting her eyelashes blink against his warm cheek. "Butterfly kisses."

Addie stared at her like she'd grown a new head. Somewhat understandable since she'd done nothing but gripe about this guy for nearly half the girl's lifetime. "Mom, you just kissed Dad. And gave him butterfly kisses. What's gotten into you?"

Alicia flicked a glance up to Addie, before resting her gaze on Conor. "I don't know, Ads. I guess he kind of wore me down. Kind of crazy, huh?"

Addie's look said her statement went way beyond crazy. "You need some serious rest." She rounded the bed and put an arm around her mother's shoulders. "If you want to go home and get some sleep, Kim and I will cover here. We'll call if anything happens."

"And leave him?" Alicia sent Addie a look of astonishment. "Not a chance."

Addie frowned and leaned down, her voice a whisper. "Mom, you left him a long time ago, remember? You've been divorced for nearly nine years."

"Addie." Keeping Conor's hand firmly in hers, Alicia turned. "I'm not delusional, I'm not on drugs, I'm not crazy. Your father and I have managed to mend some of our differences, that's all."

Addie straightened, mouth open, eyebrows arched. "That's all?" She said the phrase as though uttering the biggest understatement known to man.

Alicia nodded. "Yes. And of course I want him to recover fully. He's got the checkbook, right? And who knows what he's done to me in his will."

"Mom." Addie remonstrated her with a one word hushed whisper.

The nurse cleared her throat. Alicia stood and smoothed a hand from Conor's cheek to his shoulder. Gentle, she let her fingers rest there and leaned down. "Get better. Hurry. You and I have a wedding to plan, remember? And a house to fix, a dog to walk, not to mention a bookstore to open. And stop trying to steal my help."

Addie frowned, stepped forward, kissed Conor's cheek, whispered something in his ear, and grabbed her mother's arm. "You're dangerously psychotic."

Alicia grinned at her. "Probably the closest to normal I've been in a long time, honey."

By late afternoon both girls had dozed off in the less than comfortable waiting room chairs. Conor's brother had driven in from Pennsylvania. He seemed surprised to find Alicia waiting, his demeanor saying ex-wives should be relegated to end of the line status when it came to visiting rights. Worse, he was right. Kim held next of kin honors now. Alicia was nothing more than a former family member.

The whole notion of that ticked her off.

A shuffle at the door drew her head up from the magazine she pretended to read so she could ignore the baleful glances from her former brother-in-law. An old man hobbled in, his gait uncertain, his mode of dress three shades below casual. A woman accompanied him, tall and attractive. She glanced around the room, unsure, but the man met Alicia's gaze head on. "You must be the Missus."

Alicia frowned, confused, but stood.

The old man came her way. "How's Conor doing?"

This man knew Conor? Alicia studied his face, her mind flipping through pages of memory, trying to age-enhance someone from their past, maybe some long lost, distant relative with really bad taste in clothes. Nope. Nothing. She moved to the man's side and shook her head. "Not well, I'm afraid."

He shifted his gaze to the girls curled up at the end of the room and kept his voice soft. "Them girls doing all right?"

Alicia shrugged. "They're scared."

The old man worked his jaw. When he did, the scruffy beard twitched left, then right, in Santa Claus style. "They'll be okay once he's okay. How about you?"

Something in his voice, or maybe in his look, told Alicia there was more than polite interest behind the old guy's question. She shook her head. "Not so well, I'm afraid."

He nodded as if he understood. "Making things right ain't easy, 'specially after so much time, but it's doable. Long as you're breathing, it's doable." He stared at the double doors that blocked them from Conor. "They don't let you in much, do they?"

"No." Alicia breathed the word on a rush, then paused, brushing a strand of hair aside. "Five minutes every hour. And only two. Did you want to see him, Mr...?He shook his head, eyes shadowed. "Name's Sarge, and no, I don't need to see him. You just tell him I came by, that my smoking partner brought me out here so's I could pay my respects to you and the girls. Tell him I'll see him in New York when he's feeling better."

"I will, Sarge." The name clicked in, along with Conor's reaction to the dog's name the day previous. Alicia motioned to the double doors, a hint of insight nudging open a well-rusted chamber of her brain. "They'll be calling for us soon. Why not stay a few minutes? Tell him yourself. I'm sure he'd love to hear your voice."

The tall woman smiled her approval. The old man's fingers gripped the placket of his jacket, his motion insecure, his eyes tender and gruff, an intriguing combination. "Well..."

Alicia took his arm and led him to the chair closest to the double doors. "Sit here. Conor needs his friends right now. We'll tell them you're his father."

Looking tired, the old man did as she asked, then walked to Conor's room with her a few minutes later, leaving Conor's brother sputtering something objectionable about the scant five minutes he'd had the hour before.

When she and Sarge emerged a few minutes later, Addie and Kim were awake and obviously privy to their uncle's distress. As soon as they spied the old man on Alicia's arm, they hurried across the room.

"Sarge. How are you? I'm so glad you could come." Kim gathered the old guy in a gentle hug, eyes closed as though relishing the contact.

"My turn." Addie stepped in, bumped Kim out of the way, and grabbed the old man with all the finesse of a first string linebacker. "I miss you, Sarge."

The old guy's eyes misted. "Me, too, but I hear you're doing well in school. Kicking the old man's butt, hey?"

Addie grinned. "And proud of it. You saw Dad?"

He nodded. "Nurse said his temp's down a bit more. That's a good sign."

Alicia noticed he deliberately didn't mention Conor's renal failure from the stress on his body to fight the pernicious bacteria. Sarge clapped a hand to Addie's shoulder. "He's strong and young. He'll be fine. And tears make him nervous, so mop your faces before you go in there and scare him to death, looking all mopey. You'd think you never saw a sick person before. Sheesh."

"Yes, Sarge."

"We will, Sarge."

The old man turned to Alicia, his hand out. "This old man appreciates your kindness, Missus."

"Alicia." Alicia accepted his hand and shook it with care. "Call me Alicia, Sarge."

A smile lit his face from within. "I'll do that. Thank you."

"Mom, this is Cassie Barnes. She's a—"

"Friend of Sarge's as well," supplied the woman, interrupting Kim's introduction, her hand extended.

Sarge sent the woman a look of appreciation while Alicia shook her hand.

Foster appeared in the waiting room door as Sarge turned to leave. The old man nodded and moved

forward, obviously acquainted with Conor's houseman-
slash-butler-slash-well-paid friend.

Alicia watched the houseman dip his head as they
talked, an easy hand on the old man's shoulder.
Something Sarge said brought Foster's gaze to hers,
his eyes thoughtful, his expression surprised but
accepting. As Sarge headed toward the elevators,
Foster crossed the room. "Mrs. Bradstreet." He
reached out a hand. "I'm so sorry. How can I be of
help?"

"Foster." Alicia reached out for him. He hugged her,
the years melting away like April snow, quicksilver
wet. Alicia mopped her eyes, laughed when Foster
presented a hanky, then hugged him again. "I'm so
happy he has you," she whispered.

Foster stepped back in recovered decorum, nodded
and met her eye. "And you, I take it. Now." Being
Foster, he stood straight and tall, chin up, expression
even. "I need to keep busy. Assign me a task."

Assign him a task? What a Fosterism. Alicia put her
hand against his arm. "There are two things, actually,
if you don't mind."

"At your service."

She smiled, his words taking her back to before she
was a total twit. "Conor has acquired himself a dog in
the last twenty-four hours."

Her head had a hard time believing that it had only
been a day since she and Conor trucked the canine to
the veterinary hospital.

Foster nodded. "I see."

Alicia ignored the fact that Conor's brother was
avidly listening while the girls exchanged looks at her
side. "The dog was neglected. We found him chained in
the back corner of our old carriage shed."

"Where we kept our soccer equipment," Kim
declared.

Alicia included her with a nod. "Yes. This poor dog
had been in there for weeks."

Foster's expression said he understood the rest. "Which veterinary, Madam?"

Alicia gave him the name. Jotting it down, he started to step away, then swung back. "And the other thing?"

"Oh, Foster, don't worry about that. If you can just go and check on the dog, I'm so grateful."

Foster stood his ground. "The second thing, Mrs. Bradstreet."

Alicia met his gaze and saw nothing recriminatory or critical. Just Foster, wanting to help, ready, willing and able, a trusted employee, a true friend. What a blessing to have his stalwart presence. "I need clean clothes. I don't want to leave again while he's this bad, and I just threw on yesterday's clothes when I woke up in the middle of the night, not the dog smelling ones, of course, that would be awful, but I knew something was wrong, so I called Conor and he didn't answer his cell, so I called again, and you know Conor, Foster, he always, always, always, answers his cell." She was babbling, she knew it, the words free-falling from her brain to her tongue in slip-shod shape, tumbling over one another in her haste.

Tears she hadn't allowed herself began streaming down her face. Foster put out a hand for her keys as Kim embraced her.

Foster's expression stayed firm and calm in spite of her histrionics. A neat trick. He nodded, his gaze a comfort. "You're quite right. He does always answer. You got to him in time, Madam. You did the right thing."

Did she?

No. She knew she should have stayed, she'd felt it in his suite of rooms, as if the Holy Spirit himself had nudged her to sit and keep watch by his bed, but she hadn't listened to the tiny, inner voice.

What if she had? Would he suffer as he did now? Would he linger at death's door if she'd gotten him help six hours before?

Foster dipped his chin, surveying her outfit. "I think comfortable would be the best choice for today." He sent a disparaging and utterly British look to the vinyl seating and barely suppressed his shudder. "Something not... sticky."

His tone reminded Alicia of how capable the houseman had been during Jon's illness, the many things he'd done to help with two half-crazed adolescent girls and frantic parents on the verge of losing their son.

"God bless you, Foster." Never had she meant a blessing so much.

He met her gaze, his eyes compassionate. "Oh, he has, Madam. He has."

A familiar man walked into the waiting room on Monday afternoon. "Mrs. Bradstreet?"

Tired, Alicia stood to meet him. "Yes?"

He moved forward and motioned her back to the chair. "No, sit, please, sit down. I didn't mean to disturb you."

She shook her head, still unable to place the visitor. "You didn't. Not really."

He extended a hand from his well-cut suit. "Reggie Preston from Garlock Estates."

Of course. The zoning board chairman. Alicia nodded, remembering how miffed she'd been when he and Conor let business interrupt the planning of Kim's wedding. Stupid men. "How are you, Mr. Preston?"

"I'm fine, but I'm concerned about your husband. The word is he's quite ill."

"The word is correct."

"Mrs. Bradstreet," he sat forward, his expression earnest, "Conor and I had discussed some plans projected by a team of local developers."

"Of course." Why wouldn't development take precedence over Kim's wedding? Duh, Alicia.

"Because he's directly involved in this venture, I wanted him to know that the sale is complete as of this morning. His sound insight and our legal team were able to work things out to everyone's satisfaction."

Except the poor bloke who lost his shirt in the deal, no doubt. Alicia tried to muster a smile of acceptance and failed. "And you think this is important enough for me to share with him while he fights for his life?"

Reggie's expression switched to one of confusion. He paused a moment, puzzled, then shook his head. "I'm sorry. I wasn't aware you were unapprised of the situation, considering Conor's request."

"Request?" Alicia wished her brain were working better. Short sleep for the past two days had things mis-firing. "What request?"

"We're building a campground, Mrs. Bradstreet, a special needs camp for gravely ill children."

His words brought Alicia more upright. "Oh?"

Reggie nodded. "When Conor heard about the project, he called and offered a substantial donation with one stipulation."

"My bookstore." Suddenly her timeline for the bookstore approval became much clearer. "He bought you."

Reggie laughed out loud. "I thought the same thing at the time, but no. That wasn't his intent. At least, not his sole intent. The only thing he asked for was to have something in the campground named for your son, Jonathan."

Conor did that? Her Conor? Alicia's chest tightened. Her throat went thick. Words came hard. "And?"

Reggie handed her a pamphlet, full color, a rendering of a kids' camp at mid-summer best, the

brace of background trees green and full against a
deep blue sky. "I know how you like horses. Conor told
me that Jon did, too. I thought this would be
appropriate if you approve." He pointed a finger to the
centered picture on the third wall of the glossed
pamphlet.

"The Jon Bradstreet Stables." Her chin quivered as
she ran a finger across the name of her son, their son.
She nodded, overcome, tears welling, then spilling. She
pictured Jon as he'd been, snugged onto the saddle,
helmet in place, his beautiful brown eyes full of trust.
"I love it."

Reggie offered a wad of tissues from the never-
ending box that understandably lived in the waiting
room of the ICU. "Good. And Conor would approve?"

"Yes." She nodded, grabbed more tissues, mopped
her eyes and blew her nose, not caring that this rich
man watched. "Conor will approve."

"And, about the bookstore..."

Alicia stiffened. "Yes?"

Reggie contemplated her a long moment as though
searching for words. "Your proposal should have gone
through the first time. Both the presentation and the
location were fine as offered. Unfortunately there are
times when outside variables take on too much weight.
That was the case with your project. I'm glad we had
the opportunity to look at it again, reassess our
decision."

"Because Conor made a hefty contribution?" Should
she hate the man she'd called her husband for years
for engineering things in typical style or love him to
pieces, glad to have a champion on her side again?

Reggie shook his head. "While his contribution in
both advice and dollars proved stellar for procurement
of our camp land, Conor wasn't the causative factor in
the vote change. Sometimes government officials trip
over themselves to make certain people happy at the
expense of others."

"Shipton Books."

He smiled but wouldn't commit. "Once we realized our mistake, we backtracked. Princeton is a community that stands by its own. We forgot that for a minute."

Alicia gave him a watery smile. "Thank you."

He stood. Winked. "Of course, seven-figure checks aren't exactly chicken feed, you know."

"Should have held out for eight," Alicia told him. She stuck out her hand. "I appreciate your efforts and your candor."

He nodded, then indicated the ICU doors. "And we'll keep you in our prayers. I think the good father had tears in his eyes when they prayed for Conor during Mass today."

"I saw that too." Alicia's smile grew. "I think it's because he fears getting wet."

Reggie cocked a brow.

Alicia grinned. "A little wager they had going. Father lost."

"And Conor won."

She nodded. "So typical. Now he just needs to live long enough to enjoy his victory."

"Amen."

"I think I've got him, Leash," Conor muttered, eyeing the scrawny dog in need of medical help. "Yes, look, he's right there, behind the bush. No, not over there, Leash, to the left. My left. Yes, right there, you've almost got him, great job. Leash? Alicia? Leash, where are you?"

The weights yanked again, pulling him back, disallowing movement and speech. With a quick twist and a yell he disengaged whatever blocked his airway, croaking the dog's direction to Alicia, sure she could find the bedraggled mutt if given the chance.

The waiting room intercom buzzed the next evening. Addie hit the button, looking fairly good for someone who spent the last three days sleeping on chairs. Youth factor, Alicia reasoned. "Yes?"

"Mr. Bradstreet's family, please."

Addie's face drained at the frantic note in the nurse's voice. "Speaking."

"Mr. Bradstreet has pulled out his vent tube and is calling for someone named Lisa, or Alyssa, something like that. Is there a person with that name here? He's quite distraught."

Alicia growled. "Tell them to open the door."

She cruised through the opening before the automatic doors swung wide, banging her elbow on the hard, polished metal, but felt nothing. She raced down the hall, banked a right and practically flew into Conor's room. "I'm here, Conor. It's me. Alicia." She pulled a breath, wanting and needing to calm her nerves so she could present a brave front. The guy had been through plenty the last seventy-two hours. Her job was to make things better, not worse. She picked up Conor's hand and pressed it to her cheek. "I'm here, Conor. Right here."

"Leash."

A sigh whooshed out of her at the sound of her name on his lips. "Yes, Conor."

"I saw him, Leash."

The nurse met Alicia's gaze across the bed and cocked a brow while someone else tried to make sense out of the equipment Conor had pulled free. Alicia leaned close. "Saw who, Conor?"

"Jon."

The name came out a valiant whisper over roughed up vocal chords, as if Conor himself couldn't quite believe his words. Alicia laid her second hand to his forehead, definitely cooler. "Rest, Conor."

The fingers in hers wiggled impatience, a not unfamiliar Conor trait. "He was bigger, Leash, not like when he—"

"Conor."

"—died."

The nurse's expression turned to one of comfort. She nodded to Alicia to let him go, let him talk.

"Oh?" Alicia clung to his hand, not wanting to have this conversation, not now, not ever.

"Tall, like me." Conor's air pushed out as he struggled to speak, the effort costing him. "And still blond. But your face, Leash. My brown eyes. I'd have known him anywhere."

Alicia closed her eyes and sank into the chair. "Did he look good?"

"Wonderful."

A peaceful expression stole across Conor's features. Alicia dropped her head to his arm, her tears wetting his sheets. "I'm glad, Conor."

"Hey."

His left arm struggled to move. Alicia lifted her head to accommodate him. He brought the hand to her face, touching the skin, feeling the tears, his eyes closed tight like a newborn pup. "You're crying."

"A little."

Conor frowned. "Don't."

His order made her smile. "Yes, sir. That better?"

His breathing tightened as he groped her face, his hands clumsy. "Some. I'm tired, Leash."

"I bet. Rest. I'm here. The girls are here. We're not going anywhere."

"Promise?"

She smiled against the skin of his hand. "Promise."

"Leash."

"Conor. Shh... You should be sleeping."

"Been sleeping. Over-rated. Leash...I'm sorry." The words had slowed to a half-croak.

"Conor..."

"I'm trying, Leash..." His air broke. He pulled for breath. The nurse stood nearby with an oxygen mask, watching him, ready to intervene, but allowing him to say what he seemed so determined to say. "Can't die..."

Alicia's heart spiked, then dipped. She raised her head. Palmed his face. "You're not going to die, Conor. Too much to do."

"...without telling you."

Sudden insight offered Alicia means to help. She leaned closer, her lips against his cheek. "That you love me?"

He sighed and relaxed into the pillow. "Yes."

Oh, man. She studied his face, the familiar lines, the planes of his cheeks, hollowed and gaunt from his ordeal. "You've been telling me, Conor, in so many ways. Your work. Your charity. Your kindness." Alicia gnawed her lower lip, watching his muted reactions. "I was too mad to listen."

An understatement if ever there was one. Conor's face flexed, then relaxed. "And now?"

Hmm. A loaded question. One she might need a little time on. She moved forward and laid her lips against his face again, the kiss whisper soft. "Now you need to rest. Let the medicine and the staff do their jobs. Get better. We've got lots of time as long as you don't decide to check out on me, leaving me with a wedding to plan, a store to open and a dog to take care of all on my own. Then I'll be ticked off all over again. We don't want that, do we?"

Conor shuddered as if calling to mind the last eight years. "No." His expression shifted to confusion. "Dog?"

"Mm hmm. The one we found, remember?"

His eyes blinked open, then closed. He twitched his nose as though smelling something foul. "Oh, yes."

Alicia smiled. "Well, he's doing much better and smells good now."

"Sarge."

"You do remember. Good."

"Leash."

"Yes, Conor?" The nurse made a quieting motion. Alicia nodded agreement. "One more thing and then you need to sleep, okay? We can talk more later. What?"

"I killed... the fleas... for you."

Fever ramblings. Alicia smiled and batted eyelashes against his cheek. "You did, and I thank you. Go to sleep now. I'll be here when you wake up."

"You're sure?"

She grasped his hand and gave it a light squeeze. "I'm positive, Conor."

CHAPTER SIXTEEN

Alicia strode into the private room on the fifth floor of the hospital and whistled softly. "Holy flowers, Batman."

Conor snorted. "Get me out of this place."

"Um...How, exactly?" She let her gaze rest on the PIC line, then re-directed her attention to the dozens of floral arrangements. "Does anyone on earth need this many flowers?"

"The nurses will shift them to other patients just as soon as we take out the cards so we can send thank-you notes."

"We?" Alicia perched on the edge of his bed and gave him an arch glance. "No one sent me flowers, Conor."

"No?"

"Uh uh. Not one single blossom has come to my door in too many years to count. Be grateful."

He reached out a hand to her cheek, IV tubing draped along his arm. "Oh, I am."

His smile inspired hers. She raised a hand to his forehead and nodded at the distinct drop in temperature. "Much better. And I have to say I'm glad to have you out of that stupid—"

"Bad word, remember?"

She grinned and made a quick substitution. "Goofy ICU where they wouldn't let me come in to see you until Kim put me on the list of approved visitors."

"Really?" Conor's smile deepened. "Held you at bay, did they?"

"It wasn't one bit funny at the time."

Conor made a phony attempt at a serious face. "Of course not."

"Conor." She poked him, then felt almost bad when he winced, but not quite. "You deserved that. Being shut out of your room was demoralizing. Degrading."

"Deserved?" He hiked one brow and for a moment looked like the Conor of old, cocky and quite self-assured, although pale.

"You—"

Conor leaned forward and placed two fingers against her mouth, successfully preventing the bad word at the edge of her tongue. "I have a distinct feeling that anything you're about to call me goes well beyond the realm of stupid, so I'm going to save you from yourself."

She sputtered.

Her sputter inspired a deeper smile from him. The fingers against her mouth turned into a gentle caress of her cheek, then her hair. He leaned even closer. "I'm sorry they have goofy rules downstairs about ex-wives in the ICU. I'll sue them for you. How does that sound?"

To Alicia's surprise and ultimate mortification, her eyes filled with tears.

"Hey, hey." Conor reached for her with his other arm. "Leash, what's up? What's wrong? Why the tears? Don't do that, okay? You know they make me crazy."

"I..." sniff, "was..." sniff, sniff, "so..." sniff, "scared."

"Really?"

The hint of humor in his tone comforted her, and she had no idea why. Maybe because it boded well for his full recovery? Or maybe because she'd been afraid to lose him before she got to know this new and improved Conor Bradstreet, the one who befriended tired old men and had parks named for his deceased son, the one who headed up a huge foundation that offered a life with a semblance of dignity for those down on their luck.

"So..." He played with a lock of her hair, twisting it around his finger, then watching the curl fall back into a ringlet along her neckline when he released it. "You'd miss me?"

Alicia sucked in a breath and tried to gain control of her roller-coasting emotions, first up, then down, then up again on a sliding scale of one to at least a cool hundred. Whether the mix of emotions was spurred by age-related hormone fluctuations or Conor's influence, she didn't know, but most likely the hikes and dips came from the sudden meeting of the two dissimilar and opposing forces clashing together, kind of like Gulf air moisture meeting an Arctic clipper over Nebraska. At that point, someone better be praying for Nebraska, 'cause the storm of the century was about to dump snow, freezing rain and the occasional tornado on the unsuspecting state.

Conor tweaked her chin. "So. Would you miss me, Alicia? A little?" He tipped her chin with one finger, his voice soft and low, his look shifting from her eyes to her mouth as he angled his head and moved forward.

A light knock at the door interrupted the moment. Part of her wanted to lean into him and taste the kiss he'd offered, but he'd already straightened, his look to her apologetic.

"Conor, you had us worried, old man." George Bleu stepped into the room, scarcely giving Alicia a glance. "How are you doing? You've looked better. And how soon can we expect you back? I'm covering your list, but you know there's no one that does it quite like Conor Bradstreet."

Alicia eased off the bed and started to step away. Conor grasped her hand, tugging her back. "George, you remember Alicia, don't you?"

George turned full benefit of his ultra New York smile on her. "Of course, of course. How are you, Ms. Bradstreet? Glad to see our boy here getting better?"

"Very much." She squeezed Conor's hand and wiggled her fingers from his, a move that wouldn't have worked had he been healthier.

A second man strode in the door, waving a folder, his face creased in smiles. "Heard you were out of ICU so I thought I'd bring you a little work on Ehrmentraut to pass the time."

Conor groaned. "I hope that's a joke, at least for a day or two."

Anger bubbled inside Alicia. Didn't these two present day Neanderthals understand what Conor had been through? How sick he really was? How capricious this turn around could be if the Legionella bacteria got the best of the antibiotic? She stepped forward to save Conor from himself when a woman strode into the room, long and leggy, wearing a power suit, power shoes and hair that flowed soft, silky and blonde across her shoulders. Total class act, New York prime, smart, sophisticated and slim as a reed.

Obviously Alicia's cue to go. While Conor was distracted greeting the newcomer, Alicia moved toward the door.

"Leash?" His voice held question and concern. "Where are you going?"

She turned at the door in full "zone" mode, emotions buried, face shielded. "Got a bookstore to open. You take care, Conor."

The confused look on his face nearly broke her resolve, but even as she contemplated that, another member of Conor's elite New York tribe moved past her, as if she were nothing. A non-entity.

Pushing Conor's hurt expression aside, she left the room, realizing the accuracy of the assessment. She was a non-entity in Conor's life. The mother of his children, but no longer a person with a vested interest in the man himself. Hadn't the ICU made that abundantly clear?

Yes. Better she realize this now, while Conor's room filled with New York money movers whose pictures graced CNBC on a regular basis. Conor is, was, and always would be a man whose destiny brought him untold millions, proximity to some of the swankest and toniest parts of the world, two beautiful daughters, an amazing array of available women and one cranky ex-wife.

So be it.

Conor looked up when Kim came through the door of his hospital room the next evening. He frowned and growled, not bothering to hide his disappointment. "Where's your mother?"

"I have no idea." Kim met his scowl with one of her own. "And stop frowning. You'll get wrinkles. And then I'll get them because I frown back at you."

His glare deepened. He waved a hand. "I tried her cell. She won't answer my calls."

"What did you do?"

"Not a thing," he exploded, pushing up, out of the chair alongside the bed, grabbing the tails of his hospital gown as he climbed back into bed. "She was here yesterday, all nice and sweet, then some other people showed up and she took off without even saying goodbye."

Kim gave him one of those special, *The-Doctor-Is-In* looks made famous in Peanuts' cartoons. "And you can't add that up? Put two and two together?"

"She left because they came?"

"Got it in one. Good job, Dad."

"But that makes no sense," Conor complained. His throat hurt from talking, his back ached from his inability to find anything remotely close to a comfortable position, his body yearned for food, but his weakened digestive system wouldn't allow solids as yet, and Alicia wouldn't return his calls, leaving him crabby, sore, starved and frustrated.

"To you or her?"

Conor glowered. "Your mother has enough chutzpah to hold her own with a room full of my co-workers."

"Does she know that?"

"Of course she does," Conor blustered. "She..." A dawn of realization came over him.

Kim met his look and nodded. "Exactly. She's doing better with you when you guys are on *her* turf. Yours? Might take a while on that one."

Conor bit his lip to keep from swearing out loud. Kim was right. He understood that now, but it wasn't like he had the strength or the option to go to Alicia, wear her down. Or maybe in this case, build her up.

"The nurse's station says you've had a steady stream of hob nobbers the past two days."

"Some good, some bad." Conor nodded. "I need to get out of this place, Kim. I have stuff to do." *Like find my ex-wife, pull her close, and kiss her senseless. Right before I take on the ills of corporate America. After my next nap, that is. Piece of cake.*

"I believe the requirements for that are a solid diet, clear lungs and movable bowels, sir." Foster came into the room looking very New York British, a look only the Fosters of the world could pull off. He set his bowler hat aside and eyed his employer. "At the moment, sir, you are batting zero."

"With the advent of spring comes Foster and his amazing baseball analogies," Conor retorted, feeling more than a little peevish because the one person he wanted to spend time with was refusing his calls. Again. "I'm sorry the poorly-planned timing of my near-fatal illness requires you to miss spring training." Foster had canceled his annual trek to Florida to watch the Yankees test their mettle with the advent of a new season.

Foster ignored the barb in Conor's voice. "There will be other springs, sir. There's always another season when it comes to baseball. Kind of what attracts me. Can I get you anything?"

"My wife."

"Um, well, yes, sir, I've actually just had dinner with Mrs. Bradstreet. And the dog."

Conor leaned forward. "Sarge? How is he? How's he doing?"

"Remarkably well as I'm instructed to tell you. He's eating home-made chicken and rice, and *his* bowels seem to be working just fine, much to Mrs. Bradstreet's chagrin."

Conor remembered Alicia's gentle manner with the unclean animal, how she ignored the smell and the general foulness of the poor creature as she stroked his neck, his back. A smile tugged his cheek, picturing her in the vet's office, her stance tough, her touch gentle. "She'll be fine." His brain must have become more fully engaged because he hadn't missed the meaning behind Foster's casual words. "She's sending messages through you again, Foster?"

The houseman's eyes dimmed, but he kept his countenance even. "Yes, sir."

"Of all the—" Conor sent a mulish look to both Kim and Foster. "I need to get out of here."

Kim put a hand to his arm. "Soon, Dad. She's not going any place. It's Mom, remember? Once in Princeton, always in Princeton."

Conor recognized the truth in that, but he needed to see Alicia, talk to her, for his own peace of mind. Having his New York office descend on his hospital room pushed her over some unseen edge, but he couldn't do anything about the situation if she deliberately stayed away.

He wondered if she got the flowers he'd ordered the day before, if she liked the mixed bouquet.

"And Mrs. Bradstreet would also like me to express her gratitude for the lovely floral arrangement that arrived at her door late yesterday. The ones the dog didn't chew up and spit out all over the living room Aubusson are perfectly lovely."

"The dog ate her flowers?"

"Only some."

"Did she go ballistic?"

Foster frowned as he tidied up the room, which appeared much larger now that thirty-one floral arrangements had found other lodging within the hospital. "Oh, no, sir. I believe her words were to the effect of: 'It's nice to see someone enjoy Conor's efforts as much as I do.' End quote."

Conor straightened his shoulders and pressed his lips into a line. "She said that? About a dog eating a bunch of flowers that cost nearly two hundred dollars?"

"A stellar arrangement, if I do say so myself, sir, but they went a mite heavy on the pinks. You may want to note that for next time. I believe Mrs. Bradstreet prefers bold, sassy colors."

"And I believe Mrs. Bradstreet—"

"Dad." Kim's warning came in the nick of time.

Conor glowered her way. "I need to see your mother before this gets out of hand."

"Well, without dragging her here, that's quite impossible, so I suggest you put a sock in it, stop grumbling and growling at everyone, concentrate on getting healthy and getting out of here, and then you can go see Mom, and put this whole stupid thing to rest."

Grayce's little voice gasped from the door. "Stupid's a bad word, Kimmy."

Kim sent Conor a rebellious look that reminded him of her mother and turned to greet Brian and Grayce. "Oops. I know. Sorry, Graycie. I won't say it again."

Brian brought Grayce to Conor's bedside and dipped her close for a kiss. Her tiny hand trailed along his cheek, feeling his unshaved skin. "You've got prickles. Like the Christmas tree."

"I do."

She gave him a look to melt his heart. "I miss you, Grandpa."

"I miss you too." Conor patted the bed beside him. "Climb up here, Kid. Let me see you."

"You sure?" Brian gave him a warning look. "She wiggles."

"She'll be fine," Conor said. "They've got me almost unhooked and they've ordered soft foods for later this evening."

"Well." Brian grinned and doffed an imaginary cap. "Aren't you The Man?"

"As long as I control the checkbook, I am," Conor retorted. "Have you guys heard anything on that little matter we discussed before I took sick?" He meant his offer to Chloe Martin, Grayce's biological mother.

"No." Kim shook her head while Foster left the room in search of fresh water that didn't come from an unfiltered tap. "Not a word."

"And you've gotten over the idea of taking out a contract on your only father for extending the offer?"

"Yes. Once I realized you were right. Didn't necessarily make things easier," announced Kim with a side look at Grayce, "but your reasoning made sense. Which only served to annoy me."

Conor huffed a sigh. "You are your mother's daughter. Sometimes."

She smiled and leaned down to kiss his cheek. "And yours."

"Yes." Conor flashed her a smile. "A good combination, all in all."

"If you throw in the all important checkbook," Brian added.

Kim leaned across the bed, over her father's weak, inert body and glowered. "Knock off the checkbook jokes or there will be no wedding. Got it?"

Brian pretended remorse. "All of them?"

"Every one."

"But—"

Conor kicked Brian in the leg, just enough to get his attention. "Word to the wise: Women like to be loved for themselves and themselves alone, not for the proximity to their parents' monetary funds."

"Got it, sir. Thanks for the reminder." Brian rubbed his leg in punctuation.

Grayce reached over to give Conor a hug. "I miss you, thiiiiiiiiis much, Grandpa. When are you coming home?"

"Soon, Kid. Real soon."

"Good. Grandma 'Licia misses you, too, and wants you to take your doggie home."

Conor glanced from Kim and Brian. Kim shrugged. "No clue, Dad."

"How do you know this?" Conor eyed the little girl who'd stolen a huge part of his heart.

"'Cause the doggie ate the flowers and made a mess on the floor and she told me it's okay to cry, even if you're a grown-up, 'cause even grown ups get sad sometimes. But I don't like it," Grayce announced.

Conor was having a hard time getting past the image of Alicia's beautiful flowers strewn about by the neglected animal he'd foisted on her because of his poorly timed illness. On top of that, the thought of dog messes in her picture-perfect home seemed more than slightly out of place when she'd just committed her time and efforts to the rush of putting together her own business and her daughter's wedding. She had every reason to hate him. His timing couldn't have been worse.

Brian looked at Grayce, his face puzzled. "What don't you like, honey? The dog?"

"No, Sarge is special," Grayce explained. "'Licia said so. I just don't like to see 'Licia cry. It makes me sad."

Her woebegone expression chugged Conor's heart to his throat. Here he was, tied to this stupid bed, in this stupid room, in a stupid hospital that hurt Alicia's feelings, and he couldn't get to her, make things better.

Brian whisked the little girl up and off the bed. "Well, enough cheering up Grandpa for the moment, hey?" He held Grayce up and gazed into her eyes. "You could have just given him a paper cut and poured some lemon juice in it, Kid. Easily as effective as your tried and true methods as witnessed thus far."

Grayce looked utterly confused. Kim shook her head and leaned in to kiss her father. "Do what the nurses say if you want to facilitate your release. Got it?"

"Yes."

"Love you."

"I love you, too. Tell your mother to come see me."

"Right. I'll get right on that." The look she threw him said plainly that she'd leave him to tidy up his own messes, canine and otherwise, once he was set free from the restraints of hospital life.

"Bye, Grandpa."

"Bye, Kid."

"Love you."

"Love you more."

She smiled and blew him a kiss. "I know."

"Things are looking much better, Mr. Bradstreet." Dr. Montoya nodded his encouragement the next afternoon. "Everything appears to be fully functioning. We'll discharge you tomorrow. Here is a list of instructions. Will you be staying in Princeton, or returning to New York?"

That decision had been weighing on Conor's mind for the past forty-eight hours. He glanced at Foster who kept his expression carefully blank. "I'll be here for a few days. Then New York."

Conor couldn't be sure, but he thought the houseman gave the slightest of approving nods.

"If you have further troubles while you are here, please call me," Dr. Montoya instructed him. "My emergency service will contact me immediately if I am out of the office. Once you are in New York, you should see your own doctor. I sent him your records so he can review the treatment step by step."

Conor reached out a hand. "Thank you, Doctor. For everything."

Dr. Montoya gave a brisk nod. "It is my job, yes?"

Conor smiled, acknowledging that. "Yes."

His cell phone rang about an hour later. He scanned the display and fumbled the phone, his fingers clumsy. "Yes?"

"Mr. Bradstreet?"

"Yes."

"This is Nurse Barnes from Crossings Adult Care."

"Yes, Miss Barnes? How's Sarge?" Conor said the words, but his heart read the writing on the wall from the over-quiet tone of her voice.

"He's nearing the end, Mr. Bradstreet. I'm sorry to have to tell you this. I know how ill you've been, and how difficult this is, but your orders were to call you, regardless."

"Absolutely." Conor pushed his legs to floor and stood up from the chair, grasping its arm with his free hand. The room spun, but nowhere near as bad as the previous day. Bit by bit. "I'm still in Princeton, but I'll head that way directly."

"Use the side entrance," she instructed. "The guard there will let you up."

Side entrance. Guard. Simple enough. "Thank you, Ms. Barnes."

She sighed. "You're welcome."

Foster came into the room as Conor struggled into his pants. "Sir?"

"It's Sarge. He's dying. We've got to head up there."

Foster, bless him, broached no word of argument. "I'll help you dress then bring the car around."

Conor clapped a hand to the other man's back. "You're a good friend, Foster."

"As are you, sir."

"Do you think we'll get there in time?"

"That depends solely on how quick you can convince those nurses to let you sign out of here and God's eternal plan. My driving abilities should not be brought into question."

Conor knew the truth in that.

He hated leaving things unresolved with Alicia. That thought stabbed his gut, but right now Sarge needed him, if nothing more than to hold the old man's hand as he crossed that final bridge. Conor could do no less.

Soft lighting welcomed Conor as he stepped into Sarge's room. Cassie Barnes glanced up, nodded and stood, then crossed the room and helped Conor into a chair alongside the bed without making him feel weak or foolish. Good woman. "How's he doing?"

Her eyes misted. "Standing at the edge. I think he was waiting for you."

Her gentle words stretched Conor's heart a bit more. He leaned over his old friend, called his name.

"Hey, Sonny."

That weak, thready voice couldn't come from the Sarge he knew, but it did. Conor held a small box aloft. "I brought you some fresh smokes."

A tiny smile twitched beneath the whiskers. "Give 'em to the nurses, boy. My smoking days are over. Unless they sell Marlboros in heaven."

Conor shook his head. "No smoking zone. I saw it on Fox News."

Sarge struggled to open his eyes. Once open, he worked harder to focus. "You take care of that wife and them girls, you hear?"

Conor fought the thickening in his throat. "You have my word."

The hint of a smile flickered once more. "You're one of the few who keep their word these days, Sonny. Kinda surprised me with that, back in the day."

"Really?" Conor leaned close, holding Sarge's hand. "You didn't think I'd come back?"

"Most don't. You're..." Sarge's lids fluttered, his grip tightened, then relaxed. "...one of a kind."

Conor thought of the myriads of crazed businessmen lining the streets of New York, vitally important pencil pushers, just like him, frenzied with the rush and bustle of wheeling and dealing. "Just one of the crowd, Sarge."

"Hah." Again Sarged huffed for breath, his chest rising in silent protest. "Shows what you know. You got things under control down here? Feeling up to the task?"

Conor nodded. "Yes."

"Then I'm heading on home."

"You do that, Sarge." Conor stood, leaned down, and gave the old man a gentle hug goodbye. "You do that."

"Mom, this looks totally awesome." Kim made a full turn as she scoped out the nearly ready bookstore two weeks later, her gaze sweeping the balance of historic colors, wainscoting, crown moldings and the curving stair, center-stage, elegant and timeless. Golden oak library shelving lined the walls, with round oak tables arranged for quiet or communal seating throughout. To the far right stood a coffee bar, set apart by tiny, clear, globed lights. Coffee signs done in black script on brightly painted thin boards dangled from the ceiling in multiple lengths and languages, while the wall behind featured eclectic artworks. The coffee machinery gleamed metallic as early morning sun streamed through, tiny rainbows dancing their way across the honey-finished oak bar. "Absolutely wonderful. Who thought of all this?"

Alicia smiled. "Actually...me."

"Seriously?"

"Well, Jerome suggested the colors for upstairs. By the time he was done showing me what could be done with color and room spacing, I had some fun down here."

"I'll say." Kim nodded and gave Alicia a hug. "It's great."

"So." Alicia angled Kim a look. "I didn't exactly expect you down this week. I know you had to take a lot of days off with your father's illness."

Kim nodded and shrugged. "Between that and the funeral, it's been a crazy few weeks, but I felt like I was neglecting you. Amazing thing, guilt."

Alicia nodded. "Awful and wonderful, depending on the levels applied. Who died?"

"Sarge. Dad's friend."

Alicia's hands stopped in the middle of showing Kim how well the coffee set-up worked. "When?"

"The day Dad left the hospital and went back to New York. The nursing home called him, said Sarge was nearing the end and Dad hopped into his pants and had Foster get the car."

Kim's explanation painted a glib picture, but Alicia had seen Conor a few days previous. There was no way he hopped into anything, pants or otherwise. "That's why he went back so quickly?"

Kim met her look. "Yes."

Alicia worked her jaw, feeling dense and foolish, take your pick. "I thought..."

"That he'd hurried back to work because he's crucially important to the ongoing success of New York litigation as we know it?"

"Um. Yes."

Kim moved forward. "You wouldn't answer his calls."

Alicia shrugged and didn't look up. "He hasn't called in nearly two weeks."

"Why call if the person you're calling refuses to speak to you?"

"Kim, I—"

Kim held up a hand for silence. "No. Let me just say this, get it out there. The guy made some bad mistakes in his life. You know it. I know it. But were his any worse than those the rest of us make?"

Alicia thought of her ongoing anger, her constant refusal to try things new, to see things Conor's way. He'd made a serious mistake in the wake of losing his child, one she refused to forgive, carrying a grudge she fed for years. Did the gravity of his mistake weigh heavier than hers? Not if you figured in the longevity of grudge-holding and the negativity it spawned.

If life were a balance scale, her side tipped dangerously low.

"Dad has worked really hard to turn himself around, to be the kind of guy any girl would be proud to call her father," Kim announced, her tone flat. "He cares about everyone and everything. If someone needs help, Conor Bradstreet's their 'go-to' guy, and half of New York knows it even though he keeps things low-key."

Kim's words stung. After all of Alicia's empty promises to herself about being a better person, less judgmental, less critical, she'd gone and behaved in typical Alicia fashion the minute Conor's attention was divided. She'd stormed out, pouted, whined and fussed like a pre-schooler welcoming a new baby.

At that moment she hated herself.

Kim waved a hand to the new bookstore, the soft glow of the freshly finished wood, the clean lines of unchipped paint, the jazzed and upscale coffee bar. "I love that you're doing this. I really do. I think it's a great step up from hiding in the library."

"But?" Alicia met Kim's eye and refused to flinch.

"I wish it didn't mean quite so much." Kim glanced at her watch, made a face and headed for the door. "I've got to meet the florist in ten minutes. See you later."

See you later?

Alicia watched her leave, then sank onto one of the leather-topped coffee stools and looked around her. Really looked.

The store, slated to open in a few days, stood nearly ready, everything fresh and new, a mix of books and giftware, an eclectic but welcoming shop for the average buyer. She hadn't gone high-end Princeton, but middle-of-the-road, tried and true.

A tiny full-spectrum rainbow danced across her clenched hands. She eyed the colorful movement, then stood and moved to the window, seeking the source.

Slanted sunlight bounced through prismed corners of windows marching along the old church wall, their picture-painted panes open for whatever reason. Spring cleaning? Lemon-oiling the aging pews?

The sun's position must have been just right, because the beams shot into her storefront, dancing and moving with every shift of the propped windows in the brisk spring wind.

She had no idea how long she sat there, eyeing the combination that had to be perfect, a sight she might never see again depending on the day and the angle of light through glass.

Even as she pondered that, the sun moved higher, its rays less oblique. The rainbows thinned and faded, the colors muting. Within moments the spectral visitors fled, leaving a fleeting memory of magical dancing light and rainbow parties.

She stared across the road at the beautiful stone church and wondered why it took so long and so much to teach her the basic fundamentals, what made her so stubborn and willful?

Conor hadn't left because he wanted to. He'd left because he needed to, and as a woman who loved words, she understood the difference between those two verbs better than most. Putting a call through to her store manager, she made arrangements for the other woman to oversee the final days of prep work at the bookstore while Alicia tackled the somewhat unnerving idea of cruising to New York with a full grown German shepherd in her Range Rover.

CHAPTER SEVENTEEN

Conor peered at his laptop screen, ruing the waves of exhaustion that swept with no warning.

Being back in New York should have felt normal and good. Comfortable, with Foster at his beck and call. But comfort had taken on a whole new meaning in Princeton, at least he thought so. Before he decided to tempt the Grim Reaper, that is.

He missed Alicia. Missed her spark, her fire. He thought he'd made her laugh a time or two before he took ill, and in his best possible scenarios, he was sure he remembered some rather invigorating conversation just before he went down for the count.

Or maybe he dreamed the whole thing.

A glance at his watch made him frown. He needed to drive to Princeton, claim his dog, and re-negotiate terms of the truce with Alicia. She'd gone scurrying back to her hiding place because New York had swooped in, snatching his time and attention.

So be it.

He didn't have to work in New York. The firm would go on, with or without his presence. Corporations would continue to make foolish mistakes in the name of greed or arrogance, and corporate lawyers would consequently rake in millions. Kind of the law of the land. But the law of the land didn't exist exclusively in New York. If she needed him in Princeton more, he'd be there.

If she needed him at all.

Staring at Ehrmentraut figures that seemed destined to fell a huge company from within, Conor pressed a hand to his face. Too much computer work gave him headaches, but they were less intense these last few days.

His cell phone rang. Conor glanced at the display, frowned and answered. "Conor Bradstreet."

"Mr. Bradstreet?"

The female voice sounded familiar and uncertain. Conor straightened in his chair. "Yes?"

"This is Chloe Martin. Grayce's mother."

"Yes, Ms. Martin, how are you?" Interest heightened, Conor sat back in his chair, keeping his tone gentle.

"I was wondering..." she hesitated, her voice soft.

"Yes?"

"That offer you made. Is it still available?"

Conor breathed a sigh of relief. "Most assuredly. Are you ready for this step, Ms. Martin? Because if you and I blow this, my son-in-law will have my head on a platter, and that's a less than comfortable position for me to be in."

"I know. I..." Her voice hesitated again. "I called last week. They told me you were sick."

"I was. But I'm recovering well."

"Good." Once again she paused. Her breath hitched up. "It scared me that I might not get the chance you offered."

"I know." Conor nodded. He'd been afraid a time or two. He recognized the symptoms. "But the offer is on the table, Ms. Martin."

"Chloe."

He smiled. "Chloe. I've got several rehab facilities with the ability to take you. All you have to do is say the word and I'll have my limo pick you up within the hour."

"Consider it said, Mr. Bradstreet."

Tit for tat. "Conor," he told her. "Like it or not, we're family, and I'm totally, absolutely, irrevocably in love with your daughter. She's one of the most fascinating creatures on earth."

"Is she smart?"

"Very."

"Like Brian."

Conor objected. "I see both parents in her. She's definitely a born performer. Very expressive. A natural for the stage. Or corporate law."

Chloe laughed out loud. "Luckily we've got a few years to fight that one out. So... You'll send the limo?"

"It's on its way. And, Chloe?"

"Yes?"

"Thank you."

She breathed deep, then sighed. "Do you pray, Conor?"

"Yes, ma'am."

"Put me on the list, okay?"

He smiled. "You've been there for months. I think we're at payoff time. Now go. Get ready. My driver will know what to do."

"Okay. I—"

"Chloe. Enough already. Go."

She laughed. "Goodbye."

He hung up, feeling good. The figures beneath the Ehrmentraut file swam before his eyes. Time to walk away from the screen for a bit, let the ibuprofen do its job.

The apartment seemed more empty than usual after the foray of visitors. Foster had muscled most of them away, but the give and take at the door had been both disturbing and commendable. Of course if he were poor, the stream of well-wishers might have been more abbreviated.

Kim was down to calling once a day and stopping by on alternate days, trying not to hover.

Addie called once a day the first week, decided he'd live to a ripe old age on or about Thursday, and he hadn't heard from her since. Typical Adelaide.

Alicia?

Alicia forwarded plain, unadorned and somewhat boring dog reports, when what he wanted was to sit her down, gaze into her eyes and see if what he'd dreamt was true or the leftover visions of a fever-racked brain.

Probably the latter, but he felt pretty sure the image he carried from the short minutes they shared at Benedetti's was old-style Alicia. Did she really give him that 'come hither' look, the one that brought him to his knees? Tease him about food and timing?

Not likely. A more likely scenario had his fevered dreams mixed with depressing reality. Perfectly understandable although most disappointing.

He stood and made his way to the window, eyeing the famous park, its footprint a stamp of snow-covered green and gray against concrete and stone.

The doorbell sounded. He stiffened, then relaxed. Foster would handle whomever, whatever.

A strange combination of sounds drew his attention toward the foyer. A four-footed sound clackety-clacked across the floor, followed by a huge, *"Woof. Woof. Woof."*

Conor stepped forward as a glorious black and tan German shepherd trotted into the room, head high, ears perked. The dog's profile stood magnificent, despite short spots in his thick, wooly coat. "Sarge?"

"Yes, it's him. And me," puffed Alicia, unknotting a long scarf from around her neck. "Did someone fail to tell New York that it's March? Hello? Like they don't have a calendar handy in this whole, big city? Where's spring when you need it?"

A tiny spark began to burn somewhere in Conor's belly. He shifted his look from Alicia to the dog and back again. "I can't believe you're here."

Alicia handed off her scarf, hat and coat to a waiting Foster, ran her fingers through a bank of dark auburn hair, and huffed. "We got more than a little tired of waiting for you to come back to Princeton."

"We?" Conor took a step forward, an eyebrow up.

"Well, him, mostly," Alicia answered, tugging off gloves. She tossed them onto a sofa table. "I kept telling Sarge you'd be back soon, we'd go through the whole story, each and every morning, didn't we, fella?" She reached down and patted the dog on the head. "But that's been my story for weeks, and he got tired of waiting, so..."

"You brought him here."

"Yes."

"To New York."

"That is where you live, right?"

Conor nodded and moved closer, near enough to smell the hint of spice in her cologne. "Although I plan to exercise more options in the future."

"Really?" Alicia copped him a smart aleck look that took him back to that fateful night at the Italian restaurant, very Billy Joel-friendly.

"See, I bought this house in Princeton."

"Our house."

The spark burned a little brighter.

"And I've got this great carpenter who's agreed to fix things up."

"Any way I want, right?"

Conor frowned. *Traitor.* Wait 'til he got a hold of Jerome Biltman.

"Stop scowling, Jerome didn't breathe a word, he's as thickheaded as the rest of you men," Alicia announced as she closed the distance between them, her footsteps confident. Sarge followed. She ran a hand across his head, the dog's, not Conor's. Immediately the pooch relaxed on his haunches, arching his neck, no doubt enjoying her touch, her caress. Conor had the strangest urge to stand in line, see if she'd do the same for him.

Alicia patted the dog, then took one more step. "You owe me."

"No doubt." Conor tried to read her expression, see how much was play, how much was passion, but she kept her intentions sheltered in a casually off-hand manner. "How much?"

Alicia angled a look at him. "Hmm?"

"How much were the vet bills?"

"Conor, I'm perfectly capable of taking care of Sarge's vet bill. Do you have any idea how much you pay me each month?"

He did, actually. If he weren't filthy rich, the very thought would cause him undue pain. He winced anyway, hoping for sympathy. "Yes."

"Then you know money's not a problem."

"But..." Conor paused, thinking back. "You said I owe you."

"Oh, yeah." This time she looked up. He read her eyes, the look in them, and wondered if he might still be sleeping, lost in a dream. "Big time, actually."

The dog moved to a firm second place on his agenda. "Because?"

"You made me some promises a few weeks back."

"Oh?" Two could play this game. He moved in, crowding her space, watching emotion swim in her eyes, those beautiful eyes, dark blue with gray rims and amber flecks. Behind her he saw Foster remove his coat from the foyer closet and head for the door. Smart man, that Foster. "About cabinets?"

"Yes."

"And dogs?"

Alicia swept a hand toward Sarge, all soap and water clean, his eyes bright, his body lean but muscled. "Done."

"So?"

"See, it's like this." She smoothed a slow hand through her hair, letting the curls fall back on her shoulders. "I've decided to put my house on the market."

"You... What?" She wanted to talk real estate at a time like this? Conor hoped he heard wrong.

She nodded. "It's too big, for one thing."

Like this was news? The stupid house hadn't grown in the twelve years she'd been there. *Oops, there was that word again, watch it, Conor.*

"And I always liked living right in town."

Conor's heart went to full pause mode. "Oh?"

"I figured we could board the horses at any one of several fine choices."

"Sensible."

"And who needs two houses in a town the size of Princeton?"

"Two?" The import of her words struck him. He looked down at her, his heart expanding that last little bit, wondering if she meant... "What do you need, Leash?"

She stared up, into his eyes, lips parted, her breathing unsteady but her gaze secure. One hand snaked around his neck, pulling him down. "Us," she whispered as his lips met hers, the touch soft and warm, heady with invitation. "I need us, Conor."

Somewhere in the back of his head he heard the dog whine, then make the customary three-circle spin before curling up in a ball on the living room rug, ready to wait them out.

Obviously the dog was as smart as the butler.

The End

AUTHOR BIO

Born into poverty, Ruth Logan Herne likes to be called "Ruthy", she loves her mid-life crisis writing career, and thanks God (after pinching herself!) for this dream come true. Mother of six, no *seven* kids (Ruthy may or may not have stolen her goddaughter and made her a daughter of her heart while her sister wasn't looking), grandmother to twelve, she and her husband Dave live on a small farm in upstate New York . She works full time but carves a few hours each day to write the kind of stories she likes to read, filled with poignancy, warmth and delightful characters. She loves God, coffee, chocolate, country, dogs and family and thinks kids are the best miracle ever. You can visit her on Goodreads, or at ruthloganherne.com, her blog www.ruthysplace.com or hang with Ruthy and other inspirational authors at www.seekerville.blogspot.com , or www.yankeebellecafe.blogspot.com a fun cooking/child raising blog she shares with other regional authors. She loves company and loves to talk so come prepared... ☺

OTHER BOOKS
BY
RUTH LOGAN HERNE:

From Love Inspired Books:
North Country:
Winter's End
Waiting Out the Storm
Made to Order Family

The Men of Allegany County Series:
Reunited Hearts
Small-town Hearts
Mended Hearts
Yuletide Hearts
A Family to Cherish
His Mistletoe Family

Kirkwood Lake Series:
The Lawman's Second Chance
Falling for the Lawman
The Lawman's Holiday Wish (December, 2013)

From Summerside Press:
Love Finds You in the City at Christmas (October 2013)
Two novellas featuring Ruth Logan Herne's "Red Kettle Christmas" and Anna Schmidt's "Manhattan Miracle"